I'LL GO TO TEXAS

THE CHEROKEE YEARS

BY Anne Odom

DEDICATION

To all my grandchildren, Maddy, Zach, Zoey and last, but definitely not least - Jimmy (who's name is really James). And also to my great-grandson, Daathe, an unexpected miracle. They are the loves of my life and my life's inspiration.

Acknowledgement

My sincerest thanks to Brandy Woods, an amazing young artist from Canada, for doing the cover art for this book. I gave her an idea of what I wanted and she ran with it and did a magnificent job!

I'll Go To Texas - Part 1
(The Cherokee Years)
By Anne Odom

Chapter 1

When Amanda Whitworth woke, the sun still hadn't risen and she was unsure of the time. Amanda had always been a light sleeper and easily awakened. She quietly lay in bed beside her sister Leticia, listening. Something had awakened her, but she couldn't figure out what it was. There - she heard it again. A bump on the outside wall of their house near her parents room next door. Amanda was afraid, but her innate curiosity got the best of her. She quietly slipped from her bed and crossed the room to the window.

There were no curtains on her second floor window. She looked outside through the glass at the yard dimly lit by a full moon. Indians! She saw three bucks climbing her father's ladder to the second floor of the house. She must have heard the ladder hitting the side of the house. She almost screamed, then thought better of it and ran to her parent's room next door instead, with her hand clasped over her mouth.

Amanda ran through the door to her father's side of the bed. She shook his shoulder and when he startled awake, she put her finger to her lips to hush him. She pointed to the window with a shaking finger. John Whitworth was instantly alert. Their farm had been attacked by the Cherokee before. He slid out of bed and grabbed his pants from a nearby chair.

He struggled into them then grabbed his long rifle and shot bag from the corner.

John motioned for his daughter to get back away from the window. He wanted her to run to her room and hide, but didn't take the time to try to sign that information to her. He needed to concentrate on preventing the Indians from gaining admission to their house. John went to the window and stood carefully by the side so he could see out, but no one could see him. What he saw scared him badly.

There were three heavily armed bucks already on the ladder and several more on the ground. The ladder was leaned up on the wall just below the window he was looking out of. He heard a noise behind him and turned to see his wife, Rhoda, sitting up in bed with her arms around a shaking Amanda. He signalled for them both to be quiet and turned again to the window.

The window was closed against the chill October night, but there was no lock on it. A lock would have made little difference as the Indians would just knock out the glass with one of their tomahawks. John tried to ease the window open, but it came open with a low squawk despite his best efforts. The first Indian on the ladder looked up at the noise. John stuck his rifle barrel through the window opening and fired.

He hit the Indian in the shoulder, but he didn't fall off the ladder. John was frantically trying to reload when the big Indian's body came bursting through the window, his shoulder bleeding down the front of his deerskin shirt. Glass went everywhere as Amanda and Rhoda screamed in unison. John finally got the rifle loaded, but it was too late. The other two Indians were in the room and grabbed the gun from his hands.

One of them hit him in the head with the rifle butt and he fell to the floor unconscious, amidst the broken window glass.

The first Indian who had come through the window looked at the two screaming females on the bed. He calmly walked over to the bed and grabbed Amanda. One of the other bucks came over and back-handed Rhoda across the face. Her screaming stopped abruptly, but Amanda's just got louder. She cowered back from the Indian and put her hands up to protect herself and her mother.

The Indian grabbed her hands and pulled her away from her mother and up onto the floor. Amanda dug in her bare heels on the rough wooden floor and struggled to keep from being pulled from her mother's clutching hands. Although splinters were gouging her heels, she still used all her strength to resist. Her puny sixteen year old arm strength was not nearly enough to keep the man from pulling her to him. He wrapped his arms around her, picked her up, threw her over his shoulder, and started for the window.

Seeing that the Indian intended to take her daughter, Rhoda jumped from the bed and ran across the broken glass barefoot to try to stop him. One of the other men grabbed her by her hair and drug her back onto the bed. She rose again and he shoved her so hard, her head made contact with the heavy bedpost and she passed out.

The Indian holding Amanda looked at the unconscious woman on the bed, but didn't break stride. Still holding Amanda tightly around the legs, he threw his leg over the window ledge, his foot quickly finding the top rung of the ladder. Amanda pounded on his back with her little fists, but he didn't even seem to notice. He quickly started down with his squirming burden.

Amanda was not a big girl, but she had thought she was strong from working alongside her parents and siblings on their farm. She struggled with all her might to get loose from the man's iron grip, but it was to no avail. He just tightened his hold even more. It felt like the circulation was almost cut off in Amanda's thighs as he agilely backed down the ladder holding on with only one hand. When he was three or four rungs from the bottom, he jumped the rest of the way landing lightly on the balls of his feet.

During all this, Amanda hadn't stopped screaming. Once they were on the ground, the Indian man put Amanda on her feet. While holding her with one hand his other hand covered her mouth to shut her up. Her green eyes looked up at him in fear and fury and she tried to bite his hand. He laughed at her spirit and then handed her to another Indian while he went to get his horse. Amanda had started to scream again, but the second Indian just put his hand over her mouth while holding her around the waist with his other hand. She was soon unceremoniously dumped into the first Indian's outstretched arms. He pulled her up on the horse in front of him to sit across his legs and covered her mouth again. They rode away quickly into the dark cold night.

The other Indians spent a couple of minutes seeing what they could steal from the farm yard and barn, then followed quickly. They didn't waste too much time because lights were coming on in the house as the other Whitworths woke to the sounds of the scuffle and the one shot John had been able to get off. When the other Indians caught up to Amanda and her captor, she saw they had taken some sheep skins that had been drying in the farm yard and a couple of bags of grain from the barn. It looked like Amanda was the main prize for the night.

As Amanda looked around her, she counted eight mounted Indians. It was a small raiding party out to steal anything they could, she guessed. Amanda was more frightened than she had ever been in her life. Living in the outlying areas of western Tennessee, far from any settlement or town, Amanda was well aware of the dangers of frontier life. One of her brothers, Jesse, had been attacked by a bear not three months ago and was just recovering from the bites he had taken to his arms and shoulders. Another of her brothers, Jacob, had been bitten by a snake the year before and almost died. But being abducted by Indians was the most horrifying event that could happen to a settler, especially a woman. She was pretty sure she would be raped or killed or both, and started to cry.

Again, the Indian who had captured her seemed amused. She saw nothing amusing in the situation and gave him a dirty look which also seemed to amuse him greatly as he actually laughed this time. Finally she was cried out. She just lay in the man's arms bouncing along on the horse and feeling utterly exhausted and horribly cold. Her feet also hurt from the splinters of wood in her heels, but that was the least of her worries right now.

It seemed to Amanda they had ridden for many hours when they finally stopped near a creek. She could tell that it was near daybreak because the sky was lightening a little in the direction behind them. The Indian man who had taken her threw his right leg over his horse and slid to the ground, still holding Amanda. He stalked over to the creek and set her down on the bank. Then he went back and brought his horse up to the edge of the water to drink. He motioned for Amanda to drink as well. Amanda was too cold and frightened to be thirsty, but she knew it might be a long time before she had another chance to drink. She hobbled further down the creek bank as far from the horse as she could. Kneeling on the ground, she cupped some of the cold water in her hand and drank it. She drank three times and then stood up shaking the cold water from her hand.

Only wearing a thin flannel nightgown, Amanda was very cold. She stood with her arms wrapped around herself trembling from the cold. She hadn't noticed how very cold it was before because both the Indian's body heat and the horse's had warmed her to some extent while they were riding.

The Indian man she had been riding with noticed she was cold and took the blanket off his horse and came over to her. He wrapped the blanket around her shoulders. Although the blanket was rough and smelled like horse, she was very glad to have its warmth.

Her Indian, as Amanda was beginning to think of him, also drank from the creek as did the others with them. Again her Indian mounted his horse and another man picked her up and handed her to him. He settled her in front of him again with the horse blanket still wrapped around her. Between the man's warmth and the warmth of the blanket, Amanda, though still frightened, was eventually lulled by the steady pace of the horses and after some time drifted off to sleep.

Chapter 2

When Amanda awoke, she didn't open her eyes right away. She could tell through her closed eyes that it was daylight. Amanda smelled smoke and sat up straighter. When she opened her eyes, the group was coming out of the woods into a clearing. Amanda sat up straight and looked around. There were several mud houses built in a rough circle in the clearing. Smoke was coming from the conical roofs of all the small houses. There were even smaller buildings built beside each of the larger ones that looked just like the larger ones, only there was no smoke coming from them. There was one really big house sitting in the center of the circle.

Amanda was surprised to see all the houses and the amount of activity in the little town. Indians seemed to be everywhere. Some were standing together talking, some were sitting around a fire outside the largest house, and there were others working at various jobs around the town.

When the horses stopped beside the largest building, again Amanda's Indian threw his leg over his horse's neck and slid to the ground still holding her. He walked to the entrance of the large building and ducking a little entered the doorway. The house was large, about forty feet long and maybe thirty feet wide. Inside, it was dark and smoky from the fire burning in the center of the dirt floor. Several older Indians were sitting around the fire talking. All talk stopped when Amanda and her Indian entered.

One of the oldest Indians stood and addressed Amanda's Indian. She couldn't understand a word, but from the tone, the older man was upset with her Indian. The Indian who had abducted Amanda didn't seem to care that the older man was upset. He set Amanda on her feet and pulled the blanket from around her. He pointed to her and said something to the older Indian and then he smiled broadly.

Amanda had not had a really good look at the man who took her until now. He was tall and athletically built. He had broad shoulders with a large chest and heavily muscled arms. His legs were bare and they were heavily muscled as well. He wore only a deerskin shirt that came halfway to his knees and a leather breechclout belted at his waist that hung a little longer than the shirt. On his feet were long deerhide moccasins that almost reached his knees. His moccasins were heavily beaded and had feathers and animal fur attached to them.

He was young, maybe in his early twenties, and had long, very dark hair, parted in the middle. The two tails were held on each side of his face with leather thongs, leaving the hair to spill down the front of his bloody shirt. His face was a coppery color with a strong beaked nose and high cheekbones. His eyes were very dark and set in deep eye sockets. His brows were thick and black. He was handsome in an exotic, but frightening way. He also had on jewelry, long earrings of bone with feathers and beads on them and a gorget at his throat made of bone with a wolf carved in the center and tied to his throat by a leather thong. He was quite a sight to see.

Amanda had forgotten he was wounded. He had shown no sign of weakness or pain since the whole ordeal had begun. Amanda was amazed at herself that she thought him handsome. She felt guilty because of it. How could she admire him and ignore the fact that he had taken her from her home against her will and hurt her parents? What was wrong with her? She mentally shook herself and tried to understand something of what was being said by the two men.

It was useless. Their language was totally incomprehensible to Amanda. There were no words that even sounded remotely like English. Finally, the older man seemed to give up on whatever he was telling the younger one. He sat down abruptly and waved the younger man away. Again, the younger man laughed. He took Amanda's hand and started to lead her away from the group sitting around the fire. She dug in her heels again and strained backward away from him. Her actions again made the big man laugh. He just walked back, picked her up in his arms, and strode away with a smile on his face.

The man walked to one of the houses, ducking down, he entered through the skin hanging over the open doorway. An older woman was cooking something over the fire in the center of the room. The little house was only one room and was about twelve feet by twelve feet. There were crude benches around the walls along with reed baskets and clay pots and jars. There was a small pile of skins in one corner of the room and a larger pile in another corner. There were herbs and wild onions hanging from the ceiling. The interior was dark and somewhat smoky from the fire.

The woman looked up when they came in. As soon as she noticed Amanda, she rose quickly and started to speak rapidly in their guttural language, but Amanda couldn't understand a word she said. She pointed her finger at the man and then at Amanda, then shook her head and left the house, still muttering angrily as she went.

The man set her down and pointed to one of the benches. Amanda supposed he wanted her to sit down, so she hobbled over and sat. He then went to the fire and stirred the pot that was bubbling over it with the same large wooden spoon the old woman had used. He looked at Amanda and made a sign as if he was eating and then he pointed at her. She was very hungry, but she didn't want to eat whatever was in the pot. She had no idea what Indian's ate. She was afraid to eat it, although it smelled really good. Maybe she would starve herself and he would let her go, she thought.

She was still very frightened, but now that it looked as if no one was going to kill her, her fear lessened. If they had been set on killing her, she would already be dead. Instead of being frightened, now Amanda got really angry. Her volatile temper had always been kept under control by her very strict parents, but Amanda had been known to lose control on occasion. Usually with one of her several siblings. Her little brothers especially liked to push her to the point where she was screaming and throwing things at them, but not in sight of their parents.

There were no parents here now and the longer Amanda thought about how this man had had the audacity to come to her home and steal her in the dead of night, the more angry she became. She had been staring at the fire while her temper had been coming to a boil. She saw the man move from the corner of her eye and looked up. What he saw in her eyes must have pleased him because he laughed again as he had several times before. It was just too much.

Amanda launched her small body off the bench and started to yell at him at the top of her lungs. "You despicable cur. How dare you come to my home and spirit me away in the middle of the night. And you hit my father with a rifle butt. You may have killed him and my poor mother may be dead too. You filthy Indian, I would very much like to claw your eyes out with my fingernails." Upon those words, Amanda raised her hands like claws and propelled her small body right at him still limping from the splinters in her heels.

For the first time, the man didn't laugh. He watched her come toward him with her outstretched claw-like hands until the last second. He reached his long arms out and caught her hands in his much larger ones. She continued to scream at him and began to twist her body trying to get out of his grip. He held her effortlessly, but seemed genuinely surprised by her sudden ferocious actions. When Amanda couldn't break his hold on her hands, she began to kick him with her small bare feet. Surprised at her vehemence, he called out in his native tongue and the flap over the door opening was pushed aside.

A man walked in who didn't look Indian. Amanda stopped struggling right away and turned her head to look at him more closely. He was dressed much as her captor was. However, his hair was light brown, almost blonde and his skin was only lightly tanned. Most telling of all, his eyes were blue. Amanda felt a rush of hope. Maybe he was there to rescue her. She looked toward him and shouted.

"Watch out for him. He's dangerous. He stole me from my home and hurt my parents. Please do something and get me away from him before he hurts me too.", she begged while beginning to try to free her hands again.

The new stranger looked at her then turned to her captor and spoke to him in the guttural language she had heard earlier. Amanda was shocked into stillness. Was he some other type of Indian? One with light hair and eyes. The only Indians she had ever seen were dark skinned with dark hair and eyes. After speaking to her captor for a moment and hearing his answers, the stranger turned to her.

"Waya wants to know your name. What is it?", he spoke calmly as if this were an everyday happening.

"My name, why does he want my name? And why are you interpreting for him? Why don't you help me get away? I told you he stole me from my home and hurt my parents. Why aren't you helping me?" Amanda screamed hysterically at the man.

"Screaming and fighting will not help your case, Miss. Waya will not put up with that behavior much longer. Actually, I'm surprised he hasn't taken you to hand already. My advice to you is to be quiet and do as you are told."

Amanda was so shocked by what the man said, she became still almost instantly. She stared from one of the men to the other. She felt as if she were in a nightmare. Here she had thought this man was there to help her and it seemed he was there only to interpret for her captor.

When Amanda became quiet and stopped fighting, her captor smiled and said something to the other man. It sounded to Amanda that he had called the other man Charles, but she wasn't sure.

Amanda turned to him and asked, "Is your name Charles?"

Without looking at her, he nodded his head affirmatively and said, "That is my birth name. Waya only uses it when I am speaking English to someone. My Cherokee name is Mohe." He spoke again to her captor, but didn't speak to her again until after her captor replied to him.

"Waya wants to know if you are hungry." he said with very little animation in his speech.

"Why do you interpret for him? How did you learn his language? Who are you?" The questions tumbled out of Amanda's mouth before she could stop herself.

"I interpret because that is my job here, as well as many others. I suppose some would consider me a captive like you, however I do not. I have been here many years, I'm not sure how many, but it has certainly been long enough for me to learn the Cherokee tongue. You will learn it in time too." Charles said haltingly, with the same lack of inflection as before.

It was almost as if he hadn't spoken English in a long time and had trouble expressing himself in that language. Again, he looked steadily at her and repeated, "What is your name?"

"Amanda Whitford, daughter of John Whitford. Please tell him," Amanda said pointing at her captor, "that my father will be looking for me. He won't stop trying to find me, no matter how long it takes."

Charles spoke to her captor and again he laughed. He said something to Charles and then pointed at Amanda. He obviously wanted his words repeated to her.

Charles turned to her and said, "Waya says your father can look all he wants to, but you belong to him now and he will never let you go. Are you hungry, or not?"

Amanda was so frustrated by now that she stomped her foot which hurt quite a bit, crossed her arms over her chest and plopped back down on the bench. She refused to answer

Charles or look at the one called Waya. After a few minutes, Charles brought her a bowl of the stew that had been cooking when they came in. The bowl was clay and had been painted all over in yellow with a pretty design on the outside in red and blue. The spoon she was handed was carved from wood with the figure of a wolf on the handle.

Amanda almost threw the bowl of steaming stew at the tall smiling Indian, Waya, but then thought better of it. She hadn't eaten since supper the night before at around six. She was very hungry now, so she ate the surprisingly tasty stew. She knew she had to keep up her strength to try to escape. When she was done, Charles asked if she wanted more. She said no, but that she was thirsty. He went to a large clay jar in the corner and dipped some water out of it. Amanda saw the water he brought her was in a gourd that had been carved and decorated. It was also brightly painted and was quite pretty. Amanda drank deeply, emptying the gourd. After she handed it back to Charles, he replaced it in the jar and started to leave them.

"Wait, don't leave. I don't know how to talk to him. You can't just leave me alone here with him," Amanda said pointing at Waya.

Waya looked at her quizzically, then turned and said something to Charles. Charles looked a little surprised, but then he said to Amanda, "Waya says I should stay so he can communicate with you more. So, I will stay."

"Fine then.", huffed Amanda. She was not very happy that her request would have been ignored, but whatever Waya wanted, he seemed to get.

"Do you have to do everything he tells you to? Do you belong to him or something?" Amanda asked with asperity.

"I don't belong to Waya, I am not a slave. He is my brother. I was adopted by his parents many years ago when I was a small child. I have lived as a Cherokee all these years, but our parents wanted me to keep my English so I could translate for the tribe when needed. It has been very hard to keep all the words because I use it so little. Maybe with you here, I will be able to speak English without always having to think of the words first in Cherokee and then in English."

"I'm not going to be here that long. My father and the rest of my family will be coming for me. Do you want to go with us when they come? I'm sure they would be happy to help you too."

"Why would I want to leave? These people have been very good to me. They treat me as they do any other person in this town. My birth parents died of some disease when I was very young. Waya's father found me and my sister nearly starved near our old home. He brought us here and took care of us. He had my sister and I speak English to each other all the time so we wouldn't lose the ability to speak it. My sister is married to a chief in another town near here and has been gone for four years. I, myself, have a wife and two children in this town. Why would I want to leave my family?"

"But you aren't Cherokee, you're white. Don't you want to live with your own people?"

"These are my people," Charles replied with alacrity. "I am Cherokee now, not white. I have no desire to live with the whites. To them, I would be an object of pity. I would not be able to take my wife and children with me. They would be objects of ridicule in the white world. I am happy here and I have no desire to leave. You may also become happy here if you will just give it a chance."

Waya was watching the conversation very closely although he didn't speak English. He could tell from the tones of their voices that his new woman was not happy to be with him. He didn't care about that, she would come around in time. He had no doubt that he could make her happy. He told his white brother, Mohe, to tell his new woman that his mother would come back in a little while with her some new clothes. After Mohe told her, they both left the house.

Chapter 3

Waya went to his mother's house to ask that clothes be prepared for his bride to be, Ah-man-da. Her name was not too difficult to say. It almost sounded Cherokee. Waya's mother, Ninovan, was not pleased that he had taken a white woman for a wife. She had hoped he would marry the chief of the next town's daughter, Salali. Unfortunately, Salali looked too much like her namesake, the squirrel. She had very full cheeks, a tiny nose and bright inquisitive eyes. Her face was not pleasing to him and she was very meek, although she chattered like a squirrel sometimes too. He wanted a woman with fire.

After leaving his mother's house, Waya went to the edge of the woods and sat on a log to think. There was much to do before he could marry Ah-man-da and Waya needed to plan carefully.

Now, Ah-man-da, she was very beautiful, he thought. She had bright green eyes that tilted up on the corners, long wavy dark brown hair with streaks of red in it, and a sweet heart-shaped face. And she had a lot of fire. Waya had been watching her for several moons. He knew she didn't have a husband because she still lived at home with her parents. He knew she had fire because of the way she acted around her many brothers. They tried to tease her, but she was very quick to get angry when it seemed they had gone too far.

Several days ago he had gone to the tribal grandmother and asked her permission to steal the white girl. She refused. She wanted Waya to marry either Salali or another chief's daughter from another town who had no sons. Waya could then become chief of that town when the chief got too old or died. Cherokee men were not allowed to marry a woman from their own village. When the couple married, they had to live with the wife's family. That would not be possible for he and Ah-man-da. Her family would never consent to having a Cherokee son-in-law.

They would have to live in his village as his brother Mohe and his wife, Tsula, did. Mohe's wife had no parents. They had been killed by the white man and her town had been destroyed before she and Mohe had married. She had been visiting her brother and his wife in this town when the white men came calling. When word came that her town was gone, Mohe had asked permission to marry her and continue to live in his own town. The grandmother had granted permission, but grudgingly.

When Waya asked for Ah-man-da, the grandmother answered with an emphatic no. He had been very disappointed, but had decided to abide by her ruling. Then he and his friends had gone on a hunting party and he couldn't resist going to see his pretty white girl just one more time. He had lain in the woods watching her house all day. He had seen her come out of the house and go to the barn to milk the cows they kept there, both early in the morning and late in the afternoon. She had been in and out all day - gathering eggs, washing clothes, hoeing in the fields. She was a hard worker. That he liked. She worked as hard as a Cherokee woman. The more he watched her, the more he wanted her.

Finally, in desperation, he had talked his friends into going on a raid that night to steal her away. He told his friends, not to kill anyone. It wouldn't be right to kill members of his new wife's family, as they would soon be his own kin. They had found the ladder leaning on the wall of the barn. He had seen the whites at the house use these wooden legs to get hay down from the top of the barn that same day. When he and his friends moved it to the house, they realized it was just a little too short to easily reach the window. Waya wasn't sure which of the rooms she was in. They decided to just pick one and try to sneak into it and see if the girl he wanted was in it. They had chosen the wrong room. Her parents had been in the room, but so had his little white girl. He had taken that as a sign that she really did belong to him.

When the girl's father had shot him, he thought at first he wouldn't be able to get her. Then, when he didn't fall from the wooden legs, he knew that truly was a sign and he was right to steal her away. If the white man's bullets couldn't stop him, then nothing could. His shoulder hurt, but he was determined to get his bride. He had sprung off the top rung of the ladder through the flimsy glass covering the window feet first and gotten his girl. Now that his adrenaline had ebbed, his shoulder had really started to hurt.

Waya went again to his mother's house. He told her he had been shot. His mother, Ninovan, had been so angry with him for stealing the white girl, she had not noticed his bloody shirt earlier. She had him remove his shirt while she pounded some herbs to make a paste. She examined his shoulder and found that, happily, the bullet had gone all the way through. She took the paste and rubbed some on each side of the wound. She used a very small stick to push some of the paste into the wound both back and front. That was very painful, but Waya neither moved nor made a sound. When she was done, she put leaves on the wound both back and front. The leaves had been soaked in another herb that helped to kill pain. The liquid would help the leaves adhere to his shoulder. Ninovan wrapped a piece of cloth around his shoulder to hold the leaves. Waya's shoulder finally stopped throbbing from her ministrations and began to feel a little better. He put his shirt back on. Before he went out to care for his horse, he told his mother that Ah-man-da was limping and might need splinters removed from her feet.

Waya found Mohe already taking care of his horse for him. Mohe was a good brother. Waya was very glad to have him in his family. When Waya's father, Degataga, brought the two small white children to their town, Waya was very young, but still a little older than Mohe. Their parents were older than most of the other parents in the town. They had tried to have children for years, but only Waya had survived. His mother lost several other children, both before and after Waya was born. It was good to have siblings like the other children in the village, even if they were white. Soon Waya forgot that Mohe and Inola were white. They acted just like the other children and they soon picked up the Cherokee tongue.

Waya had been surprised that Degataga insisted that Mohe and Inola keep talking the white talk. Later when they were all older, their ability to speak the white man's tongue came in handy when the tribe was dealing with trappers or other white men with whom they traded their furs, produce, and game for tools and weapons.

Since his horse was already being cared for, Waya went back to his house for a clean shirt. The one he wore was torn now and ruined with blood. When he walked through the door of his house, he saw Ah-man-da still sitting on the bench where he had left her. He was struck anew at how beautiful she was. Waya walked over to his pile of furs and skins. He took off his soiled shirt and sat down on the furs reaching behind his bed for his roll of extra clothing. He unrolled the clothes and looked at his best shirt, the one he saved for celebrations.

His mother had made the shirt for him. It was of buckskin and had long fringes on the shoulders, down the front two panels and along the outside of the sleeves as well as at the bottom. There were beads and shells on the shirt as well as an intricate pattern made of porcupine quills on the front and back. The shirt came almost to his knees and was beautifully made. He would wear that shirt to be married in, he thought. He chose another every day deerskin shirt like the one he had taken off.

When he stood and turned toward Ah-man-da, she was staring at him. She looked frightened again. She wrung her little hands together and edged farther back on the bench. Waya couldn't understand why she looked more frightened now than when he walked through the door. He looked down at himself and suddenly understood her fear. He was naked except for his breechclout. She must think he was going to rape her. "Oh, how wrong she is," he thought. "When we are married, I will make love to her, but I would never rape her. That is what white men do, not Cherokee."

Waya put on his shirt and went out of the house. He needed Mohe again. He had to let Ah-man-da know that they would soon be married and no harm would come to her. Waya found Mohe at his own house playing with his small son. Mohe was pretending to be a bear and growling and running at the small boy. The boy, Kanuna, would shriek with pretend terror and run laughing to his mother, Tsula. Tsula would scoop him up and they would both run a few feet from Mohe laughing all the while.

When Mohe saw Waya, he immediately came to his brother's side. Waya told him how Ah-man-da was acting and what he thought the reason was. Mohe was not surprised. He knew that white women always thought Indian men would rape them. It was rare that that happened with the Cherokee. Mohe went immediately with Waya to his house.

The white girl was still sitting on the bench in her nightgown. The nightgown was dirty and had a tear in the side near the bottom. Her hair, once braided neatly down her back, was partially loose from her braid and curling wildly around her face. Her face was pinched looking and very pale. Her large green eyes showed relief when she saw Mohe enter after Waya.

Mohe went to stand near the girl. He spoke quietly to her. "You have nothing to fear from my brother, Waya. He will not harm you. He means to marry you as soon as the feast can be planned. He will not touch you as a man touches a woman until after your wedding."

Mohe had meant to comfort her with his words. He was surprised when the girl leapt from the bench and began to speak so quickly he had trouble understanding her.

"Married, I can't marry him. He's a heathen, a, a Indian, a wild man. I can't get married anyhow. I'm too young. My pa said I couldn't marry until I was 18. I just turned 16. That's way too young. My Ma married my Pa when she was 18 and I have to wait., " the girl was almost hysterical by this time. Mohe was having a hard time understanding her, especially at the end of her tirade.

Mohe turned to Waya and explained the girl thought she was too young to marry. Waya asked, "How old is she then?"

"She is 16 summers.", Mohe replied.

"16 summers. Your sister married when she was only 15 summers and your wife wasn't much older when she married you. Why do these white people wait so long? She is plenty old enough for a Cherokee. Tell her she is old enough, Mohe."

Mohe again tried to reason with the white girl. He explained that Cherokee girls married much younger than white girls. Since she was marrying a Cherokee, her age didn't matter.

Again, the girl began to get hysterical. She walked around the house in circles limping and twisting her hands while shaking her head. "Tell him," Amanda said pointing to Waya, "that I can't marry him. I don't know him. I have to marry a white man. I can't marry an Indian. My folks wouldn't like it. My Pa wouldn't allow it."

Again Mohe translated her speech to Waya. Waya just laughed which seemed to antagonize the girl even more.

Chapter 4

Finally she wore herself out limping around the little house and sat down again on the bench. She continued to fidget, moving her feet and twisting her fingers. It occurred to Mohe that she might need to relieve herself. He asked Waya if the girl had been allowed to take care of her needs on the trip from her home.

When Waya answered negatively, Mohe turned to the girl and said, "Do you need to make water?"

"Make water, I don't know how to make water. Water comes from the sky or creeks or rivers. I don't know how to make it." The girl said while she looked at Mohe as if he was crazy.

"Not actually "make" water. Do you need to relieve yourself?"

Amanda was so embarrassed her face flamed red. She had been needing to go for hours, but didn't know where Indians did that sort of thing. She hadn't found a chamber pot in the little house and had been afraid to leave. There were way too many Indians moving around outside when she peeked through the door hanging. She could hear them talking and laughing as they passed by the door of the little house. Amanda looked at Mohe and shook her head affirmatively.

Mohe translated for Waya. Waya looked kindly at the girl and came to her offering his hand to help her up. She looked at Mohe questioningly.

"Waya means to take you to the place where you can relieve yourself. His mother will have clothes ready for you soon. You will need to be purified before you can put on your new clothes. After you take care of your needs, Waya will show you to the purification house. By the time you are done there, your clothes should be ready. Our mother will also take care of your feet"

"Purification house? What is that? I don't have a disease." Amanda said with asperity.

"The purification ceremony is done whenever a new person comes to our town. Waya will also have to have the ceremony because he has left our town, as will all the men who went with him. Anyone coming into our town from the outside world needs to have the purification ceremony. It is the Cherokee way."

"But I'm not a Cherokee. I keep telling you that. Why don't you listen to me? I don't want to be a Indian. I just want to go home." Amanda said starting to cry again.

Mohe just stood helplessly looking at Amanda as if she was crazy. He shook his head and translated her words to Waya. Waya just gave a short bark of laughter and offered his hand to her again.

Finally, in desperation, Amanda stood and took Waya's hand. She really had to relieve herself. She just couldn't wait any longer.

The pair walked out of the house and Waya lead her toward the woods. They walked several feet into the woods. Waya pointed to some bushes and then at Amanda. She understood she was supposed to go behind the bushes. She was reluctant with him still standing so near, but the uncompromising need of Mother Nature won out.

When Amanda was finished, she came back around the bushes to find Waya patiently waiting for her. Then he led her to the edge of the river and made motions of her washing her hands. She knelt down on the bank of the river and washed her hands. Since she was already there, she decided to wash her face as well.

When Amanda had finished her ablutions, Waya led her to a small hut beside the largest house in the town. He motioned for her to go in. Mohe had been waiting for them and also entered the hut behind Amanda. There was a rather large fire, surrounded by rocks, burning in the middle of the hut and it was extremely hot.

Mohe explained that she would need to take off her clothes for the purification ceremony. She immediately became very agitated again. Amanda said somewhat hysterically, "I'm not taking my clothes off in front of you or that Waya person either. If you think I am, then you're just crazy as he is."

Mohe explained that the town grandmother would be conducting the ceremony, she wouldn't be seen by anyone but the grandmother and Waya's mother.

Still Amanda protested. She didn't want anyone to see her naked. No one had looked upon her body since she got old enough to bathe herself. She backed away from Mohe, but there wasn't much room. About the time she hit the back wall, the flap over the door opened and two old women came into the hut. Amanda recognized Waya's mother, but the other woman, she had never seen. The second woman was really old. She looked ancient. Her back was bent, her hair a grizzled gray. Her face was incredibly wrinkled like old parchment paper. Her skin color was a faded copper and her fingers were bent like claws. Amanda was instantly afraid of her.

When the older woman walked, or rather hobbled, into the little hut, she barked something at Mohe in their guttural language. He hurried out of the hut before Amanda could even say anything to stop him. The old woman hobbled over to her and reached out for Amanda's nightgown. There was no more room to back up, but Amanda did her best to jerk away from the old woman's hands.

Waya's mother came over to them and quickly bent to grab the hem of Amanda's nightgown. In one swift movement, she jerked the nightgown up and over Amanda's head. Amanda cowered back against the rough wall of the hut, putting one arm across her breasts and the other over her nether regions. The skin all over her body turned a bright red. The two women paid little attention to Amanda. They went to the fire and began to throw herbs on it, smothering the flames and chanting. The older woman took a long feather out of her bun and started to waft the herb smelling smoke around the hut. Waya's mother motioned for Amanda to come to the fire to join them.

Amanda hesitated a moment, but didn't see how either of the old women could be dangerous, so she complied. It felt very strange to sit naked on the cold dirt of the hut. Amanda could feel every little pebble and dirt clod under her. She didn't sit cross-legged like the older women, but sat with her legs to her side. She still kept her arm across her breasts and her other arm in her lap.

The heat in the little hut began to become stifling. Although the old women had thrown herbs on the fire and smothered some of the flames, it didn't help much. Amanda noticed that there were rocks inside the small fire circle also. They were so hot, they glowed red. The rocks seemed to be generating most of the heat. The hut was now filled with the herb smoke. It smelled good, but it also somehow made Amanda sleepy.

As the old women chanted in a low rhythm, the combination of herbs, heat, and the lulling chant were soon too much to take and Amanda nodded off. She was roughly shaken awake by Waya's mother. A blanket was wrapped around her and she was lead from the small hut, addled by sleep. The old ladies lead her quickly to the river.

The older one pulled the blanket from around her shoulder and dropped it on the river bank. The two old women then waded into the cold water like it was nothing, dragging a reluctant Amanda with them until they were chest deep. They cupped water in their hands and poured it over Amanda's head, all the while chanting in their language. She protested while she shivered, but either they didn't understand or didn't care what she was saying. The older one stepped a little closer to Amanda and then ducked her under the water like a baptism.

Amanda came up sputtering and shivering. The river was extremely cold. She was also very frightened because she didn't know how to swim. She looked around and saw that the old women were wading out of the water. She quickly followed them. On the bank, she saw a pile of clothes she hadn't noticed before. Waya's mother motioned for her to come to her where she stood beside the clothes.

Amanda went to her and dried her body and her hair on the cloth handed to her. She then dressed herself in the unfamiliar clothes she was handed with some help from Waya's mother. There were only two pieces of clothing, a wrap around skirt that went to Amanda's calf and tied snuggly around her waist at the side. There was also a long, loose shirt that was worn on the outside of the skirt. It had long sleeves and was made of deer skin, as was the skirt. There was some fringe on the shirt, both down the sleeves and at the bottom. There was also had a braided deerskin belt that tied around the waist. For her feet, there was a pair of soft deer hide moccasins. Amanda slipped them on as well although her heels still hurt badly. There was a leather tie that ran around the edge of them to cinch the moccasins snugly to her feet.

After Amanda was dressed, Waya's mother took a bone comb from her pocket and handed it her. She finished taking loose her braid. Her hair had almost completely come loose from it already. She ran her fingers through her waist length hair to take out the worst of the tangles and then used the comb to smooth the rest. When she had the tangles out, Waya's mother parted her hair in the middle and pulled the two sides over her shoulders securing them with leather thongs. Her hair was still quite damp, but it wasn't dripping on her new clothes. She had towelled it thoroughly when she first came out of the water. Amanda's hair was naturally wavy and a very pretty shade of mahogany brown. There were red highlights in it that the sun picked up. Waya's mother ran her hand over the waves and actually smiled at Amanda, to her surprise.

Amanda was also surprised at how comfortable the Indian clothes were. She normally wore dresses that had fitted bodices and sleeves that fit snugly to her wrist. The skirts were gathered at the waist and full and she wore them over at least one petticoat. She had only had three dresses at home, two for every day and one for special occasions. They were all made from calico and she had to wear a corset under the nicest one. She didn't wear a corset every day, but she had to wear a chemise always, even on the hottest days of summer. She felt strange not having anything under her clothes, but it was somehow freeing.

Chapter 5

Amanda was distracted from her musings by Waya's mother, who touched her arm. The woman said something in their language that of course Amanda didn't understand. She looked quizzically at the old woman and shrugged her shoulders. Amanda looked around, but didn't see Mohe or Waya. The three women were the only ones on the riverbank. Amanda was grateful for that, but she was also at a loss as to what was being said to her.

Finally Waya's mother grabbed her hand and started up the river bank. Amanda had no choice except to follow. She was lead back to Waya's house. He was standing outside talking to Mohe. When he spotted Amanda, he smiled broadly and started toward her. His mother said something to him, but didn't stop. She lead Amanda to another house farther away. She motioned for Amanda to go through the door hanging. Amanda wasn't sure what was going to happen next and became anxious again. She stood just inside the entrance wringing her hands.

This little house was an almost exact duplicate of Waya's in design, but had a lot more baskets and jars than his. There was piles of skins in two corners, crude benches along the walls, and a large collection of woven baskets, clay jars and pots standing between and under the benches and even hanging from the ceiling. There were a lot of herbs, wild onions and wild garlic hanging from the rafters too. In the middle of the room, there was a fire pit with a small fire burning in it. A tripod hung over the fire with a clay pot hanging on it. Something smelled very good and Amanda's stomach growled loudly.

Waya's mother heard the small noise and looked at Amanda and smiled. She motioned Amanda to come over to one of the little benches. When Amanda was seated, the old woman retrieved two bowls from one of the baskets nearby along with two spoons. She dipped some of the stew into each of the bowls with a decorated gourd. When she brought Amanda a bowl, Amanda automatically said, "Thank you."

The other woman didn't understand the words, but it seemed she understood the sentiment because she nodded her head and smiled at Amanda again. Amanda smiled back at her and timidly began to eat. The stew was very good. Amanda thought the meat was either squirrel or venison.

She was accustomed to eating both meats at home. Her parents rarely killed an animal of their own for food if they could help it other than pigs. Her father and brothers hunted every few days and her family ate whatever they were able to kill. The meat in this stew was very tender and was accompanied by what Amanda thought were onions and squash of some kind. It was flavored with some herbs she didn't recognize, but she definitely tasted garlic in it. The thick stew tasted wonderful.

While Amanda was finishing her stew, she heard a man's voice at the doorway. She thought it was Mohe and she was very glad. She had so many questions for him. Waya's mother said something in their language and Mohe entered.

"Mohe, my son, it is good you have come.", said Ninovan. "This white girl doesn't understand anything I tell her. You must start to teach her our language. She cannot live in our town not knowing how to speak properly."

"Yes, mother, Waya has asked the same of me. I will try to teach her at least a few words every day until she starts to understand. I will start with teaching her how we wash dishes at the river if that is alright with you. She can learn our words and also do something useful. I see you have finished your meal. Do you have other things to wash other than these bowls and this pot?"

"No, my son. This is all. It is good to teach her something useful while she is learning to speak correctly. But wait, the white girl has something wrong with her feet. Waya said something about splinters. I will take care of her feet before you take her to the river"

Mohe turned to Amanda, "When you have finished your meal, I will take you to the river and show you how to clean these dirty dishes. While you are learning that small chore, I will teach you the Cherokee words for things. Before we go, my mother will take care of whatever is wrong with your feet"

Amanda hastily finished the stew. She was more than ready to get the splinters out of her heels. They were very uncomfortable and her legs were hurting from walking on her toes so much. She was also overjoyed to be going outside and being allowed to speak English with Mohe. It was very difficult for her not being able to talk to anyone. Everything was so new and strange here. She wasn't sure about learning their language. She was sure her father would be here soon to get her.

The thought of her father lead to thoughts of her mother and brothers and sister. Her heart hurt knowing how worried they would be about her. She missed them so much, especially her sister, Leticia. They were very close and were almost a year apart in age. Leticia had just turned seventeen a few days before Amanda was taken from their home.

When Amanda had finished her meal, Ninovan took a basket of herbs and brought them to the bench Amanda was sitting on. She had Mohe instruct Amanda to take off her moccasins. It took her a few minutes to extract all the splinters from Amanda's heels. Then she made a paste of some of the herbs in her basket. She applied the poultice to Amanda's heels and then wrapped them in clean rags. Amanda put her moccasins back on and then she gathered all the dirty dishes into a basket that Ninovan handed her. She smiled at the older woman and thanked her again. Mohe thought the words for thank you would be a good start for Amanda's lessons for the day. He turned to her and said, "Thank you in our language is wado and my mother's name is Ninovan."

Amanda thought, "That's not too hard." She smiled at the older woman and said, "Wado, Ninovan."

Ninovan smiled at Amanda and said, "Osdv"

Amanda quickly looked at Mohe and he said, "My mother said good."

Amanda smiled at Ninovan again and followed Mohe outside. He lead her back to the river bank, but not to the same spot she and the women had used before. The bank went down very gradually here to a small sandy beach.

Mohe said, "This is the area the women in our town use for cleaning dishes. The sand is used for scrubbing the dishes. Then they are rinsed in the river. The Cherokee word for bowl is atlisdodi. Now you say it."

Amanda tried to say the word, but kept mispronouncing it at first as atleastdoodi. Mohe tried hard not to laugh and kept repeating the proper pronunciation. Finally after several attempts, Amanda could say the word. Next he taught her the word for spoon, adidodi. Again she tried several times, but mastered spoon a little sooner than she had bowl. However, when he tried to teach her agvsquosdi, the word for wash, Amanda just couldn't seem to get the pronunciation correct. She became more and more frustrated.

Finally Mohe told her no more lessons for right now. She had mastered three words and his mother's name. Maybe she would do better tomorrow or later today. While Mohe had been teaching Amanda the words, she had been scrubbing the dishes. She finished the pot and put the dishes back into the basket.

"Mohe, do we have to go back to Ninovan's house right now? I would like to ask you some questions."

"That will be fine. We will take the dishes back to Ninovan and then I will take you to my house to meet my wife and children. My wife has a few words of English she learned from my sister and me. She may be able to help you learn Cherokee."

Chapter 6

They walked back to Ninovan's house. Outside the door, Mohe called out in his language. They heard Ninovan answer and went in. Amanda took the basket of clean dishes and set it beside the fire. Ninovan asked Mohe how the lessons had gone.

Mohe replied, "She mastered about four words today. I am taking her to my house to meet Tsula. I think she may be able to help since I have taught her some English words."

"A very good idea, my son." Ninovan said, smiling.

Mohe and Amanda walked the short distance to his house. Amanda wasn't limping as much as she had before being treated by Ninovan. Tsula was outside playing with their little boy. When she saw Mohe, a huge smile lit up her pretty face. She noticed Amanda and stood from her game with her son. She waited for them to come closer and then spoke to Mohe, "Is this the white girl Waya has taken for his bride?"

"Yes, Tsula, this is Amanda. I am trying to teach her our language. I thought maybe since you have some English words, you could help me."

"I will be happy to try, but I don't know a lot of English words.", Tsula said looking worried. She turned to Amanda and said, "Hel-lo."

Amanda's face was wreathed with smiles as she replied, "Hello. I am so very glad to meet you. I hope you can help me. I feel so lost here."

Tsula turned to Mohe with a quizzical look on her face. She had not understood much of what Amanda had said. "I don't know what she said, Mohe. This might not work so well."

Mohe laughed, then turned to Amanda. "You spoke too fast, Amanda. You will have to speak slowly to Tsula. She only has a few words of English."

"Oh, I'm so sorry. I was so happy to hear her say hello in English, I just rushed on. Mohe, what is the word for sorry in Cherokee?"

"There is no one word to apologize in our language. Just be sure to speak slowly to Tsula and you will be fine."

Amanda was mystified as to why the Cherokee had no word for apologizing. Did they think they were always right? She couldn't figure it out, but decided to wait to ask Mohe about it at a later time.

While the adults had been talking, Kanuna had been inching closer and closer to Amanda. Kanuna was only two and had never seen a white person before. When he was close enough, he sat down by Amanda's legs and wiped his little hand down her leg. Amanda jumped and let out a little screech.

She had thought an insect or animal had touched her at first. When she saw it was a little boy, she knelt down beside him so she would be more on his level. Her screech had scared him a little, but since he was an inquisitive little fellow, he inched toward her again. He reached his little hand out and touched her skin again, this time on her face.

Kanuna looked up at his father and asked, "Isvwanige?"

Mohe laughed and scooped up the small boy. He held him in front of him and said, "No, Kanuna, Amanda does not have flour on her skin. Her skin is naturally that color. She is not Cherokee, she is a white woman."

"Unegv ageyv?" he asked.

"Yes, Kanuna, Amanda is a white woman."

Kanuna studied Amanda for a few moments and then turned to his father, "Uwoduhi".

Mohe laughed again and said to Amanda, "My son, Kanuna, thinks you are pretty, but he thought your skin was covered in flour before."

Amanda laughed and Tsula joined in. Kanuna couldn't understand what was so funny. He held his arms out to the pretty white woman. Amanda took the child and held him snugly against her. She thought he was delightful. Kanuna was a combination of both his parents. His skin was much lighter than his mother's, but he had her beautiful large brown eyes. His hair, though not black like Tsula's, was nowhere as light as Mohe's. It was a medium dark brown with a hint of a wave in it. However, he had inherited Mohe's facial features and slim build.

Amanda had always loved children and had been a lot of help to her mother with her younger siblings over the years. The Whitworth family was quite large. Amanda had one sister and eight brothers. Two of her brothers, John and Jesse, were older and already married and living on farms of their own. Leticia was due to marry next year. She was marrying a neighbor's son, William Wells, and they would live with his family on their farm.

Tsula and Mohe were surprised that Kanuna had been so taken with Amanda so quickly. He was not usually so trusting of strangers. Maybe it was because she looked so different or maybe he just had a child's intuition and knew instinctively that she posed no threat to him.

Kanuna spent the rest of the afternoon staying very close to Amanda. She played games with him, laughing at his antics. She and Tsula couldn't actually talk to each other, but between hand signs and the few words of English Tsula knew, they seemed to be getting along quite well.

Tsula soon had Amanda helping her with some sewing. She had to show Amanda how to thread and use the bone needles and deer sinew she was using to make winter clothes for her small family. Amanda soon caught on though, as she had been sewing at home for years. Although there no actual patterns for the clothing items they were working on, they were not difficult to cut out and sew. They were designed to be loose fitting so no measurements were needed for them to be made.

Mohe left Amanda with Tsula and went to visit Waya. He had a message to deliver to him from Ninovan and he wasn't looking forward to it. When Mohe arrived at Waya's house, he found him sitting outside on a bench using his whetstone to sharpen his knives. Waya was well known in the town for the knives he carried. He carried several different styles and sizes of knives. When away from home he never had less than six knives secreted on his person. Either he or Ninovan had made him knife scabbards from deer hide in several sizes. He even had a scabbard sewn into the necks of his shirts to hold his largest knife. He could reach for it and throw it before most people even realized it was there.

Though most warriors preferred to fight with throwing hatchets made of stone with wooden handles and, of course, with bows, Waya used predominantly knives. He had a bow for hunting and war, but his real love was knives. When Waya had first seen the steel knives of the whites, he had been determined to have one of them as soon as he could. He had trapped last winter, even when it was the coldest of times, until he got enough hides to purchase a large knife with a steel blade from the white man's store in Paris. It was the pride of his collection. It had a blade almost ten inches long and the handle was carved from a deer antler. Waya kept it sharpened to a razor's edge at all times.

When Waya saw Mohe coming toward him, he stood and walked to meet his brother. When he didn't see Amanda with him, he became worried.

"Has something happened to Ah-man-da, my brother? I thought you were going to try to teach her our language today after her purification?

"I worked with her earlier. She is at my house with Tsula now. They are sewing and Tsula is trying to teach her some more words. Our mother has sent a message by me. She wanted me to tell you that Amanda will be living with her until your wedding day. She and the Grandmother have decided you will be married at the First New Moon of Spring Ceremony. That way your marriage will have a propitious start."

"Spring, why do I have to wait until spring to marry? One of the seven sacred ceremonies is not required for a wedding. Why do those old women want me to wait so long?" Waya was very upset and began to pace in front of his house. "That old woman," he thought, "She's just getting back at me because I didn't obey her and stole the woman I wanted against her wishes. I'm surprised she didn't try to make me take her back."

Mohe watched Waya pacing and knew his brother was very angry. There was nothing to be done however. When the Grandmother said a wedding had to be at a certain time, the tribe listened. He knew Waya was headstrong, but even he wouldn't go against the Grandmother on this. Perhaps she had seen signs that made that particular ceremony the right time for Waya to marry his white girl. Mohe also knew Waya was upset about Amanda having to live with his mother all those moons as well. Traditionally, a bride lived with her family until the marriage. Since Amanda had no family here, Waya's mother was taking the role of her family.

Mohe guessed Waya had planned to marry right away and make Amanda his wife quickly in every way. Mohe could understand his frustration. When Tsula was to become his bride, she had lived with her brother and his family until the actual wedding day. They were allowed to see each other whenever they wanted, but there could be no intimate relations until after the marriage. His marriage had been put off for many moons as well, but it was because of Tsula's mourning time for her parents.

Waya walked with Mohe back to his house. He was pleased to see Ah-man-da getting along so well with Tsula. He thought she looked very beautiful in her Cherokee clothes. He would ask his mother and Tsula to help her make her wedding dress. From the looks of it, she could sew, but he didn't know how she would handle the fancy bead work and quillwork that usually went into a Cherokee wedding outfit.

In keeping with tradition, on the day before their wedding, he would kill a deer and bring her some of the meat. If she cooked the meat for him, they would marry the next day. If she didn't, he didn't know what he would do. By tribal law, she was free to turn him down. As upset as she had been about him stealing her from her family, he would have to work hard to win her over before the wedding. When he decided to steal her, he hadn't thought about how the tribal traditions might affect their relationship. Maybe that was why the Grandmother had decided they had to wait. Although this explanation made sense, Waya was still very frustrated. He wanted his Ah-man-da now, not five moons from now.

Chapter 8

Amanda kept waiting for her father and brothers to come for her. She waited and waited, but still they didn't come. She tried to be patient and bide her time. She did whatever she was told to do because she was so sure her family would arrive any day to get her back. She didn't want to anger the Cherokee in hopes they would turn her loose if her family came for her. She couldn't figure out why they couldn't find her. On the night she was taken, she knew they had travelled for many hours. Maybe that was why, but then again, couldn't they have tracked all those horses. There had been eight of them after all. It seemed to Amanda that eight horses should have been easy to track.

The days turned into weeks and before Amanda knew it, two months had gone by. She had been keeping a calendar of sorts on a tree at the edge of the woods. She found a sharp shard of rock and after she had been in the Cherokee town for two days, she started to keep track. It took that long for Ninovan to let her go alone to relieve herself.

She knew she had been taken on the night of October 28th, so she started the calendar on the 29th. It was now December 29th and she was still at the Cherokee town. Amanda was very depressed. Christmas had come and gone. The Cherokee, being heathens, didn't celebrate the birthday of Christ. When she asked Mohe about it, he didn't have any idea what she was talking about. She tried to explain it to him, but couldn't seem to get the idea of her religion over to him. Waya was worse. He didn't want her talking about her time before he had stolen her. When she tried, he would just turn away and he even walked away on occasion.

It was very cold now. She and Ninovan had moved out of the bigger house into the tiny house that sat beside it. They had moved there after the first bad cold spell because the smaller house was easier to heat. True, it was easier to heat, but it was also less than half the size of the larger house and always very smokey because of the fire. The roof on the smaller house was clay like the walls and only had a small smoke hole in the top.

Since it was so cold, there was little they could do outside now. Going to the woods to relieve herself was agonizing to Amanda because of the cold. Ninovan had helped her make herself some winter clothes, but they didn't completely keep out the cold when she was outside.

Amanda had learned enough of the Cherokee language to communicate with the others, but she still couldn't really hold a conversation with anyone except Mohe. She was so very lonely. Everything she had ever known and loved had been ripped away from her. She often cried herself to sleep at night. She tried to be quiet, but sometimes she saw how Ninovan looked at her the next morning and knew she had been overheard. When Waya would see her red eyes, he would just turn away.

She got no sympathy or understanding from anyone in the town. They all seemed to expect her to just accept that she was now a Cherokee and forget her home and family. But she wasn't an Indian, she was white and she wanted to go home. Amanda began to try to think of some way she could escape and make her way home alone since her family couldn't seem to find her.

She had no idea where she was and that was the biggest problem. She cursed herself daily for not paying more attention to the direction Waya had taken her on that fateful night in October. She had been so scared and cold, her mind had shut down. She remembered there was a full moon that night and when they left her house they had headed what she thought was west into the wilderness. After that, though, she had no idea.

She did remember that when they stopped at the creek the sky had been getting light behind them, so they must have headed due west, but she couldn't be sure. If she ran away and headed east, would she find someone to help her, or just more Indians? She had no way of knowing. She definitely couldn't leave now though, it was so cold, she would freeze to death without a horse and heavier clothing. Her deerskin shirt, skirt, and leggings kept her relatively warm inside the little hut, but whenever she was outside she was always very cold.

Amanda saw many of the tribe had fur coats and blankets that they wrapped around themselves when they had to be outside. Waya and Ninovan each had such a coat, but no mention was ever made of making Amanda one. Tsula and Mohe had them as well, even the children had rabbit fur jackets and boots. Little Hialeah, Mohe's daughter, had started to walk now and she wore tiny fur boots while she toddled around their tiny house. When she asked Mohe about one for herself, he was strangely reticent to talk to her about it. She didn't dare bring it up to Waya, since apparently it was he who decided what she could and could not have.

When she had been in the Cherokee town for a couple of weeks, Waya had presented her with a small skinning knife. He gave it to her in a beautifully decorated scabbard to wear on her deer hide belt. Mohe said it was a great honor to receive such a gift so soon after being captured. Usually captives weren't allowed a knife for several months for fear they would turn it on the residents of the town. Amanda guessed no one saw her as a threat. She knew she was small, so maybe that was why they didn't worry about her hurting any of them. They were all bigger than she was.

As Amanda sat with Ninovan sewing more deer skin shirts and leggings, she paid very little attention to what she was doing. She could sew in the Cherokee way without even thinking about it now. It seemed that was all women did here, sew and cook. The men hunted and made war when they were attacked by another tribe or the whites. So far, there had been no attacks. Mohe told her there rarely were in winter. It was a very simple life the Cherokee lived.

Amanda was told by Mohe that the Cherokee women spent most of their time growing, preserving or gathering enough food to survive on. Mohe had told her when spring came, she would be required to work in the fields where the tribe raised their corn, beans, and squash. The tribe worked as a group to grow and gather enough food to see them through the year. What was raised was supplemented with whatever the men found when hunting. The food seemed to be plentiful still. Ninovan had a lot of corn, beans, and squash dried and stored in the bigger house. Waya was also a very good hunter.

Amanda had been surprised at the amount of dried fruit that Ninovan had stored in the jars and baskets in the large house. There were tiny, very sweet strawberries, and even cherries, and persimmons. She also had grape juice in clay jars that tasted wonderful. Blackberries were also apparently abundant because she had several baskets of them which she sometimes mixed with meat. Amanda had never had meat with berries, but it was actually quite tasty.

She was learning more every day about Cherokee cooking. They used a wide variety of herbs and spices that grew wild in the area and were harvested and then dried. The big house smelled wonderful from all the different herbs and foods that were stored there. They no longer built a fire in the big house, so it was very cold and a good place to store food, but it was a chilling experience to be sent there to bring over supplies. Since the smaller house was so very small, they went to the big house every day or so to get what they needed. It seemed to be Amanda's job more and more to do that chore alone. The cold really bothered Ninovan so she rarely left their little house, except for necessities.

One day when Amanda was in the big house to get herbs and corn meal, she accidentally knocked over a stack of baskets in the corner. It took her quite some time to gather all the squash and beans that had been stored in them. As she was about to put the baskets back on top of each other, she noticed the bottom basket didn't have food in it. Instead, she saw some beautiful furs. She ran her hand over the soft fur and thought how good it would be to have a cloak or coat made from the fur.

Then she had an idea. Since she was sent over here so often, why couldn't she sew these furs into a cloak for herself while she was here? She could do a little each day until she had it complete. With a warm cloak her escape would be a lot easier. She could also start to stockpile some food in the woods. She knew just the tree she could use. It had limbs she could grab to climb up into it and a hollow about halfway up the trunk. No animals would get into her stash of food if she put it high enough in the tree. She could wrap it in a deer hide. Since it had only taken one night to get here from her house on horseback, she figured it would take her two or three days travelling on foot.

Amanda began to get very excited. She knew she would have to wait a few more weeks, but if she could get everything together in say, four weeks, she would be able to escape well before she had to marry Waya. She didn't want to get married to him or really, to anyone yet. She didn't feel she was old enough to marry. She just wasn't ready.

She was afraid of what happened after you got married. Leticia had told her what Mama had said was going to happen after she married William. It sounded disgusting to Amanda. She didn't want anyone touching her there or doing any of the other awful things Leticia had mentioned. Amanda had never kissed anyone and couldn't understand why Leticia got so excited when she talked about kissing William. She even said he put his tongue in her mouth. "Ugh" thought Amanda, "how disgusting."

Thinking about all the things her older sister had said just helped Amanda make up her mind to start doing anything she could to make her escape plans a reality. She very carefully took the basket of skins out from under the beans and corn. She took it to a different corner of the house and hid it behind some large jars of grape juice. Then she took one of the cured deer hides they used to make clothes and put some dried meat and fruit into it. She folded the hide and slipped it under her shirt in the back.

Then Amanda gathered the things she had come to the big house for and returned to the small hut. Ninovan made no comment about the time Amanda was gone. She waited an hour or more while helping Ninovan prepare their evening meal. After the meal, she gathered the dishes in a basket and headed to the river to wash them. When she finished, she headed to the area the town used as a latrine. No one paid any attention to her. She went a little farther into the woods away from the latrine to the tree she had in mind to store her food. She jumped up and caught a lower limb with both hands. She put her feet on the bark of the tree trunk and walked up the trunk until she could swing her leg over the limb. She easily climbed up the tree.

There was a large hollow in the tree. At first she was afraid some animal might have a nest in the hollow. She broke off a limb and poked around in the hollow. It was apparently an old nest, but no creature was using it now. She took the skin out of the back of her shirt and lay it in the hollow. She was beginning to worry about the time she had been gone and shimmied down the tree as fast as she could.

Amanda hurriedly walked back to where she had left the basket of clean dishes. She had just bent to pick it up when she heard her name being called. She hurried to the edge of the woods to see Tsula headed toward her. Tsula had become her friend since she had been brought to the town, but Amanda knew she couldn't confide her plans to her. She would tell Mohe and Waya if she thought Amanda was planning to escape.

Tsula was wrapped in her fur coat and was still shivering. She said, "How can you be out here so long in just those clothes? Aren't you freezing? Ninovan said you had been gone quite awhile."

Amanda was shivering so hard her teeth were chattering. "I went to the river to wash the dishes and when I was on my way back I realized I had to go to the latrine. I thought I would never get through. Hurry, let's get back to Ninovan's before I freeze to death."

The two young women hurried across the small town and entered Ninovan's tiny house to find both Mohe and Waya there before them. As soon as the girls entered, Ninovan said, "Ah-man-da, I was worried about you. You took a long time to just wash a few dishes."

"I had to stop at the latrine on the way back from the river. Here are the clean dishes." As Amanda handed the basket to Ninovan she realized she had a long scratch on her hand. She tried to hurriedly hand off the basket, but Ninovan saw her hand.

"What happened to your hand?"

"Oh, it's nothing much. I must have scratched it on a bush at the latrine. I was so cold I didn't even notice it until now."

"You should let me clean it for you. It might be from a poisonous vine." Ninovan said.

"I don't think it was a vine, probably just a branch. I was in kind of a hurry because I was so cold. It's not deep." Amanda replied.

During this exchange, Waya watched Amanda closely. He didn't know why, but he suspected she wasn't telling the truth. It wasn't anything in particular, but there was just something in her offhand manner that didn't ring true. He didn't say anything then, but later, he told Mohe they needed to keep a close watch on Amanda. He thought something was off, although he didn't know what.

Mohe agreed and for the next few days he and Waya made sure to be near Ninovan's little house around meal times. Most meals Waya ate with them anyway. If he didn't eat at his mother's house, he ate at Mohe's. Now he took all his meals with Amanda and his mother. When Amanda would go to the river to wash the dishes, Waya came with her. The only place he didn't follow her was to the latrine.

That was a good thing because she steadily slipped food out of the bigger house and took it to her hiding place in the tree. She learned a less easily seen route to her tree from the latrine and learned to climb the tree really fast. When she went to the big house to obtain food, she would hurriedly sew a few more pieces of the fur together. It might not be her best sewing, but she thought it would hold together long enough to get her away from the Cherokee town.

Amanda really wanted to steal a horse for her escape, but she was afraid of being caught. Her best bet was to wait until Ninovan was deeply asleep and then slip out in the middle of the night. She could easily slip into the bigger house to get her cloak and then to the tree for her food.

Amanda was able to complete the cloak in three weeks. She thought she had plenty of food to last several days. She wanted enough to last in case she got caught in a snowstorm or had to hide from other bands of roving Indians. Amanda had decided to take all her clothes with her. She would layer them one on top of the other for extra warmth. She had been able to make herself a pair of fur socks to go inside her knee high moccasins. With three layers of clothes, the fur socks and the fur cloak, she should be warm enough to get home.

Amanda had made sure to be outside early enough to know exactly what direction east was. Unfortunately, east went right across the river. She didn't remember them crossing the river to get to the little town, so she figured there was a way around it. She remembered where they had entered the village and planned to start her escape in that direction and then turn in a more easterly direction as soon as she could. She planned to travel only at night and hide during the day.

Amanda knew the nights were much colder than the days. Moving at night would help to keep her warm. She should be able to find somewhere to hide in these dense woods during the daytime. Finally, she was ready. Tonight was to be the night.

When Amanda was sure that Ninovan was really asleep, she slipped from her furs and picked up her moccasins. When Ninovan was at the latrine earlier, Amanda had tied all her clothes together and hidden them behind her pallet. Now, she carefully picked up her bundle along with her moccasins and carefully slipped out the hide door. She looked around, but saw no one. She slipped over to the big house and quietly went to the corner where she had hidden her cloak. She put her extra two shirts and skirts on, as well as her extra pair of leggings. It was bulky, but she could still move. She wrapped the fur cloak around herself and quietly left the house.

Chapter 9

She made it to the tree where her food was stored with no problem. She had trouble climbing the tree with all the extra clothes on, but she finally made it. She reached into the hollow of the tree and found the food wrapped in the deer hide. Now she was ready to go. She slipped the deer hide full of food into her shirt and climbed down from the tree.

Amanda skirted the town quietly and took off in the direction she had first arrived from to the Cherokee town over three months ago. She walked as quietly as she could on the dark trail. It was extremely cold, but as long as she kept moving, she knew she would be alright. She couldn't see much, even after her eyes became accustomed to the dark. She knew she would have to stay on the trail or become hopelessly lost. She could hear the river to the right of her through the woods. She hoped she was going in the right direction.

After what seemed to be about three hours of walking, the trail she was walking on intersected another trail. The other trail went to the right. Amanda chose that one because she thought it was east. Amanda kept walking for what felt like another three hours. Finally, she was so tired, she felt she had to sit down for awhile. She found a deadfall not far off the trail and sank onto it with relief. Her feet were sore and her legs were beginning to cramp from all the unaccustomed walking. Amanda rubbed her legs through her leggings and they began to feel better. She hadn't been sitting long when she heard a noise in the brush to the right of her.

Amanda became very still and carefully turned her head to look at the brush. She saw the brush moving like something was crawling or walking through it. She was so frightened, she could hardly breathe. She sat perfectly still with her heart beating so hard she wondered if the animal or whatever it was could hear it. About when Amanda thought she would scream from the tension, the head of a small wild pig came through the brush not five feet from her. Apparently it didn't smell or see her as it just kept ambling along across the trail and into the brush on the other side.

When Amanda was absolutely sure the pig was gone, she let out her breath and rose from the log. Her legs were stiff and her first steps were faltering, but she made herself keep moving. She finally worked the stiffness out of her legs and lengthened her stride.

When the sky started to lighten towards dawn, Amanda started to look for somewhere to hide during the day. She kept her eyes open and finally spotted a clump of very dense evergreen bushes growing about twenty feet off the trail to the left. Although she didn't know it, Amanda had been walking for over eight hours. She was totally exhausted. When she crawled into the dense bushes, she went far enough that she didn't feel she could be seen from the path.

Amanda removed the bundle of food from her shirt and ate a couple of strips of dried venison and a handful of berries. She hadn't thought about bringing water and she was thirsty. It was getting too light to go look for water now. She would just have to wait until dark and find a stream somewhere. She could no longer hear the river. She thought she would turn due east when she left her hiding place that evening. It only took Amanda a very few minutes to fall asleep after she finished her meal. She rolled herself into her cloak and using her food bag as a pillow, closed her eyes.

Amanda woke several hours later. She was roused by a noise, but kept her wits about her and didn't move right away. She lay in the bushes barely breathing, listening to what she thought were horses on the trail. She listened intently hoping to hear the people talking. She would know then if they were white or Indian. She waited what seemed to her a long time, but heard no conversation between the horsemen. She could tell there were several horsemen in the party , but not how many. Amanda wished she could see, but was afraid to raise her head enough to look. She knew any movement she made would be easily noticed by someone in the group. She remembered how she had seen the motion of the pig moving in the brush earlier and it had been fully dark then.

Finally the horsemen had passed her hiding place. She could no longer hear any horse sounds at all. Still she lay in her hiding place. It was still daylight and from what she could see of the sun above her through the tree branches, it wasn't very late. The sun was just a little past being directly above her. She figured it was between one and two in the afternoon. At this time of year, darkness fell completely around six.

Amanda's stomach growled. She very carefully rolled onto her side and pulled the food packet from under her head. She extracted some more dried meat and some dried strawberries. She lay watching the leafless branches blow in a light wind while she had her lunch. After she finished eating, weariness again found her and she fell asleep.

Amanda woke again just before dark. She was very sore and stiff. She didn't dare get out of the bushes yet. She wanted to wait for full dark before she rose. When it was finally completely dark, Amanda rose slowly. She was very sore, but she knew she had to keep moving. She got back to the trail and started walking as fast as she could.

When Amanda had been walking about an hour, she heard water not far from the trail. She followed the sound to a small creek. She was so very thirsty, she drank and drank. Amanda couldn't believe she hadn't thought to bring a small jar or bladder to carry water in. At least it wasn't hot. Since she wasn't sweating, she could go longer periods without water.

After drinking her fill, Amanda went back to the trail she had been following. She walked another few hours and came to another crossroads. This time, the trail went in three different directions. She took the one on the right, which she judged to be in an easterly direction. Amanda had only been walking a few minutes when she saw what looked like a campfire not far off the trail. She immediately left the trail and crept under some nearby bushes.

Amanda could hear voices, but she couldn't understand what they were saying from her position. She was too far away. She was so frightened, she was shaking all over. She was afraid to stay where she was, but she was even more afraid to move closer to the fire. She lay under the bushes for quite some time. It was so cold, she was shaking now from both fear and the cold.

Finally, she could stand it no longer. She very quietly crept forward, keeping near the ground, until she was closer to the firelight. She could see several men, she thought there were five of them, but she wasn't sure. She thought they were white men, but again, she couldn't be positive until she heard them speak. She wasn't close enough to see their faces and could only vaguely see their hair. Most of them had long hair, but that wasn't a determining factor since most men of the day wore their hair long. Also, most men, white and Indian, wore buckskins, so she couldn't tell from their clothing if it was safe to call out to them. Amanda was afraid to get any closer, so all she could do was wait.

About the time she was convinced they were white, she heard one of them call to one of the others. "Oh, no," she thought, "they aren't white, but I don't think they are Cherokee either." Their language sounded very different from the Cherokee tongue. Amanda slowly crept backwards away from the fire.

When Amanda thought she was far enough back not to be seen, she very carefully stood and made her way as quickly as she could away from the men at the fire. She stayed off the path and moved from tree to tree. She soon found herself at the three-way crossroads again. She chose the path straight forward this time. She wasn't completely sure where it would lead her, but she knew she would be able to tell better when it became daylight. All she could think of right then was putting as much distance as she could between herself and the men she had almost walked up on.

Amanda again walked through the night. When the sun started to rise, it rose to her right. If her calculations were correct, she was headed south. Amanda had no knowledge of what was south of the Cherokee town where she had been for over three months. She also had no idea how far she had traveled on foot after leaving Ninovan's house. Again, she was angry with herself for being so frightened when Waya brought her to the town. She was angry for not paying more attention to what direction they had come from and which direction they had gone.

Amanda began to look for a place to spend the day. Suddenly, she heard horses moving toward her from what she thought was the south. There was little cover near, so she moved as quietly as she could off the path toward the east. There were no bushes near, but there were plenty of large trees. Amanda squatted behind one of the largest oaks she could find making herself as small as possible. Again, she trembled with fear. Her only hope was that whoever was riding the horses would speak while she was in listening distance.

It seemed to Amanda that she squatted behind the tree for a long time, but in reality it was only a few minutes. She heard what she thought were several horses coming up the trail. She didn't hear the telltale jingle of harnesses or the sound of wagon wheels on the earth, so she assumed there were only riders in the group. She wanted so badly to stick her head out and look, but her fear kept her as close to the huge tree as she could get. The horse's hooves didn't make a lot of noise as they hit the hard packed trail. That made Amanda think the horses were unshod, probably Indian horses, then.

Amanda stayed hidden until she could no longer hear any sounds except the normal forest noises, the sound of the wind in the trees, night birds beginning to rustle again in their nests and the occasional bark of a fox or some other animal. She very slowly left her hiding spot and edged to the trail she had been walking on. She peered down the trail the way she had come from to see if anyone was still visible. She only caught the sight of the last horse's tail as it passed a bend in the trail. She didn't see a saddle, just the edge of a blanket on the horse's back. Definitely Indians then. Amanda was very glad she hadn't made her presence known.

Amanda wondered why so many Indians were about. At home, they rarely saw Indians at all. Sometimes in the small trading post close to their home, there would be a few Cherokee, but even that was rare. The Indians usually stayed quite a bit west of where the whites had settled in West Tennessee. Seeing so many Indians made Amanda think she was still quite a ways west of where she wanted to go. She was disheartened, but she was also even more determined to try to make her way home.

The sun was now completely up and it was full daylight. Amanda had to find a place to spend the day and soon. She eased her way through the woods toward the sun looking for any kind of shelter she could find. Finally, after over an hour of searching, Amanda found some thick catalpa bushes she could edge through, trying unsuccessfully not to catch her clothes or hair on the branches.

At last, she found a spot large enough to lie down in. There was a thick layer of leaf mold under the bushes that made a very comfortable bed. Amanda was worn out. The walking, as well as the jumps of adrenaline coursing through her body, not once, but twice during the night and very early morning had served to make Amanda beyond exhausted. She took a couple of strips of meat and some dried berries from her sack and ate them quickly. All she really wanted to do was sleep. She rolled herself in her cloak with her head on her bag and was soon deep in a dreamless sleep.

Chapter 10

Amanda awakened stiff and sore. She was extremely thirsty. She hadn't found water before she lay down and now her thirst was all she could think of. The sun was almost down, but it wasn't dark yet. However, the cold was worse this evening than it had been since she started her journey. The twilight sky was filled with dark menacing clouds. To Amanda, they looked like snow clouds. Since it was still February according to the calendar she had been keeping, snow was certainly not out of the question. It was surprising they had had so little snow so far this winter.

After waiting for dark to fall, Amanda edged out of her catalpa shelter and headed in the opposite direction from where the sun had set. After walking as fast as she could for what seemed hours, she finally found a small creek. As she was easing her way down the steep embankment of the creek, her right mocassin slipped from under her on the slick leaves and she felt herself falling. She tried to catch hold of one of the small shrubs that grew on the embankment to no avail.

Amanda's right hip struck the cold ground hard. Before she knew it, she started to roll towards the creek. She reached out blindly trying to stop her swift descent. The creek was only about ten feet wide, but Amanda had no way of knowing how deep it was. She couldn't swim and was deathly afraid of the water. Right before she hit the water, she was able to grasp a small bush. It stopped her descent, but she couldn't stop her feet from going into the freezing water.

Amanda quickly bent her knees pulling her feet up, but the damage was done. Her moccasins were soaked. As quickly as she could, she got onto her knees and scooped some of the cold water into her mouth. She drank until her stomach hurt.

When she had drunk her fill, she started looking for a way to climb back up. Then the thought hit her that she needed to cross this creek to continue in an easterly direction.

Figuring that her moccasins were already wet, Amanda decided to try to wade the creek. She looked for a limb to put into the water to try to gauge its depth. After ranging along the creek for quite some distance, she actually found a deadfall that went partially across the creek.

Amanda stepped on the fallen tree with one foot to test its strength. It held her slight weight without giving, so she brought her other foot up. There were still bare branches on the fallen tree. Amanda held onto the branches as she inched her way across the log. She would have to jump about four or five feet from the end of the tree to the bank of the creek. Amanda was very worried because as the fallen tree went across the creek, less and less of it was visible in the half darkness. She feared her weight would make the end of the log go under water, but there was nothing she could do, but go forward. Going back was out of the question now.

Just as Amanda was about to take the last step before trying to leap from the fallen tree to the bank, the part of the tree she was standing on dipped into the freezing water and the other end came up behind her. She went in up to her knees. This time, not only were her moccasins wet, but so were her leggings. Her teeth started to chatter and she shivered uncontrollably. Amanda stood in the freezing water for just a few seconds. She knew she had to take the chance and jump to the bank. There was no choice.

With a deep inhalation of breath, Amanda bent her knees and leapt towards the bank. Her left foot made it, but her right foot went into the creek. She fell forward onto her hands and knees, scrabbling to try to get up the bank. She caught hold of a small bush and pulled her weight up as far as she could. It was getting darker by the minute. Amanda couldn't see very well, but she pulled herself slowly up the embankment, bush by bush, anyway.

When her hand went over the edge, she let out a great sigh of relief. Amanda finally made it over the embankment and collapsed face down on the creek bank to catch her breath. Finally she sat up to assess the damage. Her moccasins and leggings were wet up to her knees. The bottom of her cloak was wet too. She couldn't chance trying to make a fire and besides, she didn't have any way to light one anyway.

Amanda stood and tried to brush off as many leaves, twigs and as much mud off her clothes as she could. She would just have to walk her clothes dry. She stared at the sky to try to determine which way she should head, but there was no moon. The sky was very dark as were the trees and bushes around her. When she could hesitate no longer, she just faced away from the creek and started to walk. Her wet moccasins rubbed her feet and she could feel blisters forming on her heels and some of her toes. Her leggings were weighing her down as was her wet cloak. She was already weakened from all the walking she had done on very slim rations for the past couple of days. It was her third night of walking and Amanda had no idea whether she was close to help or not.

Chapter 11

Amanda was very tired and discouraged, as well as being colder than she had ever been in her life. At this point, she was sorry she had decided to escape. If she was in the Cherokee town, she would be warm and dry in Ninovan's house. Her stomach wouldn't be empty and she wouldn't hurt in almost every part of her body. As she tramped through the thick woods, all she could think of was how miserable she was.

Just as the sky was beginning to lighten slightly, it started to snow. That was the last straw. Amanda felt the tears start and she couldn't stop them. "Now, I'm going to freeze to death." she thought. She couldn't stop yet, her moccasins, leggings and cloak were still very damp. Amanda was afraid to lay down yet for fear her clothes would freeze to her body.

There was no sun to guide her this morning. The sky was only a little lighter than it had been hours ago and the snow was getting harder. Just as Amanda was about to give up and just lie down where she was, she saw a cabin in the distance. The windows were dark and there was no smoke rising from the chimney, but it was the most beautiful sight Amanda had ever seen.

She approached the small cabin very cautiously. She knew Indians usually lived in towns or villages, not alone in the woods. She was fairly certain that whoever owned this cabin was a white person. Of course, that didn't exclude them from being dangerous. There were bad people of all races. She truly hoped whoever owned the cabin was gone, but had left some blankets or quilts behind. She needed to get out of her wet clothes and try to get dry before she froze.

There were no windows in the cabin to speak of. There was a small opening on each side that had shutters covering them on the inside. Amanda crept up to the opening closest to her and very carefully looked over the edge. It was even darker in the cabin and it smelled really bad. Whoever lived there was certainly not very clean.

Amanda wrinkled up her nose and tried not to be sick from the awful smell.

Finally, feeling totally desperate, Amanda walked around to the door and tried to open it. No matter how hard she pushed on the door, it wouldn't open. There must be a bar across the door or something was against it on the inside. Again, she went around to the window opening. The smell was just as bad as before. When Amanda pushed against the shutter, it gave some. That encouraged her to try even harder. She put both hands against the shutter and pushed with all her remaining strength. The shutter gave way and the splintered wood scraped her right arm painfully.

Amanda pulled her arm out of the shutter to assess the damage. Her shirt was torn and blood was running down her arm, but the cut didn't seem to be terribly deep although it hurt a lot. Now that the shutter was broken, Amanda had to find a way to climb into the opening. She tried to leverage her body into the opening by holding on to the sill and jumping as high as she could. That didn't work well at all, she was just too short.

Amanda walked around the little cabin looking for anything she could stand on to get her leg over the window sill. There was some wood stacked at the back of the cabin. Amanda took several pieces of what she assumed to be firewood and stacked it beneath the window. With the firewood stacked high, It looked like there was a stove or fireplace inside, and for that she was very grateful. She fearfully climbed onto the unsteady stack of wood and finally got her leg over the window sill. Even though she was small, her body barely fit through the opening even with a lot of wriggling.

When her feet touched the floor, Amanda gave a great sigh of relief. Finally she had found shelter from the snow. The interior of the cabin was quite dark. Amanda pulled the shutter she had come through open more fully. She was then able to see across the small room to the other shutter. She went to it and removing the piece of wood holding it closed, she swung that shutter open as well.

The two small openings provided her with enough light to see around the small cabin. It couldn't be more than ten feet by ten feet. The logs were not caulked very well and the cold wind whistled through them, as well as the window openings.

Amanda saw a crude table and a stool in the center of the room. On one wall, there were some cabinets and a dry sink.

When Amanda swung her eyes to the other wall, she uttered a sharp cry. There was someone lying on the bed. The bed was attached to the wall and was not very wide, although it was long. Whoever was in the bed didn't move when Amanda cried out. Amanda was very frightened. The shape under the bed covers looked quite large, but there was no movement from it at all. Amanda stood perfectly still for several minutes and then began to slowly edge back toward the window with the broken shutter.

At first all she could think of was escape. Suddenly, it hit Amanda that whoever was in the bed might be dead. The stench in the cabin was overpowering and there had been no sound or movement from the bed since she noticed it. She was afraid to go check, but the alternative, going back out into the snowstorm, was less attractive than looking under the covers on the bed.

Amanda crept toward the bed trying not to make any noise. She reached out her hand and very carefully pulled the covers back. She gasped and jumped back quickly. The man in the bed was definitely dead. His face was almost black and grotesquely swollen. Actually, his whole body was horribly swollen. Amanda had seen a dead person before, but not anyone who looked like this man. She had seen her grandmother's body when she died on the journey from Virginia to West Tennessee, but they had buried her right away. She and her sister Leticia had helped their mother bathe and dress their grandmother, crying the whole time.

Amanda backed up further until her leg touched the stool. Again, she jumped. When she looked down and saw what she had hit. She dropped down on the stool and buried her face in her hands. She was very upset at what she had just seen. Her eyes went back to the man's body almost against her will. She shuddered and wrapped her arms around her shivering body. Upon finding the man's body, she had forgotten how cold and wet she was.

Amanda knew she would have to get out of her wet clothes soon or she would become ill. She also knew she needed to get the man's body out of the cabin, the stench was incredible. However, she didn't quite know how she was going to accomplish that feat. She was small and the man on the bed looked quite large. There was a coarse sheet over the corn husk mattress on the bed under the man. There were what looked like two blankets and a patchwork quilt over him. She needed to figure out some way to get him off the bed and out from under the covers. She needed those covers and she needed them quickly no matter how badly they smelled.

Amanda first went to the door and took the wooden bar down that was holding the door closed. She opened the door just a little to let some of the awful smell out of the cabin. Then she slowly approached the bed again. She thought, "If I can just roll him out of the bed onto something, then maybe I can pull him outside. I know I can't lift him."

Amanda looked all over the cabin. She finally found another blanket. It was old and had holes in it, but she thought it would be alright for her need. She lay the blanket on the floor by the bed. Now the worst part was next. She carefully pulled the quilt and blankets from the man's body. When the covers came off, the smell of his decomposing body was more than she could take. Amanda ran outside and threw up over and over. Since she hadn't eaten much in the last three days, most of what she threw up was the creek water she had drunk. When her stomach finally stopped heaving, she sat on the cabin steps for just a few minutes. The snow was coming down even harder now. She had to get this done and it needed to be done now.

Amanda got control of herself and went back inside. She had dropped the covers on the floor in her headlong flight away from the smell. She picked them up and after shaking the dust out of them, lay them on the table. They smelled bad, but not as bad as the man did. She couldn't tell his age by looking at him because his face was so discolored, but from what she could see, he wasn't old. At least he didn't have gray hair. He was dressed in a calico shirt and buckskin pants. He definitely wasn't Indian because his hair was blonde. The clothes he wore weren't old and seemed to be in good shape.

Amanda approached the bed again. She reached over the man who was lying on his right side and grasped his shirt collar and the waist of his pants. She tugged and pulled and finally got him rolled over to the edge of the bed. He was so swollen she was afraid his skin might break when he hit the floor. She had the sudden thought that he might pop like a full tick and a hysterical laugh bubbled up in her throat. She fought down the laugh and the thought and rolled the man off the bed onto the old blanket.

His body hit with a loud plop. Amanda backed up quickly and headed for the door. She was barely able to stop herself from running out into the snowstorm again, she was so reviled by touching the dead man. The smell was even worse now. She looked at the bed again and saw that the coarse sheet under the man was stained and wet looking.

Amanda made herself go back over to the bed and taking just a tiny bit of the sheet corner, she pulled it off the bed and over the man's body. She was shaking from nerves and cold, but she knew she had to try to get the man out of the cabin quickly.

Amanda grabbed both corners of the old blanket near the man's head and pulled as hard as she could. She could barely get him to move. She tried again, leaning back as far as she could and slowly moving her feet toward the door in tiny steps.

When Amanda got to the threshold of the door, she edged her feet out onto the rickety steps. As she was stepping down, she lost her grip on the blanket and fell the last two steps to the ground. By now, she was so frustrated and upset, she was crying. Through her tears, she saw that she had moved the man almost far enough to get his head over the threshold. She climbed back up the three steps and grabbed the corners of the old blanket again. Amanda gave a mighty tug and the man's head came over the threshold. She moved down the steps, standing on the ground, and pulled as hard as she could.

The man's body came halfway down and his head lodged on the bottom step. He was half in and half out of the cabin. No matter how hard Amanda pulled she couldn't get him the rest of the way out. She sat down in the snow on the cold hard ground and just cried for a couple of minutes. Then she got up, went around to the window she had originally climbed through and climbed back into the cabin again.

She went to the man's body and grabbing the corners of the other end of the old blanket, she lifted the man's legs up and shoved with all her might. She was able to push the man's legs far enough to clear the doorway. Finally, he was out of the cabin although he wasn't far out of it. She knew she had to drag him farther from the cabin. Wolves or some other type of animal would smell him and she had no way to fight off an animal attack nor did she have the strength.

Amanda went down the rickety steps again. She grabbed the blanket corners again and pulled and pulled until she got the man several feet from the door. The sheet had partially come off the man's body. Trying not to touch anymore of it than she had to, she pulled the sheet over his body again. There were some low-growing evergreen bushes nearby. Amanda broke some branches off them and lay them over the man's body. The fresh smell of the evergreen gave her an idea.

When she was through piling as many branches as she could on the man's body, she gathered another armful of them and took them inside the cabin. She again barred the door and closed the shutters as best she could on the window openings. The shutter she had splintered, still hung partially open. She had to find something to put over it to keep as much warmth as possible in the cabin. The snowstorm still raged outside and the cabin was very cold.

Amanda looked around and finally found some clothes and rags in one of the cupboards. She took the rags and wedged them in the window opening along with the splintered shutter. She was able to block the wind at last. It was still quite dark in the cabin, but Amanda had noticed some matches and a coal oil lamp by the dry sink. After three tries because of her shaking hands, she was able to get the lamp lit.

Amanda gazed around the little cabin. There was a cast-iron cook stove in the corner. Amanda rushed to the stove and opened the door. It was filled with cold ashes. She frantically looked around for a bucket and shovel to remove the ashes. She found what she needed behind the woodbox. She had to get the stove lit as soon as possible. There was some wood in the woodbox, but only a few pieces. The wood outside was already wet with snow, but if she could get a good fire going, it would dry and burn.

As fast as she could, Amanda cleaned the ashes out of the stove. She didn't bother taking them outside. That could be done when she went out for more wood. Right now, the most important thing was getting a fire started and getting herself dry. She was still wearing very damp leggings, moccasins and a wet bedraggled fur cloak.

When Amanda looked for kindling, she didn't find any in the woodbox. She searched around the cabin for anything that would burn quickly to light the wood. She found some papers in one of the cupboards. She looked over them hurriedly. There seemed to be several letters from someone named Belinda. They would do. She put some of the paper in the bottom of the stove and took out the smallest piece of wood in the box. She found a knife in the dry sink and shaved some wood curls from the piece of wood. She leaned that piece of wood and another against each other over the paper. She lit the paper and fed the wood curls to the fire slowly while she blew gently on it.

When the two pieces of wood caught, Amanda watched it carefully still blowing gently on the flames. When she was sure the wood was well caught, she put another piece of wood in the stove. Finally after several minutes the little room started to warm. Amanda shrugged out of her cloak and hung it on a peg on the wall.

She looked through the clothes she had found earlier in the cupboard and found a shirt and pair of trousers. They looked way too big for her, but they were dry. She stripped out of her moccasins, leggings, skirts, and shirts and put the dry shirt on. It came past her knees. She pulled on the trousers and had to roll the cuffs up several times before she could walk in them. She didn't find any socks, but she did find a pair of shoes that were several times too big for her. She wrapped rags around her feet and slipped her small feet down in the huge shoes.

Amanda didn't want to touch the quilt or blankets, but she was still very cold. Finally, she took the quilt which had been on the very top of the dead man and wrapped it around her shoulders. She huddled in front of the stove on the stool until the fire started to burn down. She knew she had to go outside and get more wood. She couldn't let the fire die or she would die too.

There was a heavy buckskin coat hanging on a peg on the wall near where Amanda had hung her cloak. She took it down and shook the dust out of it. She put it on and her arms were several inches too short for the sleeves. Since she didn't have gloves, she decided not to roll the sleeves up, but use them as protection from the cold.

She found a hat near the coat and put that on as well. Now that Amanda was as well protected from the weather as she could possibly be, she took the bar off the door and taking the lamp, went outside to the wood pile. The snow was almost knee deep already around the little cabin. Holding on to the wall so she wouldn't get lost, she slowly made her way around to the back of the cabin for more wood.

When Amanda tried to pick up the pieces of firewood, the long sleeves of the coat proved to be an impossible impediment. She had to roll them up so she could use her hands. She stacked as much wood as she thought she could carry in one trip. Picking it up, she struggled against the wind and snow back to the front door. She left the wood on the steps and went back for more.

After five trips, Amanda thought she had enough wood to last through the day and night. She could get more tomorrow, she thought. It was a struggle to get all the wood into the house. There was too much for the woodbox, so she just stacked it on the floor near the stove. The fire had burned down a lot so Amanda put two more pieces of the dry wood on first and then two pieces of the wet wood. It took several minutes for the wet wood to catch, but the dry wood was blazing quickly from the hot coals.

Amanda's feet were wet again. She took off the big shoes and unwrapped her little feet. They were bright red and aching with cold. She sat on the stool in front of the stove and held her feet up to the fire to warm them. Her feet were very painful as they warmed, but she kept them in front of the fire. She couldn't afford to let her feet get frostbite.

Amanda knew she couldn't stay at the cabin forever. Someone would find her from the telltale smoke coming from the chimney. She would stay until the snowstorm was over and then try to head east again. Right now, though, she was warm and safe from the storm. However, her stomach was grumbling loudly. She had to get some food into her noisy belly.

There was no water in the cabin, but there was plenty of snow outside. Amanda took a pot and unlatched the door. All she had to do was bend over and scoop snow into the pot. The snow was up to the second step now. Amanda feared she might get stuck in the cabin if the snow covered the door. "Oh, well," she thought, "if I can't get out, then nobody else is going to be able to get in. I will be safe for a little while."

Amanda found her bag and put some of the dried meat into another pot with some of the snow. She set the pot on the stove and waited eagerly for it to heat. She knew the broth would be good for her and she really craved something hot right now. While Amanda was waiting for her meal to cook, she took some of the evergreen branches she had brought in and lay them on the soiled mattress. They would help cover some of the stench and give her a place to rest later.

Taking one of the blankets that had covered the man, she lay it on the evergreen branches. Then Amanda took the other blanket and the quilt and wrapped them around herself. She was finally beginning to feel warm. She wrapped some more of the rags around her feet when her meal was ready and sat on the stool in front of the fire enjoying her soup. She ate all the meat and drank the broth. It didn't taste the best in the world, but it was hot and filling.

When Amanda's hunger was sated, she set about taking stock of what was in the cabin that she could use. There were some canned beans in one of the cupboards along with coffee, flour, salt, lard, and a good sized hunk of somewhat moldy bacon. Amanda scraped the mold off the bacon and wrapped it in one of the rags she soaked in melted snow water. She hoped that would help to keep it edible for awhile.

Not knowing how long the storm would last, Amanda decided to ration her food like she had done when she was walking. She would eat only once a day, but she would drink a lot of the melted snow. She hadn't been drinking nearly enough water lately and she knew she needed it. Amanda found a coffeepot in another cupboard. She didn't really care for the taste of coffee, but she made a pot anyway. She knew the coffee would help her to stay awake.

She needed to be alert enough to keep the fire fed. She couldn't allow it to go out or she might freeze since the cabin was so draughty. There was wind and snow coming through the walls at an alarming rate. Amanda looked for something she could stuff in the biggest cracks. She still had some of the rags left and several of the letters from Belinda. She decided to keep some of the paper just in case the fire went out and put it into the dry woodbox. The wet rags she had had on her feet when she went for the firewood would work well in the larger cracks. She could tear up some of the paper for some of the smaller ones.

When Amanda was done filling as many cracks as possible, the cabin became even warmer. She could finally take off the heavy buckskin jacket. Because the walls still weren't airtight, Amanda hesitated to hang the coat back on the peg on the wall, so she lay it on the bed. She had taken special care with the cracks over and around the bed. She needed a dry place to sleep, when she finally let herself sleep. Also, she took her fur cloak down and draped it over the table, pulling the table nearer the fire to help dry it. She had already placed her leggings and moccasins in front of the fire to dry. She knew they would be very stiff when they dried out, but she had no choice in the matter. She would just have to wear them until they softened again. She knew she wouldn't get far wearing the man's over-sized shoes when she left the cabin.

There was no real way to judge the time, but Amanda thought it must be late afternoon or early evening by now. The snowstorm showed no signs of letting up. Amanda had done all she could to make her shelter as snug as possible. All her wet clothes were beginning to dry, her stomach was full, and she was warm. She sat on the stool in front of the stove and drank cup after cup of the bitter coffee. She wished the man had had some sugar or molasses. Either would have made the coffee more palatable.

Now that Amanda had some time to think, she worried about being discovered in the cabin. If someone found her, she would be trapped with no way to defend herself if they meant her harm. There was a long rifle hanging on the wall above the door, but she had never shot one. She didn't even know how to load the rifle or how to shoot it.

Amanda had watched her father and brothers load their rifles before a hunting trip, but she hadn't paid close attention. She knew her mother knew how to use the rifle. Her father had made sure she could defend their home while he and the others were away hunting or trading in town. There was always the possibility of an Indian raid or wild animals threatening their isolated farm and livestock. As Amanda sat in front of the fire, she thought back over the past few years.

Chapter 12

Amanda had lived in West Tennessee for nine of her sixteen years. The Whitford family had lived in Virginia prior to coming further west. They had a farm there as well. Amanda's grandfather, Douglas Whitworth, had a pioneering spirit. He had come to Virginia from New Jersey when that state became more populated than he liked. He and his wife, Rebecca, had ten children, six boys and four girls. Amanda's father, John, was one of his oldest children. When John married Rhoda Chisum, they built a house on some of Douglas's land just as all his children had. Douglas believed in keeping his family close.

When Douglas decided to come to West Tennessee, Amanda's family, as well as all his other adult children and their families, came as well. Even some of Douglas's brothers and their families came along. Douglas sold his land in Virginia to finance the trip. He then laid claim to several hundred acres and parceled it out to his married children to farm. John and Rhoda had a parcel of one hundred and twenty acres. Most of the land was still wooded. Clearing land was a slow process in the 1800's. Trees had to be felled, stumps burned and then dug out. Since the area, known as the West Tennessee Highlands, was heavily wooded and hilly, clearing it for farming was a daunting task.

So far, John, his few slaves, and his children had only been able to clear seventy acres to farm, as well as the two acres the house, family garden, barn, and outbuildings lay on. John had built a large house out of some of the trees they had felled. Two of his slaves were skilled in planing lumber, so their house had finished wooden walls, not rough, hard to seal, logs. "Wood was free after all, so why not use it", he thought. The house had six bedrooms to help accommodate his large family. John and Rhoda had ten children already and Rhoda was carrying the eleventh when Amanda was stolen by Waya and his friends.

The two oldest boys, John Jr. and Jesse, were married with small families of their own. They lived on adjoining acreage near their parents. Leticia was the oldest at home, followed by Amanda, then the boys had started to come one after the other. The last six were all boys. That was a great help on the farm. The girls, along with the two female slaves, and their mother took care of the youngest boys, Jimmy and Henry, the livestock, the family garden, and the house while John, his other three slaves, and his older sons took care of the farming. John and the boys did the hunting. The family lived on deer, squirrels, rabbits, and wild turkeys for most of the year. In the fall, as the ducks and geese migrated south, they enjoyed dining on water fowl as a break from their regular diet.

The Whitworths raised almost everything they ate. They traded their farm produce for the few things they couldn't raise or make, like coffee, flour, and sugar. They had a hard life, but it was a good one. They believed very firmly in God. Although there was no church or preacher near, every Sunday John would gather his family and slaves and read them passages from the Bible. Sunday was also considered a day of rest, except for the absolutely necessary chores like cooking, feeding livestock, gathering eggs, and milking their three cows. Those chores, usually done by the females of the family, were shared on Sunday and therefore were done quickly.

In the afternoons, the family would gather on their big porch, if the weather was good, and enjoy listening to John and Rhoda tell stories about their lives in Virginia or how they met. Rhoda was an inveterate reader. They didn't have many books, but every Sunday afternoon, Rhoda would take out one of them and read a few chapters to the assembled family and slaves. If the weather was bad, they would all gather in the large living room for some of the same.

The Whitworths were also a very musical family. John played the guitar, Rhoda the piano, and three of the slaves had crude instruments as well. One, Aloyisus, had made himself a flute out of a piece of cane. He would blow on the flute while moving his fingers over the holes he had drilled in the cane. The children were always amazed at the wonderful music he could coax from that simple piece of cane.

Another of the slaves, old Ben, had a banjo and Abraham had a guitar. Rhoda was teaching the girls to play the piano, but only Leticia was really gifted. Amanda loved music and had a lovely singing voice as did her youngest brother, Jimmy. Jimmy had just turned eight, so his voice hadn't changed yet. He had a high pure tenor voice which blended very well with Amanda's alto. The family spent many happy hours playing and singing together.

As Amanda sat ruminating about her family, tears streamed down her face. She missed her parents and siblings. She missed the slaves who were like her aunts and uncles. John had owned all five of his slaves since before Amanda was born. She had never known life without Dulcey and Mary or the men. They were a part of her family. She sat crying for several minutes. Finally, she dried her eyes and began to make plans for when the snowstorm ended.

Amanda was so very tired. Her head began to droop and her heavy eyes closed. The cold woke her. "Oh, no," she thought, 'I've let the fire die. I hope I have more dry wood to restart it."

Luckily for Amanda, the fire wasn't completely out. There were still some very hot coals in the bottom of the stove. She stirred them and tented two dry pieces of wood over them. After adding a little paper to the coals, they flamed up and caught the wood on fire. Amanda tended the fire carefully until she had it roaring again.

Although Amanda had decided to ration her food by only eating once per day, her stomach was growling ferociously. She decided to open a can of the beans and add it to the dried venison soup like she had made before. Her mother, Rhoda, had been teaching she and Leticia to cook since they were little girls. Amanda knew she could brown some of the flour in a little lard and make a thickening for her soup that would also add a lot of flavor. She also knew she needed the fat from the lard as she had been losing weight at an alarming rate since she started on this journey. She got busy and made her roux from lard and flour. She let the flour brown slowly, then added some of the dried venison and melted snow water. After the mixture was bubbling nicely, she opened one of the cans of beans with the knife and added it to the pot. Soon, she had a mouth-watering smell going in the little cabin.

After eating her fill, Amanda still had enough of her concoction for another meal. Since her recipe had made enough for two meals, she didn't feel as bad about breaking her own rule of one meal per day.

After her little nap and her tasty dinner, Amanda felt much better, except for her arm. She had ignored the cut on her arm from the broken shutter until now. It was starting to hurt. When she rolled up her shirt sleeve, she noticed the cut was now red and inflamed looking. All she needed was an infection to go along with her other problems.

She heated water and cleaned the cut well with one of the rags she had washed out earlier. She had found a little lye soap in a dish in the cupboard and used that as well. It really hurt to vigorously wash the cut, but she knew she had to make sure all the small wood chips were cleaned out of it. When she was done, the skin around the cut was a bright pink and it stung badly, but Amanda knew such treatment was necessary to keep away an infection. She wished she had some honey to put on it. Honey was the best thing she knew to keep away infection in cuts. Instead, she spread a little lard on it and wrapped the cut with a clean rag.

Chapter 13

With all the activity Amanda had been doing, she hadn't thought about the snowstorm since she had awakened. Suddenly, she noticed the wind wasn't howling anymore. She went to the unbroken shutter and pulled it open a couple of inches. The snow was still falling, but much slower than before. Even though it was night now, the sky looked a tiny bit lighter too. Amanda had hopes that the storm was almost over. From what she could see from the window opening, there was a good two or three feet of snow on the ground.

The thought of trying to trudge through that much snow made Amanda feel tired already. She knew she needed to move only at night for fear of being found on the trail with no place to hide. She decided to stay in the cabin tonight and through tomorrow when she would build up the fire as much as possible and sleep. If the storm was really over, maybe the sun would come out tomorrow and melt some of the snow. If so, she would leave the cabin tomorrow night right after dark.

With that thought in mind, Amanda began to gather up everything she could think of to help her on her journey. She found an old canvas sack that looked like it had possibly been used for hunting squirrels or rabbits. The inside had dried stains that might be blood. Amanda heated some more water and set the canvas bag to soak. She didn't want to put her food in a dirty bag.

She gathered all the food she could find in the cabin. Amanda scrubbed the canvas bag and put it on the top of the stove draped over a pot to dry. Then she decided she needed to at least try to load the long rifle. If she had that and the large knife she had found, she would feel much better on the trail. Amanda had found a shot bag in one of the corners. From her first cursory look, it seemed to have a good supply of powder and shot in it.

She had to stand on the stool to take the rifle down from its place above the door. Amanda took it to the table and lay it down beside the shot bag. She brought the stool over and sat down taking the rifle into her lap. She looked over the rifle noting the flintlock and the pan. The pan was where the firing powder was put and the flintlock was the firing mechanism which lit the powder in the pan and then in the barrel, pushing the shot out of the barrel at a great speed.

Amanda shut her eyes and imagined her father loading his long rifle at the family table. She could see him putting the powder in the end of the barrel, then the wadding and then the shot. Then he would ram it all down with the long rod that was stored beside the barrel. He would take a little powder and put it in the pan and then half cock the rifle. When he was ready to shoot, he would fully cock the flintlock, aim and fire.

Amanda looked in the shot bag and there was a powder horn, some squares of wadding, and several pieces of shot. She was worried about how much powder to put in the barrel and the pan. Then, she saw something else in the bag. There was a small cylindrical object. Amanda picked it up and looked closely at it. The object was about four inches long. It had an opening on one end. She tried to see if there was anything in the small tube. She couldn't see anything, but when she raised the tube to her eye, as it passed her nose, she smelled gun powder.

Amanda knew her father didn't measure his powder, but maybe some men did. It sure looked like the tube was used to put the right amount of powder in the barrel. She decided to try it. She poured powder into the open end of the tube then carefully poured it into the rifle barrel. She took a square of wadding and fit it over the barrel. She put the shot in the middle of the wadding and pushed it into the barrel as far as she could.

It was not easy. The fit was very tight and Amanda struggled for a couple of minutes to push it down past the barrel opening. She pulled the rod out and put it into the rifle barrel. Standing, she pushed down on the rod as hard as she could holding it with both hands while gripping the rifle with her knees while the stock sat on the floor, as she had seen her father do. It took her several hard pushes to get the rod all the way in. After removing and storing the rod, she held the rifle across her body and pulled the flintlock half way back. She poured a very small amount of powder in the pan. Now the rifle was ready to be fully cocked and fired. At least that is what Amanda hoped. There was no way to be sure without actually firing it.

Amanda took the rifle to the corner nearest the door and stood it up, leaning it against the wall. She took the shot bag and hung it on a nail close to the rifle, making sure the wall was dry there. She was as ready as she would ever be if trouble came.

It took Amanda another couple of hours to gather everything she was taking with her. The canvas bag was nowhere near dry, so she put all her supplies on the table. She had found two sets of clothes in the cupboard. One she was wearing and the other she was taking. She was going to put her buckskin shirts, skirts, and leggings on over the calico shirt and trousers. Everything was dry now, but her leggings and moccasins were very stiff. She took some of the lard and worked it into the leggings and moccasins to soften them up.

The leggings would help to hold the trousers up under her skirts. They were much too big in the waist as well as much too long. Amanda didn't find a belt or any rope in the cabin. Finally, in desperation, she tore some of the rags into strips and braided them together for a belt. She could put it through the trousers belt loops and tie it tightly around her waist. The legs, she would just roll up so they just touched her moccasins. She didn't want sagging trousers slowing her down if she had to get off the trail in a big hurry.

She planned to put the buckskin coat on over all that and the cloak over the coat. She knew she would feel like a stuffed sausage, but at least she would have a better chance to fight the cold temperatures. She realized now she had not had nearly enough clothes on to protect her from the February temperatures. Even being physically active, by travelling at night when it was coldest, she had almost ended up with frostbite on her hands and feet. There were no gloves in the cabin nor socks. Again, the rags came in handy. She could wrap her feet in two or three layers of rags before she put on her moccasins. As for gloves, she could wrap strips of rags around her hands. It wasn't a perfect solution, but it could work. She decided to braid her hair atop her head to help hold the hat on. It was also too large.

When Amanda was finally satisfied with all her preparations, she added as much wood to the fire as the stove would hold and readied the bed for some sleep. She had spread the evergreen branches on the mattress. She put one blanket on top of the branches and covered herself with the other blanket, the quilt, and her fur cloak. She hadn't removed any of her clothes and had kept the rags wrapped around her feet. She wasn't very comfortable with all that on, but she was warm.

As Amanda was trying to go to sleep, she thought again of Waya and the other people she had met in the Cherokee town. She hadn't been mistreated by anyone there. As a matter of fact, Ninovan had treated her very well, especially after Amanda learned to speak a bit of the language. Ninovan hadn't treated her as an enemy, but rather as something of a friend. Amanda had been given jobs to do around the little house and around the camp. When she did her work well, Ninovan would let her know and vice versa, but she had never been abused in any way, not even verbally.

The treatment Amanda had received at the hands of the Cherokee was not the reason she had fled in the night. It was the upcoming marriage to Waya that had lead her to try to find her way home. Waya had never treated her badly. Actually, he had been very kind to her. The way he looked at her made her think he cared about her, but Amanda felt she was much too young to marry. When Waya would visit her at Ninovan's house, he would sometimes touch her hand or her face. It made her very uncomfortable, as did the look on his face when he did it. She wasn't afraid of him, but she was afraid of what he would expect of her when they married. She didn't really know exactly what happened when two people married, other than that they lived together and had babies. Of course, being raised on a farm, she was not ignorant of the act of breeding. However, she had no idea how humans accomplished that feat. Her mother had never told her anything at all. What she had learned from her sister, Letitia, had been limited. It was mostly the romantic part of being married, the kissing and touching that Letitia had dwelled on. The actual act, although Letitia had told her the basics, was still a very big mystery to Amanda.

She and Leticia would sometimes talk about what it would be like when they married, but they never went much further than talking about kissing. True, Leticia had told her what their mother had explained about a wife's duties, but they only spoke of it once because Amanda got so disgusted. She just didn't want to hear about the private part of marriage. Mostly their discussions centered on the kind of house they would have, where they would live, and how they might get along with their husband's family.

Amanda had seen one of their cousins kissing a boy a couple of years ago. Not much later their cousin, Mary, had married the boy and they had moved into their own little house on his father's farm. To Amanda's innocent mind, if you kissed a boy, you would marry him. She also knew that babies came after marriage too. Mary had had a sweet little boy about a year after she was married. Both Leticia and Amanda wanted to have children some day too. Neither of the girls had been allowed into the room when their mother was having their younger siblings, but they could hear her moan and sometimes scream. Just the thought that having babies caused their mother that much pain was enough to make Amanda leery of getting married and having babies herself right now. Amanda just knew she wasn't ready for any of that. Therefore, she had to try to get home where her father would protect her and she wouldn't have to worry about getting married for a couple of years yet.

Amanda also knew how her family and all the other people she knew felt about Indians. No one she knew was married to an Indian. Most white people who had settled in West Tennessee were afraid of the Indians. They told terrible stories about how Indians would kill the men and steal the women and children when they raided. They said the women and children were never seen again. Amanda had heard her own mother say she would rather be dead than taken by the Indians. They made living with the Indians sound like a fate worse than death.

Most people called all Indians dirty. Amanda knew that wasn't true. The Cherokee town where she had spent the last weeks was kept clean, as were the people and their homes. Amanda wondered if her family and others had ever really been to an Indian town. Now that she had spent some time in one, she didn't understand their calling them dirty, but then maybe they didn't mean that kind of dirty. She had also heard her father refer to some whites as dirty white trash. She had seen some of the houses of those people during their travels from Virginia and also when they went to the little town, Paris, the closest nearby for supplies.

She understood what he meant about them. Their houses were run down and trash was strewn around them. Nobody seemed to be doing any work when they would pass those houses. Mostly, they just all sat around on their sagging porches and eyed the people passing by. Her father said they were lazy and no good.

She could understand his attitude towards that type of person, but he also said Indians were lazy and no good. Amanda didn't know about all Indians, but where she had been living, no one was lazy and she hadn't seen any sign of anyone doing bad things either. The Indian families she had seen worked hard to provide food for their families and treated each other with respect. Amanda was very confused. Finally, she was able to fall asleep.

Chapter 14

When Amanda woke several hours later, the fire was almost out in the stove. She built it up just enough to make herself some more bean and dried venison stew. She ate all of it this time, although it made her feel really full. She knew it might be a long time before she had hot food again. She also made a pot of coffee and drank as much of it as she could. It would help to keep her warm when she started out as well as keeping her alert. It was still very cold, but the snow had stopped and the sun had melted much of it. The last vestiges of the sun going down in the west could still be seen when she opened the shutter on the window opening. At least she now knew what direction east was and would walk in that direction when she left.

She was taking the matches she had found and some of the letters for kindling, but wasn't sure she would feel safe lighting a fire on the trail. Her biggest fear was being discovered and taken back to Waya's town or being caught by another tribe of Indians. The Cherokee weren't the only tribe in the area and the other tribes might not be as kind.

The canvas sack was dry. After eating, Amanda loaded everything she could into the sack. It was heavy, but not so heavy she couldn't carry it slung over her shoulder. She needed the other hand for the rifle. She put the big knife she had found in the cabin into her braided rag belt under her deerskin shirt. She still had the little knife Waya had given her too.

When Amanda had pulled on her leggings and moccasins, donned the deerskin shirts and skirts, the heavy deerskin coat and her fur cloak, she felt like she weighed an extra fifty pounds. However, she also knew she would be a lot warmer on the trail. She poured the last of the coffee on the fire to put it out. She didn't want the little cabin that had sheltered her so well to burn because of a stray spark. Some other traveller might be able to use it in the future.

She had rolled both blankets and the quilt together and tied them with more braided rags. Amanda knew she needed to take them with her. She wasn't sure how she was going to carry them along with everything else. Then the idea hit her she could drape them around her neck. They would give added warmth by covering the space between her jacket collar and her hat.

When all was said and done, Amanda firmly shut the little cabin's door and headed east again. She had food, bedding, and weapons now. She felt very positive about her ability to find her family or someone who could help her get home. There was no path heading east from the cabin so Amanda just wended her way through the trees in that direction.

After travelling for several hours, Amanda was tired, but not nearly as tired as she had been before finding the cabin. For one thing, she was warmer and better fed than she had been. She also had more confidence because of the weapons. Before she had been not only shivering with cold, but also fear. Amanda knew if she was caught by anyone, she would have been helpless to defend herself.

Amanda stopped to rest near a small creek. She drank her fill and ate some dried berries. She planned to eat a larger meal when she stopped to rest for the day, but just needed a snack to give her a little extra energy. After resting for about half an hour, Amanda started through the woods again. There was a moon tonight which helped her to find her way.

When the sky began to lighten, Amanda started to look for a place to hide for the day. The area she was in was heavily wooded and the terrain was rolling. She looked around, but didn't see any bushes she could crawl into. She kept going. There was little else she could do. She had to be hidden during the daylight hours.

Amanda began to hurry now because the sun was starting to come up in front of her. She topped a rise and saw some bushes off to the left. It was a small stand of rhododendrons. She hurried toward them as fast as she could. As she began to crawl through the thick rhododendrons, the scaly underside of the leaves caught at her hat and clothes. Amanda took the time to try to pull the stalks back upright to hide her trail the best she could. The bushes were blooming and although there was little fragrance, the bright pink color was beautiful.

Amanda crawled into the center of the small stand of rhododendrons. There was little room between the thick stalks, but she wallowed out a place to lie down the best she could. She wanted to get her bed made and her food ready as quickly as possible. She knew her movements under the bushes could be easily detected from the movement of the tops. Amanda wanted to take no chances.

As soon as her bed and food were ready, Amanda lay down and ate in that position. She moved as little as possible as she ate her cold beans and dried venison. She finished her meal with a handful of dried strawberries. Replete and comfortable, it wasn't long before Amanda was asleep.

Chapter 15

Just a couple of hours after she had fallen asleep, Amanda was startled awake by a noise near her hiding place. She carefully picked up the rifle. Raising up very slowly on her elbow, she aimed the rifle where she had heard the noise. She could detect a shadow right at the edge of her hiding place. She listened very carefully, but couldn't hear anything. She stayed as still as she could.

The shadow moved suddenly and Amanda could not control a quick intake of breath. The shadow stopped and moved back nearer to her hiding place. Had he heard her? Amanda held her breath as long as she could and then let it out very slowly and as inaudibly as she could. The shadow stood there for what seemed hours, but was actually about five minutes. Then the shadow moved away to the right. Amanda was very frightened. She had tried to conceal her entry point into the rhododendron stand, but she wasn't sure she had been totally successful. The stalks were probably still somewhat bent where she had entered.

Amanda stayed in her position until her elbow ached and her whole arm started to tremble uncontrollably. She knew the movement would make it easier for her to be found, so she very slowly lay all the way down. She didn't relinquish her hold on the rifle though. She took slow deep breaths and tried to calm her rattled nerves. This was the closest she had come to being found. Amanda had no idea who or what the shadow was. She couldn't be sure it was even human. She thought all the bears were still hibernating now, but she wasn't sure. Whatever it was, it stood upright and moved quietly. She was almost sure it was an Indian. A white man would have most likely been wearing boots. Boots made a lot more noise than moccasins.

Amanda lay in her bed with the rifle laying on top of her for a long time. She didn't dare move, even though holding the rifle was making her arms ache. She had used her bag as a pillow, but her shot bag was lying beside her close to where the rifle had been. She would probably only have one shot because she was so frightened she couldn't remember exactly how to load the rifle. She doubted she would have time to reload even if she could remember how.

The waiting was making Amanda very nervous. She listened as hard as she could, but didn't hear anything else. Finally, after about an hour, she had to relax her arms and let the rifle rest against her stomach. Suddenly someone was crashing through the rhododendron stand from the other end.

Amanda quickly rose up on her knees and tried to turn the rifle toward the threat.

The rifle was long and she couldn't turn it from her kneeling position. She rose to her feet and swung the rifle as quickly as she could. There was an Indian just a few feet from her. He had a tomahawk in his hand. She didn't recognize him or the way he was dressed. He didn't look like any of the Cherokee she had seen. He had a band around his short hair with a single feather sticking in the front. He was much shorter than the Cherokee she was used to. His skin was almost the same color, but his face was longer and thinner.

Without further thought, Amanda pulled the flintlock back all the way, aimed the rifle right at him and pulled the trigger. There was a loud explosion and when the smoke cleared, Amanda saw the Indian looking down at his chest where there was a large hole with blood running out of it. He looked up at her with a most curious expression on his face. Then he looked down at his chest again. He took two more steps toward her and went to his knees.

Amanda was in a state of shock at what she had done. When the man took those last two steps, it galvanized her into action. She reached down and grabbed her shot bag and the canvas bag, leaving her bedding. She turned around and ran as fast as the thick plants would allow. She cleared the rhododendron thicket and kept running back the way she had come.

She kept looking back at the man she had shot, but he was still on his knees and wasn't moving. The last time she looked back he had fallen forward. When Amanda turned her head again, she ran right into another man. She jerked her head up and was horrified to see the face of the man she had been trying to escape for the last four days. She pulled back as hard as she could to no avail.

Waya wrapped his arms around her and pulled her back against his chest. Her arms were pinned down as was the rifle. Amanda didn't know if she would have been able to load and fire it at Waya anyway. Right now, she was actually strangely relieved to see him. When Waya turned his head and spoke, she looked quickly to see who was with him. She saw Mohe and several other men she had seen in the Cherokee town.

Amanda's relief was short lived. She was caught. All she had gone through and she was caught. She began to cry hysterically and try to break away from Waya. There was no way she could break his hold.

Waya just held her tightly and spoke quietly to her. When she finally calmed down, she realized he was trying to comfort her. He thought she was upset about the Indian man she had shot. She almost laughed when she realized what he was saying, but thought better of it. Waya led her to where his horse, as well as others, was being held by a young Indian boy, Adahy.

Waya picked up Amanda and handed her to Mohe. He jumped up on his horse and she was handed up to him. He placed her on the horse and wrapping his long arms around her, he guided the horse back west. Amanda's whole body drooped with sadness. She had tried so very hard to get home. There was no way to know how close she had come. She knew better than to ask Waya or any of the others.

As they rode toward the Cherokee town, Amanda wondered what her punishment for escaping would be. In the time she had lived among the Indians, she had not seen anyone punished for anything except a few small children for minor transgressions, like not obeying immediately or not doing their chores well. Amanda knew what she had done was much, much worse. She had stolen food and furs and tried to return to her own people. They might kill her now, or at the very least, she would probably be beaten.

The trip back only took the rest of that day and part of the night. They arrived back in the Cherokee town late and everyone had already gone to bed. Waya slid off his horse still holding Amanda. She had fallen asleep several hours ago.

Waya was sad that his Ah-man-da had run away from him. He wanted her to care for him as he cared for her. He didn't understand what he had done to make her want to leave. He had tried to talk to her on the trip back, but she wouldn't speak to him. She just kept her head down and occasionally he would feel her tears fall on his arms or hands. Finally a few hours ago, her head had become heavy and she had leaned against him and went to sleep.

He loved this small white woman so much. He didn't know how to show her how he felt. He didn't have words to explain it to her. Maybe Mohe could help him to know what to say to her. Right now, he was tired, as were they all. He carried the sleeping Amanda to his mother's house. She had heard them ride in and was waiting by the door when he arrived. She pulled back the deer hide door covering and waved him in.

Waya took Amanda to her pile of furs and lay her down. She rolled over and curled into a ball like a small child. He pulled furs over her and walked out the door. His mother was waiting for him.

"You have been gone long my son. Ah-man-da had gotten far?"

"We found her this morning when she shot a Chickasaw with one of the white man's long rifles. I don't know where she got the rifle or how she knew how to shoot it, but he had found her hiding place in some bushes and was coming at her with a tomahawk. She jumped up out of the bushes and turned around and shot him right in the middle of the chest. She just stood there at first, but when he took another step toward her, she turned and ran like the wind. She ran right into me because she was looking back to see if he was following. At first it looked like she was glad to see me, but then she started to cry and it took her a long time to stop. Actually, she cried quietly for hours on our trip home."

"She misses her family. I have told you that, but you would not hear me. I have heard her cry many nights since you stole her away. She is a white woman, not a Cherokee. She doesn't want to be here. She wants to go home."

Waya didn't want to hear his mother's words. He knew that Ah-man-da wanted to go home, but he was convinced she would grow accustomed to the Cherokee way of life and be content to stay with them in time. In his mind, if they could just get married, he could make her want to stay. He would treat her well. She would soon learn to love him like he loved her.

Waya looked at his mother sadly and said, "I know this, but she will get used to us, to me, in time. We must get married now. I don't want to wait until the spring to marry Ah-man-da. I can guard her better after we are married."

"No, Waya, the grandmother has decided. There will be no marriage until the Spring First Moon Ceremony." Ninovan saw how this upset Waya, but there was nothing to be done. When the grandmother decided the date of a wedding, it could not be changed. To placate him, she said, "I will watch over her the best I can. Now it is less than two moons."

Waya was not happy with his mother's words, but he also knew changing the grandmother's mind was next to impossible. He would just have to try harder to make Ah-man-da be content here. His mother's next words surprised him very much.

"What punishment will you give the white woman?"

"Punishment? I had not thought to punish her at all. I am proud of her spirit. If you could have seen her when she shot the Chickasaw, you would have been proud of her too. She was very frightened, but she didn't drop the rifle. As a matter of fact, she reached down and grabbed the bag with the rifle supplies and another bag she had with her before she ran. She will make a fine wife for me. Her spirit is almost equal to mine."

Ninovan just shook her head. Her son was much too full of himself. She hoped Ah-man-da would take him down a notch or two when they married. Apparently, the girl had more spirit than she had exhibited before. Ninovan would indeed watch her much more closely in the future.

Chapter 16

Amanda awoke the next day expecting to be punished severely for running away. When nothing happened that day, she became even more afraid. Ninovan treated her much as she had before, only seeming to watch her more closely when they were not in the house. Nothing was said about the four days she had been gone. Waya did not come to Ninovan's house at all in the first few days after her return.

She also didn't see Mohe nor Tsula for those days either. She missed seeing Tsula. They had become close during the time she had been living with Ninovan. They saw each other almost every day. Amanda had become very fond of Tsula's children as well. She missed seeing them, but was afraid to ask Ninovan if she could visit at Mohe and Tsula's house.

On the fifth day after Waya brought her back to Ninovan's house, he came to eat with them for the evening meal. Waya acted like nothing had happened at first. Amanda was still quite frightened about what her punishment for running away would be. She said little and kept her head bowed when Waya first came in. As usual, she and Ninovan had cooked the meal together. There was fresh venison which Amanda had roasted slowly over the fire after rubbing it with herbs. Ninovan had cooked some squash with herbs and had even made a corn pudding with dried berries and nuts sweetened with honey.

Ninovan hadn't told her that Waya was coming to eat with them. She should have known because of the amount of food they had cooked. They generally only cooked enough for the two of them. There was rarely anything left over. Amanda had discovered that the Indians didn't waste food. They cooked only enough at each meal to appease their hunger. They rarely filled their stomachs completely full as the whites did most of the time. Amanda had thought they had cooked such a large piece of venison to store the remainder for the next day.

The pudding should have been her biggest clue. Although she loved anything sweet, she knew that Waya was very partial to sweet things. Ninovan, however, rarely partook of any sweets herself other than a handful of dried berries as a snack sometimes.

When the meat was done, Amanda took her small knife and cut off a good portion, putting it in Waya's bowl. She passed the bowl to Ninovan and she added a large portion of the squash to it, handing it to Waya. Waya had seated himself between his mother and Amanda at their fire. They had served him first as was the custom. Amanda then cut off a small portion of the meat for Ninovan and herself. She handed their bowls to Ninovan who added squash to them. She took the bowl Ninovan handed her and quietly ate her meal. Amanda didn't see Ninovan and Waya exchanging worried glances over her bent head. It was very quiet in the house as the three people ate.

When Waya was finished he set his bowl next to the fire. Ninovan picked his bowl up and added the corn pudding to it. He said, "Corn pudding, thank you mother. You know how much I like this dish. Amanda, don't you like this dish as well?"

Amanda had been so busy worrying about her punishment, she didn't hear his question at first. She sensed that something was wrong and looked up suddenly.

Ninovan said, "Did you not hear Waya, Ah-man-da? He asked you a question."

Both of them could see the fear on Amanda's face as she looked quickly from one of them to the other. "No," she said tremulously, "I didn't hear him. I'm very sorry. What did he say?"

Waya looked at her with concern, "It wasn't anything very important. I just asked if you liked this corn pudding my mother has made. I thought you liked sweet things."

Amanda had been almost cowering from him until she realized how innocuous his question was. She visibly relaxed and again bent her head to her almost full bowl. Her answer was so quiet, Waya could barely hear her. "Yes, Ninovan's pudding is very good."

Again Waya and his mother looked at each other. Waya turned to Amanda again and said gently, "What is wrong, Ah-man-da? Are you not feeling well? You have hardly touched your meal."

"I guess I'm not very hungry. I'm sorry." Amanda responded very quietly as she lay her bowl down with trembling hands. She had still not raised her head. She sat cross-legged by the fire staring down at her folded hands. Ninovan and Waya could both see that her hands were shaking badly.

Waya reached over and touched Amanda's hand gently. She jumped as if she had been struck. More brusquely than he intended Waya said, "Why do you jump when I touch you, Ah-man-da? Why do you fear me?"

Still Amanda didn't raise her head, though her body shuddered. She just sat and trembled even harder. When she finally looked up, Waya could see tears trembling on the lashes of her beautiful green eyes. He could tell she was very frightened.

Ninovan thought she knew the problem. She said in a quiet voice, "Perhaps, Ah-man-da, believes she is to be punished for running away, my son. You should allay her fears."

"Ah-man-da, I cannot punish you for showing such spirit as you did. I am sad that you want to leave me and my people, but I will not punish you for your actions. You showed much cunning and much bravery. Those things are appreciated by the Cherokee. I am not saying that I might not punish you if you did it again, but I will not do anything this time.

We will be married in two moons time. I believe you will learn to care for my people the same way you care for your own someday. It will just take time. You have only been with us a few moons. You have to give yourself time to learn our ways. We are not a cruel people."

Amanda was very relieved, but she didn't believe she would ever learn to love the Cherokee as she loved her own family. And she didn't want to get married. Why couldn't she make these people believe she just wasn't ready for marriage? However, she feared telling Waya that, so she remained quiet.

When Waya left, Amanda and Ninovan scraped the bowls and Ninovan took the leftovers out to feed to one of the tribe's dogs. The meat was wrapped and taken to the little house next door to be eaten later. Nothing was ever wasted here, thought Amanda. Her own family were not wasteful people either, but she did remember some of the younger children not eating all their food and that food being put into slops buckets for the pigs, so it wasn't really wasted at all. Occasionally too much food was prepared and if it wasn't eaten the next day, it sometimes went bad and had to be thrown away if the weather was hot. She had never seen that in the Cherokee town.

The next day dawned sunny and cold. The Cherokee town had also received snow and the last of it had just melted. Amanda carried the dirty dishes from their evening and morning meals down to the river to wash. Tsula was there also washing her family's dirty bowls. She smiled when she saw Amanda.

Tsula didn't have the children with her. They had stayed in the warm house with Mohe. Hialeah, Tsula told Amanda, had a cold and was fussy. She asked Amanda if she wanted to come see her. Amanda was very eager to do so, but feared not going directly back to Ninovan's house.

When Amanda told Tsula her fear, Tsula went with her to Ninovan's house. Waya was just coming out when they walked up.

"There you are, Ah-man-da. I was just coming to look for you. Hello Tsula."

"I was coming to ask Ninovan if Ah-man-da could come to our house to visit. The baby has a cold and is fussy. I thought Ah-man-da might make her feel better. She loves her so, as does Kanuna."

"That is a good idea, Tsula. I am sure Ah-man-da is tired of being in the house all the time with only my mother for company. I will go with you to see Mohe about some tribal business. Let me just tell my mother where we will be."

While Waya was in his mother's house, Tsula noticed that Amanda was very quiet since they had seen Waya. Mohe had told her his brother didn't intend to punish Ah-man-da for running away and she had been surprised. Most captives would have been punished severely for running away and even more severely for taking food, furs and a weapon as Ah-man-da had done. Waya must love her very much, thought Tsula. Ah-man-da was lucky, but she didn't seem to know it.

When they entered Tsula and Mohe's house, they heard the baby fussing. Amanda immediately went to her and picked her up. She held the baby snuggly and talked to her quietly. Hialeah quieted down almost immediately. She even managed a small smile when Amanda started to pull her fur moccasin off to play with her toes. Kanuna, not to be outdone, came over from where he was playing and pulled off his moccasin as well. Amanda would play piggy toes with first one child and then the next making them howl with laughter.

Waya looked at her beautiful smiling face and was more lovestruck than ever. He hoped to soon see her playing with her own children in just this way, their children. He couldn't help but smile at the thought. Mohe saw him smiling and being so in tune with his brother could read his thoughts. He hoped Waya was right, but he had grave misgivings about Ah-man-da ever being happy with them. He saw the deep sadness in her eyes from time to time and knew she was thinking of her own people. Mohe had not been surprised when they found Amanda was gone. He actually had hoped she would make it home before they caught up to her. She might have made it if not for the snowstorm. They still didn't know where she had been during the storm, but as far as Mohe knew Waya hadn't questioned her yet.

He, himself, was interested to know where she had come up with the long gun she had and how she had known how to use it. Cherokee women didn't fight and as far as he knew white women didn't either. She had had a long knife, her small skinning knife, the long rifle, and a shot bag, as well as extra clothes when they found her. Mohe didn't know who she could have gotten them from. They had seen only Indians while they hunted for her. The clothes she had were not Indian clothes. Although the coat she had was made of buckskin, it had not been made by an Indian woman. From the size of the coat it looked like a man's coat, as did the other clothes she wore.

It had been a miracle they had found her. They had lost her tracks during the snowstorm. Their party had holed up in a cave they knew about or they would have been hard pressed not to freeze themselves. Amanda had to have had shelter of some kind or she wouldn't have survived. She had lost some weight, that was clear to see, but not the amount she should have.

The other bag she had carried that held the extra clothes also held some canned beans and other white man's food. Mohe couldn't understand why she hadn't stayed with the white people she found or why they hadn't taken her home. There were many questions Mohe wanted to ask Ah-man-da, but it wasn't his place. He was not sure his brother was doing the right thing in not trying to find out all he could about where she had been. She might try it again and if she had found other white people, she would probably go right back to them. They might have to fight this time to get her back. Some of them could die in a battle with the whites. Mohe was very concerned.

When Hialeah began to fuss again, Amanda handed her to her mother to nurse. At first, Amanda had been very embarrassed when Tsula fed her baby, but she soon became used to the fact that a child nursing was not seen as something to be hidden. Nursing a baby was just a natural part of life. Waya paid no attention to the fact that Tsula had exposed her breast to feed her baby. There was no lapse in the conversation and Tsula felt no need to turn away or cover herself while her child was fed.

Amanda thought how strange the ways of the Cherokee were to her. Although she had become used to it to a large degree, she still felt some embarrassment for Tsula when it happened. Amanda usually averted her eyes at times like this. Mohe had noticed her apparent aversion to the baby being fed in her presence, but Waya took no notice. Mohe wondered about his brother sometimes. He was so caught up in his love of the white girl, he hardly knew what was going on around him most of the time. Mohe decided to speak to their mother on this subject. He was truly worried about Waya where Amanda was concerned.

Chapter 17

The next days turned into weeks and the weeks to months as they are wont to do. Before Amanda knew it, the weather had changed. The days became warm and the nights only cool, not cold. The trees began to sprout leaves and the wildflowers were sprouting shoots and putting on buds. She knew that her wedding to Waya was to be at the Spring ceremony, but she wasn't sure exactly when that happened and she was afraid to ask.

Ninovan and Tsula had been helping her to prepare her wedding clothes. Her skirt was made of buckskin that had been tanned and bleached in the sun until it was a creamy white. There was fringe on the bottom of the skirt that extended almost mid-calf as well as along the sides. The fringe was decorated with beads, feathers and small shiny stones that small holes had been punched in using a piece of bone that had been sharpened. The decorations were then threaded onto the fringe strings and a knot was placed between each decoration to hold it on. Her shirt was also made of the same creamy buckskin and it also had decorated fringes down the arms and along the bottom. Both the shirt and the skirt had an elaborate pattern worked into it with beads and porcupine quills. The hide had been worked until it was very soft. Amanda was also to have new moccasins from the same color buckskin.

The three women were almost done with the wedding clothes for her. Then they would start on the clothes for Waya. He was to have decorated leggings, shirt and moccasins as well. Since it took at least three weeks to complete a full outfit, Amanda knew she had at least that long before she would be married.

Everyone in the Cherokee town was very busy with preparations for the upcoming festival as well as the wedding, since they would coincide. There was much laughter and teasing as the people went about the myriad tasks that needed to be completed for such a big undertaking. There were hunting parties going out every day now. When they returned, the entire town would turn out to help butcher, skin and tan the hides of the animals that were killed.

The women were also preparing their seeds and tools for the spring planting. Amanda had worked in their family garden since she was very small, so she understood how much work went into planting a garden. What she didn't understand was that she would be responsible for her own plot of land. She had been given the land by Ninovan. In the Cherokee town, only women owned and worked the land. They also owned the houses. Men only owned horses, weapons, and their clothes.

When it was obvious that Amanda didn't really understand what was expected of her, Mohe took her aside and explained it all in English to her. She was very surprised that she would own her own land and her own house. Waya would help her build the house and live in it with her, but she would be the sole owner. The land Ninovan had given her for her garden had already been cleared, but the dirt would need to be broken up and made ready for planting.

Ninovan owned several plots of land. Since Waya's father had been a chief, he had received plots of land for battles he had helped win and problems he had solved over the years. Ninovan had also inherited some land from her mother when she had died. She had given one piece to Tsula when she married Mohe and now she gave another to Amanda. Ninovan was still strong, but she was not a young woman. Since both her sons were now to be married, she no longer needed to plant so much land.

Each Cherokee family planted what they would need to survive on and then planted more to be traded to the whites for the things they wanted from the trading post. With Waya, it was always knives, for which he traded skins and furs. However, Ninovan liked to buy colored beads for her clothes and hair, as well as iron cooking pots since they lasted so much longer than her clay ones. She would need only one plot of land this year to take care of her food needs. She would plant one other for trade. This left her with extra land which she decided to give to Tsula and Amanda so they would have plenty of produce to trade for the things they wanted and needed.

When this was all explained to Amanda, she was overjoyed. If she could have a really good crop, maybe she would be allowed to go to the trading post. If she could see a white person there, she could get a message to her family about where she was and they could come and get her. Although, she appeared docile, she was still looking for ways to get back home every day.

Amanda had given up hope of not having to marry Waya. There was no way she was getting out it that she could see. There was no opportunity for her to run again as she was watched constantly. She couldn't pretend she was happy about it, but she did participate willingly in all the activities leading up to the Spring celebration and her wedding. Everyone except Waya saw how Amanda really felt about the wedding. They could see she held no joy for the event. However, Waya, was blissfully happy and still convinced that she would love him in time.

One day as Amanda was hoeing up her fields in preparation to plant, she was surprised to see a group of warriors ride in with two male Negro captives. She thought, "They must be runaways." They were dirty and ragged and seemed very tired. The warriors had been riding, but the captives had been running alongside the horses. Waya was leading the group as was his custom. He smiled at Amanda as he rode by.

Amanda's curiosity was aroused. There had been no Negroes in the town since she had come there. She didn't know that Indians took Negroes captive. Her father had told them all a story once about a Cherokee woman named Nancy Ward who had owned slaves and been a guiding force for the Cherokees for many years. Amanda wondered if these two men would be made slaves or adopted into the tribe as she and Mohe had been.

Later that evening, Waya came to eat the evening meal with Ninovan and Amanda. He related the tale of how the two captives had been caught escaping from their owner. Waya and his men had been hunting and come upon them hiding in a cane break near the river. They had captured them and brought them back to town in order for the council to decide their fate. From what she could understand, the two men might be returned to their owner or might be made slaves, but the council would decide. Waya said in some towns, the men might even be adopted, but he didn't think anyone in their town was willing to adopt them since they had already run away once.

In the next few days, Amanda tried to get a chance to speak to the two captives. She wanted to know where they were from and if they could give her an idea where her family's farm was from the Cherokee town. She had not given up on the idea of running away again and thought she never would. She knew in warmer weather, she wouldn't need as many supplies. There were berries and wild vegetables that she could eat to survive. She would love to have the long rifle she had taken from the dead man's cabin, but she knew Waya had come to treasure it and was rarely parted from it.

Finally, Amanda's chance came to speak to the Negro men. When she went to wash clothes at the river on a bright sunny day, she saw her chance and took it. The captives were also there and only had one guard. When their guard was distracted by someone coming to speak to him, Amanda whispered to the man closest to her.

"Where are you from? Who was your owner and where was their farm?"

The man glanced at her quickly and then looked away. He appeared to be speaking to his fellow captive when he said, "We belonged to Mr. Carmichael at Brushy Hills Farm. I can't rightly say zactly where de farm was. We was brought there in a wagon from de east, but that was years ago. What chu doin here, white girl?"

"I was captured from my family farm many months ago. It was night and I couldn't tell which direction we travelled. I have tried to find my family once, but was recaptured a few weeks ago. I want to try to get home, but don't know which way to go. I tried to head straight east last time, but when I was captured I didn't recognize anything around me. My name is Whitworth, Amanda Whitworth, and my father is John Whitworth. Our farm is about ten miles from Paris, but since I only went there once when I was very young, I'm not sure which direction that is from here. I think Paris was west of us because the sun was behind us when we came and went."

"I'se don think I kin hep you, missy. I never heard them names a'tall. Has you heard of Mr. Carmichael?"

"No, that name doesn't ring a bell for me. Neither does the name of his farm. How far did you travel before you got caught?"

"Me an Nate, we was gone bout a week afore we's cotched. I got no idee where they cotched us. It took us all of one day and some of the night to get chere to dis place. We didn't go straight neither east or west from what I could tell. Shh, here comes that big Indian again."

Amanda had been looking down at her washing while she whispered to the captive. Now she raised her head, but didn't look directly at the guard, but up in a tree like she had heard a squirrel chatter or a bird twitter. She was despondent. She had so counted on these two men knowing where they were from and maybe having heard of her family. Her grandfather was well known in Paris and the surrounding areas, as was her father.

Amanda finished her washing and took the clothes to hang on the bushes near the river as was the custom. After she was done, she headed to the latrine. She was still marking the tree every day on her calendar. She had been here since late October and to the best of her knowledge, it was now mid-March. It was going on six months since she was captured. She knew her parents had probably given her up for dead.

Chapter 18

Ninovan woke Amanda very early one morning. She told Amanda that today was the Spring New Moon Ceremony and her wedding day. She took Amanda down to the river for a bath. It was very important that she be cleansed in body and spirit before her wedding. Amanda stood in the cold water and washed her body and hair as instructed. Ninovan couldn't see the tears streaming down her face as she washed her hair, but she knew Amanda was not happy to be marrying her son.

She felt sorry for the young white girl. She had tried to talk Waya into returning the girl to her people several times, but her son was stubborn. He loved this girl and he didn't want to hear anything about returning her to her family. He just kept saying he would make her happy and she would learn to love him too. Ninovan didn't think that was going to happen. She feared her son was going to be very disappointed in his marriage. Amanda did not look at her son with eyes of love, only with eyes of fear and dread.

Mohe also was not happy that this day had arrived. He was also convinced that Amanda would not learn to love his brother. He felt sad for both of them. Having a loving wife in Tsula, he wished the same for his brother, Waya. Mohe had tried to talk to Waya, but to no avail. Finally, he had tried to convince Ah-man-da that she could learn to love his brother and be happy as part of the Cherokee as he was. She only looked at him with sad eyes and shook her head negatively.

The wedding was to take place right before the beginning of the Spring New Moon ceremony. The morning before, Waya had brought a deer to his mother's house and left it by the door. Ninovan and Amanda had cleaned the deer and prepared it for roasting for the ceremony. Several deer, some wild pigs, rabbits, and squirrels were all being cooked for the feast after the ceremonies. The women of the tribe had made many dishes of corn, squash, and beans for the meal as well. Ninovan had made a huge corn pudding sweetened with honey, fresh strawberries, and nuts.

The women carried the food to the open area near the council house. There were several benches set up there to hold the food to keep it away from ants and other ground insects. They covered the food with woven mats and cloths. Then everyone went to dress in their best for the ceremony.

Ninovan, Tsula and Amanda had completed Waya's wedding clothes the day before and he had taken them to his house at that time. Ninovan helped Amanda dress and then had her sit before her on the ground on a deer skin. Ninovan braided Amanda's hair and dressed it with beads and feathers. Her thick chestnut colored braids hung past her waist when Ninovan was finished. She also took a necklace that was made of several strands of freshwater pearls with a round medallion decorated with beads and pearls in the middle. She hung it around Amanda's neck. Her ears were decorated with smaller medallions also covered in beads and pearls. She thought the white girl was very beautiful in her wedding finery.

When Ninovan and Amanda left the house, dusk had fallen. They went to the council area where a huge fire was burning. Waya stood across the fire from them wearing his wedding clothes. He too had bathed and washed his hair. Waya had chosen to wear his hair unbraided for his wedding. It was held back with a heavily beaded band that wrapped around his head and tied in the back with feathers cascading down to between his shoulder blades.

Amanda had seen the clothes of course, but not on him. He looked very handsome. His jet black hair was shining in the firelight. He was tall and broad shouldered. He filled out the shirt very well. He had a beaded belt tied around his waist upon which hung two very decorative knife scabbards, one on each side. He looked proud and happy. Amanda wished she felt differently about this marriage. She didn't dislike Waya. Actually, he had treated her well and was always kind to her. She just didn't love him and she didn't feel she was ready to be married.

Ninovan lead Amanda around to where Waya stood. The grandmother came out of the council house and stood before the two of them. She asked Waya if he had brought meat to Amanda's house the day before. He answered yes, then she asked Amanda if she had cooked the meat to which she answered yes, as well. Then the ceremony began.

Amanda didn't understand what the meat questions were about. Waya brought meat to Ninovan's house all the time. She looked at Ninovan with a question in her eyes. Before Ninovan could speak, Waya hurriedly took Amanda's hand and lead her to where the council was standing.

Mohe stood at Amanda's side in the place of her biological brother, Ninovan stood at Waya's side. Each of the attendants was carrying a blue blanket which was placed around the shoulders of the bride and groom by their respective attendant. The grandmother then blessed the young couple, then turning to the guests, she blessed all of them. Songs were sung and then the grandmother took away the two blue blankets and replaced them with one large heavily decorated white blanket which she put around the shoulders of both the bride and groom. She then handed Waya a Cherokee wedding vase that had a spout on each side. Amanda drank from one side and Waya from the other at the same time to signify their unity for a second time. Again the grandmother spoke and the couple were declared wed.

After this part of the ceremony, the New Moon of Spring Ceremony began. Mohe had explained this sacred rite to Amanda in this way. Fruits from the previous fall harvest would be brought to the ceremony and consumed to remember the continuation of the Creator's care and blessing. The festival initiates the planting season and incorporates predictions concerning the success or failure of the crops. It usually lasted seven days and included dancing and the re-lighting of the sacred fire by the fire keeper, one of the council members. All home fires were put out and relit from the sacred fire's coals which symbolized fresh beginnings and the renewal of life from the Earth Mother.

Amanda was amazed at the amount of ritual that was observed for this ceremony. It seemed the Cherokee took their religion as seriously as the whites. There was no Bible to read from, but the elders had memorized the ceremonies words and repeated them year after year. They would teach their apprentices the words by rote and so the ceremonies were handed down from generation to generation much as the word of God was handed down in white homes where the inhabitants couldn't read.

Amanda and Waya sat together on one blanket, but it wasn't shared with anyone else because they were newlyweds. Amanda brought choice pieces of meat and servings of squash, beans, and corn to her new husband. They ate from the same bowl, which they had never done before. Amanda was very quiet. She was dreading what she knew would come next when they went to her new house for the first time as husband and wife.

Waya wished his beautiful new wife would be happier, but he still had confidence that she would change. He was basing all his hopes on their mating later on. He knew it would be her first time and he intended to be very gentle with her. Mohe had given him some very good advice about making his new wife's first time enjoyable. He had warned Waya not to get in a hurry or he might hurt her and forever make her dislike mating. Waya certainly didn't want to do that. He was not inexperienced with women. He had had his share of bedding widows. Of course, they weren't virgins and he had not had to take especial care with them, but they had all seemed to enjoy his lovemaking. He was sure he could make Ah-man-da enjoy it too.

After hours of singing, eating, and dancing, Waya stood and held out his hand to Amanda. She looked up at him and he saw the fear clearly in her eyes. He smiled at her gently and reached down, taking her hand, pulled her to her feet. He took their white marriage blanket and wrapped it around both of them as the night had grown cool.

When the newlyweds arrived at their new home, they saw that someone had started a new fire in their fire ring. The house was warm and fragrant from the strings of drying herbs, wild onions, and garlic hanging from the rafters. Someone had also hung evergreen boughs among the rafters as well. Waya smiled at Amanda and lead her to a bench near the fire. They sat down together on the bench.

Amanda was so nervous, she was wringing her hands. Waya spoke to her quietly about all sorts of things until she began to calm down. She sat with her shoulders hunched and her head down, but he could see she had finally stopped wringing her hands. She stifled a yawn, but he saw it anyway.

"Come, my beautiful Ah-man-da. It is time for us to lie down together as man and wife. I have brought many furs to make us a sleeping place that is soft and warm. I have a bear fur that I have been saving for this occasion for a long time. It will cover both of us in warmth.", Waya said as he rose from the bench and reached for Amanda's hand.

Amanda practically jumped off the bench and backed away a couple of steps. "I, I need to go to the latrine first.", she stuttered.

"I will go with you, wife. Animals may have been attracted to all the food and the fire. I don't want you to come to any harm."

Amanda didn't want him to go, but she couldn't think of an excuse to keep him there. She slowly went out the door opening and proceeded to the latrine area. Waya stood watch while she took care of her needs. Then they walked back to their new house.

Amanda didn't know what to expect next. She was so nervous, she could hardly stand still. She wrung her hands, breathing shallowly. Waya could easily see that she dreaded their coupling very much. Again, he seated her on the bench and spoke quietly to her for several minutes. When she had again settled down, he reached for her hand and said, "Ah-man-da, you are now my wife. I love you very much. I know that you do not have such feelings for me yet. I believe that over time you will come to feel the same love for me that I have for you. You must give our marriage a chance."

Amanda looked at him skeptically, "How can you be so sure that I will come to love you? I don't want to be married. I am too young. I am very afraid of what being a wife means."

Again Waya spoke gently to her, "I know that you fear becoming my wife. I will be very gentle with you. There will be a little pain the first time, but not after that. I have spoken to Mohe and he has told me what to do. It will be fine. Come now, it is time."

Amanda had promised herself she wouldn't cry, but the tears were very close as she rose and followed Waya to their bed. Her small body shuddered as he reached towards her and untied her belt, letting it fall to the floor. Next he took down her hair and shook the braids loose around her shoulders.

He said, "I have wondered what your beautiful hair would look like loose and flowing around you. It is the color of the chestnuts that grow in the forest, dark, but with fine red streaks in it. You are very beautiful, Ah-man-da." he said softly and with much feeling.

Amanda had had her eyes cast down, but now, she looked up at Waya. His large brown eyes glowed with love. She knew he cared deeply for her, but she just didn't feel the same way. And now she had to be intimate with him. It just wasn't fair. The tears she had been trying so very hard to hold back almost flowed again, but she was able to stop them.

Waya reached for the bottom of her shirt and pulled it over her head. Then he loosened the ties on her skirt and it fell to the ground. She was completely naked except for her knee high moccasins. Amanda blushed with embarrassment and tried to cover her breasts and private area with her hands.

Waya pulled her hands away saying, "No, my little one, do not cover yourself. You are very beautiful and I want to see all of you."

He slowly reached out and picked Amanda up then lay her down on the soft pile of furs. He untied and removed her moccasins, then he began to remove his own clothes. First he untied his headband and dropped it, then his shirt went over his head. Since he only had on leggings and moccasins under the shirt, he was quickly completely nude.

Amanda hadn't planned to watch him, but her eyes seemed to have a will of their own. She was struck by the beauty of his body. She had never seen a grown man completely naked. She had seen her younger brothers many times, but seeing a boy in comparison with a man was day to night. Muscles were corded on his stomach and across his broad chest. His arms were long and the muscles were long and chiseled as well. His stomach was flat and his long legs were as muscled as the rest of his body.

When Amanda saw his penis, her eyes got huge and she scuttled to the other side of the bed hiding her face in her hands. He was huge. She knew that he was supposed to insert that into her body and she just knew it was going to rip her apart. Tsula had told her what to expect, but she hadn't said anything about how it was supposed to fit.

Amanda wanted nothing to do with that. If she wasn't naked, she would have jumped up and run from the house. She cowered against the house wall as she felt Waya lie down next to her. Waya reached out and pulled her hands away from her face. Then he pulled her close to him and just held her for several minutes.

"I won't rush you, little bird. I know you are feeling fear because you have never been loved before. I will be very gentle with you. I promise to not cause you any more pain than is absolutely necessary this first time."

Amanda didn't respond. She was petrified with fear. Very slowly, Waya ran his big hand down her arm and back up it again. He continued to slowly caress just her arm for several minutes until she relaxed somewhat. Then he moved his hand to her chest above her breasts. Again, Amanda tensed up, but again, he just slowly and gently rubbed her chest. After a few minutes, he lowered his hand to cover her left breast.

Waya slowly began to massage her breast. Then one of his fingers brushed gently on her nipple. At her quick intake of breath, he took two fingers and gently squeezed her nipple a couple of times. Against her will, Amanda was beginning to enjoy the sensation. She had had no idea that she would feel pleasure. She had only been concentrating on the pain she was expecting.

Waya moved to her other breast as he brought his head down and touched her lips with his very gently. Amanda was not expecting to like the feel of his mouth on hers, but she did. Very slowly, Waya deepened the kiss. Amanda was startled when she felt his tongue touch her lips and she gasped. When her mouth opened, she felt Waya's tongue enter her mouth and touch her tongue. Amanda was shocked to realize her own tongue had not recoiled from his, but had moved toward his instead.

Before she knew it, her tongue had touched Waya's tongue and then his lower lip. He groaned and Amanda jerked her tongue back into her own mouth. Again Waya's tongue reached out for hers and again her traitorous tongue reached to meet his. Then Amanda noticed that his hand had started a downward motion across her abdomen and then lower onto her stomach.

Again Amanda tensed up, but Waya's progress was very slow and very gentle and she relaxed again. All the time his hand was moving slowly down her body, his mouth was driving her crazy. She heard a soft moan and then realized it had come from her. She was shocked at herself. How could she be enjoying this when she didn't love this man? She had always thought only people who loved each other were intimate in this way. When Tsula had described what went on between a married couple, her eyes had shined with her love for Mohe.

Now Waya's hand touched her most secret of places. His long fingers caressed her mound and then one of them slipped inside. Again Amanda tensed up, but Waya deepened their kiss and she relaxed again. As his finger slowly made its way farther in, Amanda was torn by many emotions. Waya's kisses felt so good as did the way his hands touched her.

However, again, she didn't understand how she could have these feelings when she didn't love him. Was she some kind of aberration? Was she not a good person? She had always thought of herself as good. She had obeyed her parents, done what was expected of her, and loved God as she had been taught. Why did her body betray her heart like this?

When Waya touched the small nub hidden in her sex, she almost jumped out of her skin. The feeling he elicited sent all thoughts from her mind. Now her body responded in the age old way. She moaned again and her legs opened involuntarily to Waya. She felt a pressure in her nether regions she had never felt before. She needed something badly, but she was unsure what it was or how to get it.

Amanda writhed on the furs as Waya touched her in ways she had never known. Always she had been taught only to touch herself there in order to wash herself. She had no idea that part of her body could bring so much pleasure and so much pressure at the same time. Then one of Waya's long fingers entered her while his thumb touched the tiny nub. Again, the pleasure and the pressure increased. Waya continued to kiss her while his fingers were busy. Amanda lost all sense of who she was, where she was. She was just a mass of feelings, and all of them were good.

Suddenly, Amanda's body stiffened and she felt the most incredible feeling. Wave after wave of pleasure rolled over her body. Her body trembled and shook and she cried out as she reached the pinnacle of desire. When the waves of pleasure finally stopped, Amanda was limp in Waya's arms.

But Waya wasn't done. Again he began to gently kiss her and stroke her lower body. Almost immediately, Amanda's body caught fire again. The pressure was stronger and much quicker this time. She barely noticed when Waya changed position and aligned himself between her legs. He whispered, "This will hurt, little bird, but it won't last long and it will only be this once."

Before she could even think to respond, Waya fit his body to hers and slid his penis into her. There was a sharp pain and Amanda struggled to get away, but Waya held her tight and lay still inside of her.

"Just give it time, little bird. The pain will not last long. Just lie still and let me love you."

Waya's mouth descended onto hers and Amanda almost automatically responded to his kiss. He slid his hand between them and again gently touched the little nub nestled in her sex. Her body caught fire almost immediately. Her legs opened again on their own. Waya very slowly slid out of her body and then very slowly slid back in. Amanda held her breath waiting for the pain to come again, but there was no pain, just a slight tenderness. As Waya moved slowly in and out of her, Amanda soon found her body moving also. She matched her rhythm to his and soon the pressure was there again.

As Amanda writhed under him, Waya had trouble maintaining his control. She was so beautiful and she responded so warmly, it was all he could do not to slam his body into hers. But he was able to control his passion by thinking about anything except his beautiful wife. Finally, he could stand it no longer. His pace sped up and Amanda matched it with her own. Her cries of completion came right before he lost himself completely and fell over the wonderful, magnificent edge.

Both Waya and Amanda lay shuddering in each other's arms. They were both out of breath. As their breathing slowed, Waya raised his weight off Amanda and smiled down at her. She shyly smiled back. Amanda was embarrassed about how she had reacted to Waya, but he seemed very pleased. She still didn't understand, but she was really too tired now to think about it. Waya slid off her body and gathered her into his arms, pulling the bear skin over them and they both slept deeply.

Chapter 19

Several weeks later, Amanda was still unable to reconcile her carnal response to Waya with her feelings for him. She still didn't love him. She felt some affection for him, but she had felt that before they had been married and made love. Although she recognized that he loved her, it was obvious from the way he treated her and spoke to her, she didn't understand her own feelings or her reaction to his lovemaking. There was no one she could talk to about this. Tsula loved Mohe completely and wouldn't understand. She certainly couldn't speak to Waya about it. He seemed to think that because she enjoyed their sessions in bed, she was falling in love with him.

Finally, in desperation, Amanda decided to speak to Mohe. She was embarrassed to talk about something so private and intimate with her brother-in-law, but she couldn't think of anyone else to ask. One day when she knew that Tsula had taken her washing to the river, she went to see Mohe.

He was surprised to see her, but invited her in. He thought she may have come to see the children as she often did. He was working on braiding a rope from vines while watching his little ones. As the day was warm, no fire had been lit since the breakfast fire had been allowed to burn out. Mohe had the door flap open to allow a breeze to blow through. The children were playing on a fur spread near where he worked.

Amanda came in and immediately went to the children. She sat on the fur with them, picking up Hialeah. After playing with both children for a few minutes, Amanda set Hialeah down and turned to Mohe.

"There is something I would know, brother." Amanda said quietly in English.

Mohe thought she had some question about Cherokee life or tradition and looked at her inquisitively. She hung her head and spoke almost in a whisper, "Why is it that I can enjoy certain, uh, things married people do, but not feel love for Waya? I feel, I don't know, I feel like a bad person, like a loose woman because of this."

Mohe quickly looked at Amanda and saw her face was bright red with embarrassment. He thought his face probably looked the same. He didn't know quite how to answer her question. He already knew she didn't have the same feelings as Waya, that was obvious. However, he didn't feel comfortable discussing something like this with his brother's wife.

After several minutes, he found his voice. "Ah-man-da, I don't feel I should be discussing this with you. Is there no one else you can ask?"

Amanda's face was even redder now. She spoke haltingly, "I don't know who that would be. I can't speak to Tsula because it's obvious that she loves you very much. Waya wouldn't understand and even my asking would hurt him badly. I tried to ask Ninovan, but before I could even start speaking, she told me she was very happy that Waya and I were getting along so well. I don't really know anyone else here well enough to ask a question like this. Mohe, you're my only hope. I feel so guilty I can hardly eat or sleep."

Mohe had noticed that Ah-man-da had lost weight and had dark circles under her eyes. He had thought it was because Waya was keeping her up late at night with his needs. Waya went around with a constant smile on his face since they were married.

Again Mohe hesitated to address such a delicate issue with Amanda. He thought and thought of someone he could refer her to, but couldn't think of a single tribe member who could answer her without possibly telling someone about it. This tribe, much like many other Indian tribes, loved to gossip. Some still weren't happy that Waya had taken a white girl. They feared reprisals if her family ever found her. He couldn't see his brother become a laughing stock.

When Amanda had almost given up hope of an answer, and after a few more minutes of thought, Mohe cleared his throat and said, "What you are talking about does not make you a loose woman. A person, either man or woman, can enjoy relations with someone without being in love with that person. It is a purely physical thing. Just because your body enjoys what you and Waya do, doesn't mean you have to love him. Do you not feel any affection for my brother?"

"Yes, I feel affection for him, but no more than I feel for you or Tsula or even Ninovan. He is good to me and treats me well. But that also applies to the three of you. I have never felt that man woman kind of love. After all, I am still very young. I tried to tell everyone I wasn't ready for marriage, but no one would listen to me." Amanda said somewhat heatedly.

Before Mohe could answer, Tsula returned from doing her washing at the river. Upon coming into the house, she looked from her friend to her husband when she felt the tension in the air. She could think of no reason for them to be arguing, but if the look on Amanda's face was any indication, they had definitely been doing so.

After just a few minutes, Amanda rose to go with the excuse that she had to go prepare the noon meal. As soon as Amanda was out of hearing range, Tsula turned to Mohe and asked him what was going on.

"Ah-man-da is not happy in her marriage to my brother. She still feels no love for Waya, only a little affection. She is bitter that she was forced to marry him." Mohe said. He didn't go further and Tsula thought there was more to it, but she didn't say anything more. She knew her husband well, if he wanted her to know, he would tell her.

As Amanda walked through the town, she saw the Negro captive she had spoken to weeks ago. She hadn't seen much of either of the men. They had been taken as slaves by two of the men who had captured them. Waya had volunteered his old house for them to live in as their new owners didn't want them living with their families.

Amanda's new house was not close to where the captives stayed. Waya had built their house close to the land that Amanda worked, to make it easier for her. They lived a little outside the main area of town. Amanda had been very busy since her wedding. She had gotten her two plots of land ready to plant and planted both of them with corn, beans, squash, pumpkins, and gourds from seeds given to her by Ninovan. She was busy each day weeding, hoeing and watering her plants when the weather was dry. She also had duties at her house cooking, washing, and cleaning as well.

She had thought she did a lot of work on her father's farm, but the work here was much harder because she had no help and the tools were crude. At home, the chores were all shared by she, her mother, the slave women, and Leticia. The little boys helped in the garden and with feeding the animals as well.

Amanda was glad she didn't have animals to take care of too. As it was, at the end of every day she was exhausted. Her back hurt, her hands were stiff and sore and had callouses on them, and she felt tired all the time. Ninovan did help her with tanning the hides of the animals that Waya brought in when he hunted for them. He still provided meat for his mother as well as for he and Amanda. The tanning process was lengthy and messy. At home, Amanda's brothers and father had taken care of those duties. It had taken her some time after being brought to the Cherokee town to learn how to tan the hides correctly.

First the hide had to be soaked in a lye solution of hickory ashes and water for several days. Then the hide was stretched over a plank or peeled log and the loose hair scraped off, as well as the membrane on the other side. When the hide was thoroughly cleaned, it was rinsed in clean water and stretched with ropes. When the hide was nearly dry, but still slightly damp, the hide was rubbed with raw animal brains applied with a smooth stone to the hair side of the skin. The ropes had to be tightened several more times before the hide was supple and ready for use.

The part Amanda had the most trouble with was rubbing the hide with the raw brains. It was a nasty process and Amanda hated every minute of it. At the end of the process she was hot, sweaty, and had animal brains and blood all over her.

Every time she had to rub the brains into the hides, she rushed to the river and took a bath as quickly as she could. The other women thought her fastidiousness was hilarious and laughed at her every time they saw her rushing to the river.

Waya, however, was proud of his new wife's clean habits. The fact that she bathed regularly was not lost on him. He, too, began to bathe more often. He found that he liked the sweet way she smelled. She kept their house very neat and orderly just like she did her own body. His clothes were laundered often and she was a good cook. Waya was very happy in his marriage. He knew that Ah-man-da was not as happy as he was, but he still thought in time, things would change. Waya was not a deep thinking or introspective man. His wants and needs were simple and as long as they were met, he was happy.

Waya had no idea that his wife spent a large part of her day trying to figure out which way to run when she got another opportunity to escape. He didn't know that she had a secret spot in the small house they used for storage where she secreted dried meat, dried berries, and extra clothes. He also had no idea that she had also hidden two knives. If she could have gotten her hands on a long rifle, she would have hidden that as well.

Amanda had not given up hope of being reunited with her family. She knew they would be ashamed that she had been married to an Indian, but she wasn't sure she was even going to tell them. If anyone knew about it, any chance of her marrying a white man would be gone. She had not given up her dream of having her own home and children some day. She felt very bad about possibly deceiving her family, but she was sure it was the only way to have what she wanted in the future.

Each day dragged by for Amanda. She and Waya had been married for five months now and nothing had changed as far as she was concerned. After speaking to Mohe, her guilt was somewhat appeased, but she still felt somehow dishonorable because she didn't love the man she slept with. She knew she really had had no choice in the matter of her marriage, but that didn't really help her conscience much.

The days of August were hot and it hadn't rained in a long time. Every day, Amanda had to bring water from the river for her fields. She had already gathered her corn, as well as much squash and many beans. Ninovan had shown her how to grind the corn with stones, then dry the meal in the sun to preserve it. She had a good amount of dried beans and squash put away as well. Ninovan had shown her how to make the clay pots and jars used to store her produce. Amanda had more than enough food stored for she and Waya for the winter. Her yield had been very good from her two plots of land.

Ninovan had also taken her out into the forest to gather wild herbs, onions, and garlic as well as blackberries, strawberries, blueberries and several kinds of nuts. They had also robbed a beehive of its honey recently and Amanda now had two large jars of honey that she had strained thoroughly through a piece of calico and sealed with the beeswax she got from the combs.

Ninovan taught Amanda many uses for the herbs they found. They were used as medicine, not just for cooking. The honey also could be used as a healing agent on cuts, burns, and scrapes. Amanda was happy that she had learned so much since coming to the Cherokee town, but she was still terribly unhappy there.

Now Amanda was not only unhappy, she was ill. Every morning when she woke up, she was sick to her stomach. She wanted to sleep all the time. Since she had so many duties, she didn't have the luxury of sleeping when she wanted to. She was losing weight again and was tired all the time. Finally after two weeks of this, she went to Ninovan to ask her for some type of tea to help her stomach.

After Amanda told Ninovan her symptoms, she was shocked to see Ninovan smiling broadly. When Ninovan noticed Amanda's shocked look she said, "Oh, Ah-man-da, you are not ill. You are carrying my grandchild in your belly. When did you have your woman's time last?"

Amanda thought back. It had been over two months ago that she had last had her cycle. "Oh, no," she thought, "I can't be having a baby. If I make it back home, a baby will ruin everything. I can't deny what happened between me and Waya if I have a baby."

Seeing the look of horror on Amanda's face, Ninovan was saddened. She had hoped that Amanda had learned to love her son by now. Apparently, that was not the case. "Well,", Ninovan thought, "there is nothing to be done now. A baby is on its way and I for one am a happy woman."

Amanda was very upset about being pregnant. A baby would ruin everything. She wouldn't be able to escape if she was pregnant, unless she went right away. She still had no idea which direction to go when she ran. She couldn't just wander around in the woods until she found a town or some white people. She had to talk to the Negro man again or his friend. Maybe they could give her some idea which direction a town was or a farm. Even if they could tell her which direction they ran from, it would be something to go on.

The next day, Amanda took a dress she had made for Hialeah to Tsula and Mohe's house. The baby was walking very well now and toddled toward her laughing when she saw Amanda walking up to the house. Amanda picked the chubby little girl up and nuzzled her cheek. Kanuna spotted her as well and came running to her, wrapping his little arms around her leg. Both of the children loved Amanda. She played with them whenever she could. Amanda had always loved children. She had loved playing with her little brothers and sisters all her life. She missed them so much. She just had to get back home and soon.

After playing with the children and speaking to Tsula for a few minutes, Amanda casually walked by Waya's old house where the slaves now lived. She didn't see the man she had spoken to before, but his friend was outside sitting on a stump scraping hair off a deer skin. There were too many people around now to really speak to the man, but she did whisper to him to meet her at the river in the morning if he could. Out of the corner of her eye, she saw the man give a quick affirmative nod.

The next morning as soon as she could get away after breakfast, Amanda took her water jars down to the river to carry water to her fields. Both the slaves were at the river fishing. Amanda didn't go too close to them, but she did kneel down in whispering range from where they fished. She dipped one of her jars into the river and after filling it, she set it on the bank. She took the other jar and began filling it.

Amanda whispered as loudly as she could. "I need to talk to you about escaping from this place. I need to leave here as soon as I can. I have to know what direction to run. Can either of you help me at all?"

The man she had spoken to first, just shook his head slightly, no. The other man, however, looked at his friend and acted like he was talking to him. He said, "I'se know where Masser Carmichael's place was from where we was cotched. We's went straight wes when we run and that's the way we kep runnin'. Sos his place gotta be east. Problem is, I ain't sure which way them injuns took us to get to this here place."

Amanda had done a lot of thinking on this subject and was ready to ask some questions that might help her. "Where did you come into town? Was it near the house where you live now?"

"No'm it was crost town from there. That I do know. It was by the old woman's house, the one the injuns call grandma."

"Thank you, thank you so much. You've helped me. Please don't tell anyone I spoke to you about this. Don't you want to get away from here too?"

"No'm we's better off here. These injuns don't use no whips like Masser Carmichael done. We's got better food and the work ain't near as hard here. We's think we better jes stay. But we's won't say nuthin bout talkin' to ya."

Amanda took her water jars and walked quickly to her fields. She put a little water on all her plants and made her way home. She left her jars at the fields to be used the next day.

She was very excited. She finally had a good idea which way to go when she left. She just had to decide when to try to leave. Waya was around a lot now. He hadn't been gone overnight in weeks. He needed to be gone for her to leave since he slept with his arms around her. She couldn't get out of the house if he was there.

Chapter 20

Amanda's chance came two weeks later. One of the warriors had been hunting and spotted signs of a Shawnee war party nearby. He followed their trail until they camped and came back to get a war party. The Cherokee and Shawnee were sworn enemies, so a large group of warriors went, including Mohe and Waya.

Amanda was excited, but tried not to let it show. She helped Waya pack food into deerskin bags. She filled pig bladders with water, helping Waya to store his supplies on his horse. As Amanda seemed extra quiet, Waya thought she was worried about he and Mohe. He said, "Not to worry, little bird. Mohe and I are great warriors. We will send these Shawnee back where they belong. We will only be gone a few days."

With that, he gave her a very thorough kiss and jumping on his horse, he joined the other warriors.

Amanda had not told anyone that she was pregnant. The sickness was abating now and her belly was still mostly flat. She figured she was about three months along. She hoped she could make it home before Waya returned. From what she had heard in the town, the Shawnee were camped to the north of town. She was heading southeast. Grandmother's house was on the southside of town and the slaves had told her their old plantation was east. She thought if she headed south for about a day and then turned east, she would find a farm or settlement of whites.

Amanda could hardly wait for dark. Earlier, as she had been taking more food into her store house, she had gotten all her supplies ready. This time, she was also taking a pig bladder full of water as well as food. She remembered how terribly thirsty she had been on her last attempt. She had hoped to steal a horse, but the warriors had taken all of them on their raid.

Ninovan was suspicious. Amanda had not told Waya about the baby. Ninovan knew this because her son would have been so very proud, he would have told everyone who would listen if he knew. Amanda had been very quiet since she found out she was pregnant. The baby obviously was not good news to her. Ninovan would watch her while they were working and she could tell Amanda was deep in thought. Ninovan thought she was going to try to escape again.

If not for the baby growing inside her, Ninovan might have helped her go. She understood the girl was not happy here and wanted her family. She didn't believe Amanda would ever be happy in the Cherokee town. However, her grandchild was a different matter. She couldn't let Amanda leave while she was pregnant. If she wanted to go and leave the child after it was born, then let her. Ninovan wouldn't stand in her way. She knew Waya would never willingly let Amanda leave, but he wasn't thinking with his head, but with his heart.

Late that night, Amanda very quietly snuck out of her house and slowly went to the storehouse next door. She pulled aside the door hanging and slipped into the small space as quietly as she could. There was no light in the small house, but Amanda had hidden her supplies to the right of the door so they would be easy to find in the dark. She put her hand on the wall for guidance and walked carefully down the wall.

She had placed a large jar of corn meal in front of her cache of supplies. As she was bending over to pick up her canvas bag Ninovan spoke, "No, Amanda, you cannot leave again."

Startled, Amanda jumped and screeched. She turned to the sound of Ninovan's voice and said, "You have to let me go. I hate it here. These are not my people and I don't love your son. I need to get to my family. Please, please, let me go." she said tearfully.

"I understand that you are unhappy, Ah-man-da. But you carry my grandchild in your belly. I know you have not told my son or he would have happily spread the word all over town. I also know you don't love my son. If not for the baby, I would help you leave so he could find a woman someday who would love him as he deserves to be loved."

Amanda was heartbroken, but she couldn't be angry with Ninovan so she didn't argue any more. Ninovan was only doing what was best for her son. Amanda knew that Ninovan almost worshipped Waya. She would do anything for him. Amanda returned to her house and Ninovan followed. She stayed at Amanda's house that night. It looked like there would be no other chances to get away now.

When Waya came back from the raid on the Shawnee, Amanda told him she was carrying a child. There was no point in trying to keep it a secret any longer. She would not have an opportunity to get away until after the baby was born. Amanda was torn about the baby. She hated the fact that the baby was half Cherokee, but she couldn't hate the baby.

Waya was beside himself with joy. "Now", he thought, "my Ah-man-da will stay with me and be happy. We will have a child to help keep her tied to me." Waya knew his wife was not happy although she did seem to enjoy their time in bed. She rarely smiled unless she was playing with Mohe's children. "Having a baby is just what she needs", Waya thought.

Chapter 21

Amanda debated with herself all during the next months as to whether she would take the baby with her when she ran again. She knew that most white people would be cruel to her child and call he or she names like half-breed. Even her own family might not want the child. She wasn't sure how they would feel about her, even. They might not want her back either after she had been married to an Indian and had his child.

Sometimes Amanda thought she would just run from the Cherokee town and keep going, not even try to find her family. Those thoughts didn't last long. Her desire to see her family was so strong, she knew she would have to try to find her way back to them somehow.

Also, Amanda knew if she took the child with her, Waya would follow her forever. He knew where her family lived. Obviously, he could come and get her back anytime he wanted. He might even kill her family if she went back there. Amanda was driving herself crazy with all these thoughts as her belly slowly got bigger and bigger. She hardly ate and her sleep was disturbed almost every night with horrible dreams of her child being slaughtered by her own family or her friends' families.

Waya could see that something was very wrong with his wife. She had dark circles under her eyes. Instead of gaining weight like a normal Cherokee woman did while pregnant, she got skinnier every day. Her hair had even lost its shine and vibrancy. She seemed to go through her days like a dead woman. Finally, during Amanda's seventh month of pregnancy, Waya went to Ninovan for help.

"My mother, I need your help. My wife, Ah-man-da, is wasting away. She hardly eats and she has bad dreams almost every night. Is she sick? Do you know what is wrong with her? She just tells me she's fine when she speaks to me at all. Sometimes I have to ask her a question two or three times. It's like she's only half alive."

"Yes, my son, I know what is wrong with your wife. She is heart sick. She wants her own people. She is not happy to be having a baby. She just wants to go home. I fear as soon as the baby is born, she will take it and run away. We must watch her closely. She might not even survive having the child. I only hope that at least my grandchild will survive."

Waya was shocked. Not only at what he was told, but at his mother's attitude toward his wife. He had thought Ninovan liked Ah-man-da. When he asked her, she had this to say.

"I did like Ah-man-da until I found her trying to run away again while you were out hunting the Shawnee. I did not tell you, my son, because I still had some hope in my heart that she would change. I could not let her go while she had my grandchild in her belly, so I stopped her. She does not love you, my son. She may not even love this child. I don't know for sure either way, but I do know that I love the child and you love the child. I will raise it for you until you can find a proper Cherokee wife to help you and to have more children for you."

"But Mother, I don't want another wife. I want Ah-man-da. Why can't she learn to love me like I love her. I have treated her well. I have not beaten her or slept with other women. I bring plenty of meat home. She is well loved and well taken care of. I do not understand."

"My son, the heart is a fickle thing. No matter how much you love her, you cannot make her love you. Either she does or she does not. As for the baby, we cannot allow her to take it with her when she leaves, and mark my words, she will leave. None of us can watch her all the time."

Waya was heartbroken as he left his mother's house. He didn't go home, he couldn't face his wife right now. Instead, he went to Mohe's house. His brother had always been there for him. He needed to talk to him really badly. When Tsula told him that Mohe was not at home, he wandered around the town looking for him everywhere.

Finally he came upon Mohe with the horses. He was cleaning the hooves of his horse with a sharpened stick. Mohe had always had a way with horses. They reacted to his soft voice and gentle hands. For the first time, Waya noticed that Mohe spoke to the horses in the white man's tongue. He wondered why he had never noticed it before.

When Mohe saw Waya's face, he left off what he was doing and came to his brother's side.

"What troubles you, my brother?" Mohe asked quietly.

"I have just left our mother's house. She told me my wife tried to run away again while we were chasing the Shawnee from our lands. She says Ah-man-da does not love me and probably never will. Our mother wants me to let Ah-man-da go after she has our child, but Ninovan wants to keep the child. Do you think Ah-man-da would be willing to give up our child to return to her family?"

Seeing how miserable Waya was, Mohe took some time before he answered. "My brother, I am sorry you are having this problem, but I am not surprised. Ah-man-da has not let herself become a Cherokee. She holds herself back, not just from you, but from the whole tribe. She does only what is absolutely necessary for the rest of the tribe. She has no love for any of us, except maybe Tsula and our children. She does not want to be here and she will never be happy here unless her heart opens to allow her to be Cherokee. She needs to go back to her own kind. As for the baby, I cannot tell you what is in her heart. Only Ah-man-da can tell you what she feels deep inside."

Waya knew his mother and Mohe were right, but he just couldn't reconcile himself to the fact that his wife didn't love him and might not even want their child. Again, he felt he could not go home. He wandered down to the river and sat on a stump looking at the water for several hours. When Waya finally convinced himself he had to go home, Amanda was cooking their dinner. She barely looked up when Waya came in the door.

Waya looked at his beloved wife closely for the first time in a long time. Her belly was large, but the rest of her was just skin and bones. Her braided hair hung down to her waist, but it was lackluster and had no shine anymore. She stirred the pot of stew she was cooking in a lethargic way. Waya sat across the fire from her staring at her beautiful face.

When Amanda felt Waya staring at her, she looked up. "Is something wrong?" she asked. Her tone of voice indicated she didn't really care one way or the other.

Waya continued to stare at her for a few more moments before he spoke. "I have been told you tried to run away again when I was last gone. Why is it that you cannot love me, Ah-man-da? Do I not treat you well?"

Amanda felt a small flutter of fear. She hadn't wanted Waya to know about her last attempt to leave. It would make it harder when she got another chance to sneak away. She didn't know how to answer him. Finally, hanging her head, she said in a low voice., "I don't honestly know why I don't love you, Waya. I just don't feel it in my heart. I know you treat me well. I know my body responds to yours in our bed, but my heart is not there, just my body. I am sorry I cannot feel about you the way you want me to."

Waya was surprised at her honesty. He stared at her for some time and then spoke to her with a catch in his voice, "What about our child, Ah-man-da? Do you love the child growing in your belly?"

Amanda jerked her head up to stare at Waya. With tears rolling down her cheeks, she said, "I don't know. I have been driving myself crazy for months trying to decide whether I should take the child when I try to leave again. Part of me cannot even begin to think about leaving this child and another part wants to forget everything that has happened to me here. I fear if I take the child, he might not be treated well by my people, but then again, he might not be treated well here. Here, at least, he would have you, Ninovan, Mohe, and Tsula. With my family, there may only be me."

"I don't know, Waya, I just don't know. I have been trying not to feel anything for this baby growing inside me, but when I think of how much I love children and always wanted a lot of them, I can't believe I would even think about leaving my baby here."

With those words, Amanda collapsed into a mass of shuddering sobs. Her thin body shook so pitifully that Waya, although he was hurting so very badly himself, could not stand to see her in such pain. Waya took the pot off the fire then came around the fire. He picked Amanda up, he carried her to their bed, and lay her down. He lay down beside her and held her tight while she cried.

When Amanda had cried herself out, she fell asleep in Waya's arms. Waya didn't sleep. All he could do was try to think of a way out of their predicament. He didn't know if he could give up his child and let Ah-man-da take it back to her family. He actually wasn't sure he could willingly give up his Ah-man-da. He also knew that the child might be punished for its darker skin with the whites. He knew that there were people who would hate the child just because it was part Cherokee. He also knew that there were some Cherokee who might hate the child because it was part white.

There didn't seem to be an answer that was right for everyone. Waya felt guilty for taking Ah-man-da away from her family now. He had truly thought she would grow to love him as he loved her if he treated her well. When he found out they were having a baby, he had been ecstatic, not just to know he was going to be a father, but also because he thought Ah-man-da would be more content and might finally be happy.

The next day, Amanda seemed a little better. She ate a little more than usual at breakfast and seemed to have a little more energy. Waya was glad they had talked about her feelings, but there was still no decision made. It broke his heart to think he might have to give her up. The thought of giving up his son or daughter was also very difficult for him. Waya had no idea what to do.

Finally in frustration, he visited the Grandmother. He explained that his wife wanted to go back to her family, that she was unhappy with him, and would never reconcile herself to being without her own people. The Grandmother, knowing that the white girl was pregnant, asked Waya what would become of the baby if his wife returned to her people. He explained his mother's ideas and also Amanda's, but not his own.

The Grandmother looked at him and asked, "And what of you, Waya? What do you want?"

Waya looked miserable as he replied, "What I want, I cannot have, Grandmother. I want my wife to love me and our child. I know now that will never happen. I should have listened to you, my mother, and Mohe and left Ah-man-da where she was. I am at fault for everyone being miserable, but I don't know what to do."

"You must listen to your heart, grandson. If your heart tells you the white girl will never be happy here, then your heart must let her go. As for the child, that is a different matter. If the child is raised here, I believe it will have an easier time than if your wife takes it with her to the white people. Whites have not always treated those of mixed blood very well. I know that some have been accepted, but then again, many have not."

"There are those here who might not treat a mixed child well too, Grandmother. You know this is true."

"Yes, there are a few who might not look with favor on a half white child, but for the most part, they are few. Look at your own brother, Mohe. He has been accepted into the tribe almost from the start, as was his sister, Inola. And they are all white. No, I believe as your mother, Ninovan, does. The child should stay here. But, Waya, you are the only one who can make the final decision on this, unless the white girl runs away again taking the child with her. Then you will have to decide whether to follow her and bring her and the child or just the child back, or let them both go forever."

Waya went away from the Grandmother's house still unsure what he would do. Finally, he decided to just wait until the baby was born to make a decision. After holding his child, surely he would know what he was meant to do.

Waya went home, finding Ah-man-da sorting the beans she had picked that day. Some had dried in the shell and some would need to be shelled and dried in the sun. She looked up when Waya came through the open doorway. It was hot today and Amanda had pulled her hair up high on her head tying it into a bun. Waya was concerned at how scrawny her neck looked.

"Ah-man-da, I have been thinking much on the problems we have. I am having a lot of trouble trying to get used to the fact that you don't love me and probably never will. That is very hard for me to grasp because I love you so much." Seeing the look on Amanda's face, he went on, "I can see from your face that you regret hurting me, but I also know that I must come to terms with this situation.

"What is to be done with our child is also very hard for me. On one hand, I want to keep this child and raise it as a Cherokee. On the other hand, my heart hurts when I think of our child never knowing its mother. I have decided to wait until the child is born to make a final decision, but I will tell you now, if you want to return to your family after the child is born, I will not stop you. I will take you back to them myself. You will not need to run away. I could not live with myself if something happened to you while you were trying to get back home."

"Waya, thank you for offering to take me home. It is truly what I want. I don't think I can ever be happy here. As for the baby, I still don't know. I have tried to keep myself from feeling because I didn't know what to do and I still don't."

"Ah-man-da, I must encourage you to let yourself feel. That is the only way you can make the right decision for our child. We must both think much on this. There are still two moons before the baby is to be born. You must eat more and worry less this last two moons for the child's sake, if not your own. You are wasting away and that cannot be good for the baby.

"From now on, you must eat much and rest much. The harvest is now in. You have done much work this season and that work has been rewarded with a wonderful harvest. There will be plenty of food for us and much to sell or trade. I will trade for some calico and you can make yourself some clothes like you wore before you came here. You will need to tell me what else you will need. I will not send you back to your family skinny and not properly dressed."

Amanda had tears in her eyes as she looked at this good man. She wished she could love Waya. It would make things so much easier. She could just stay here and live with these good people forever. She was pretty sure her family believed her dead. It had been well over a year since she had been kidnapped. But she didn't love him. She had tried and tried, especially after her body reacted to him as it did. Amanda also carried some guilt for the way Waya was hurting, but she hadn't asked to be brought here and she couldn't help not loving him. Their situation was a problem with no answer. Either choice would hurt someone deeply.

Chapter 22

As Amanda's birthing time got closer, she was more and more uncomfortable. It had grown very cold in November and she and Waya had moved into the supply house to stay warmer. The smaller house was easier to keep warm with it's low roof and much smaller size. Waya had helped her to move their clothes and bedding to the smaller house. Normally, the Cherokee men didn't help with that type of chore, but Amanda's belly was huge and bending over was hard for her. She could no longer sit cross-legged on the ground, but had to use the benches Mohe had made for them instead.

Amanda had gained some weight, other than baby weight. Her skin and hair looked much better since she was eating well again. She was sleeping better also and the dark circles had disappeared from around her eyes. There was no scarcity of food. Her two plots of land had brought in a bumper crop of corn, beans, squash, pumpkins, and gourds. She had been making drinking dippers, ladles, and large spoons from the gourds since early summer. She had dried and ground corn in the early summer also, putting it away in clay jars. Ninovan had taught her how to make the clay jars not long after she came to live in the Cherokee town. She, Ninovan and Tsula had spent many hours making and painting clay vessels of all sizes.

Since the hunting season had also been a prosperous one, there was plenty of dried and smoked meat as well. Waya still hunted every few days so they could have fresh meat. It hadn't snowed yet, but it was bitterly cold. Most days found Waya and Amanda sitting around the fire in their small house. Amanda sewed or painted and Waya sharpened his knives and told her Cherokee stories. Amanda's pregnancy seemed to make her feel the cold more than usual. Waya had insisted that Ninovan help Amanda make a fur coat and cloak which she wore almost constantly while she was awake.

Going down to the river to wash clothes and dishes was also becoming very hard for Amanda to do. She slipped and fell into the freezing river one day trying to get down the slick bank to wash clothes. Tsula had been with her and screamed for help otherwise Amanda might have been washed away and drowned since she could not swim. Waya was afraid she and the baby would drown so he asked Tsula to do their wash until after the baby was born, after that incident. He took care of the dishes himself much to the amusement of the other men in town.

Tsula was very sad right now. She was also pregnant again, but it was very different for she and Mohe. They were very happy to add another child to their family. Tsula was actually due before Amanda, but being used to the heavy work required of a Cherokee woman, she had little difficulty getting around. Her belly was not nearly as big as Amanda's. Tsula worried that having such a large child would be hard on her friend. Ah-man-da had confided in her that she was leaving after her child was born, but she didn't know if she would take the child with her. The news was very hard for Tsula to bear. She had grown to love her friend. Kanuna and Hialeah would miss her very much as well. Ah-man-da always took time to play with them when she was around them and they loved her very much.

Mohe had mixed feelings about the situation Waya and Amanda found themselves in. He had been worried from the first that Waya taking the white girl would end badly. At first, he thought their town would be set upon by the whites trying to get the girl back. When much time had gone by, that worry was appeased. However, he knew it could still happen at any time. Whites were not unknown to raid Cherokee towns, killing everyone there. There were treaties, but some whites paid no attention to the treaties and killed, raped, and stole from the Cherokee whenever they pleased.

Now that Waya was completely aware of the situation, Mohe hoped his brother would begin to stop loving the white girl. From what Mohe could see, that was not the case. Perhaps, if all this had come to pass when it wasn't so cold, things might have been different. The fact that Waya spent so much time alone with Ah-man-da only seemed to make his brother love his wife more. He could see the pain in his brother's eyes grow deeper every day. Mohe wished the baby would be born soon, so some decision could be made.

Ninovan, on the other hand, was glad that Waya had this time to get used to the idea that his wife would go back to her own kind. She thought if he would just make up his mind on the baby, he would be content. Ninovan had cared for her husband, but she had never felt the almost overwhelming kind of love Waya had for Ah-man-da. She neither trusted that kind of love nor understood it. She also wished the baby would come soon, but for very different reasons. She thought if Waya once held the baby, he would not be able to let it go. Ninovan didn't want her grandchild to go away from her and its people.

One very cold day in early December, Mohe came to Waya and Amanda's little house bringing Kanuna and Hialeah with him. Tsula's time had come and the Grandmother wanted the little ones out of the house, as well as Mohe. The little houses were small enough without two active toddlers and a worried husband underfoot. Amanda rose to go to Tsula, but Mohe told her she would help her more by taking care of their children. Mohe and Waya went to sit by the council house fire to await the birth.

Amanda loved Kanuna and Hialeah, but she really wanted to be with her friend now. Also, on a more selfish note, she wanted to know what all was entailed in birthing a child. She had not been allowed into the room when her mother was having her younger siblings. A midwife had come from Paris to help, but her mother apparently needed very little help because sometimes the new baby was there well before the midwife arrived.

Amanda's experience with newborns had been limited to bathing and dressing them until her mother got back on her feet. Then her duties were to take care of the other young ones as well as all her other chores. It seemed she was always minding babies at home. Amanda had been surprised that the Cherokee women didn't put diapers on their babies. They only wore little shirts that came down almost to their knees in the winter and nothing in the summer. Tsula was forever washing bedclothes that her two babies had wet on.

When Amanda suggested putting diapers on them, her friend had no idea what she was talking about. When Amanda explained, Tsula had laughed at the idea, but after thinking about it, had acknowledged that it would save on the washing. Amanda had shown her how to fashion a diaper out of calico and how to tie it on the baby. Tsula had been amazed how easy it was and how much time it saved her. She didn't need to wash as many bedclothes or scoop up the soiled dirt in her house and take it outside nearly as often. Sometimes, there was a leak, but that was minor in comparison.

Amanda had sewn little shirts and diapers for her own baby. At first when she started working on the small garments, she had tried to pretend they were for Tsula's baby, not her own. Since she and Waya had talked, she had begun to let herself feel more. The more she opened her heart, the more she began to love the baby growing in her. Sometimes, when her baby moved, she would sit with her hand on her belly and a smile on her face. She wondered who the baby would favor. Would it have black hair and eyes or would it have her chestnut hair and green eyes or a combination of both?

When Waya saw Ah-man-da sitting with her hand on her belly and a smile on her face, his heart was glad. He could tell his wife was beginning to really care for their child. He watched as she sewed the tiny shirts and laughed when she told him what diapers were and what they were used for. He had never seen a Cherokee baby in a diaper, but he didn't tell her to stop making them. If making diapers made his wife happy, then so be it. Waya hadn't noticed Tsula's children wearing the diapers, but he saw them much less than Ah-man-da did.

When Mohe had come to their house this morning, Waya had taken his brother to the council house to smoke a pipe and listen to the elders tell stories to help take his mind off his wife's pain. Waya knew that having a baby was painful, but neither he nor Mohe had any real concept of what women went through to produce a child. Neither of them had ever been there when a woman gave birth. In the Cherokee nation, men didn't witness such things. If a couple were away from town when the time came, the woman would simply ask the man to leave and then have the child on her own. The man would come back some hours later and the baby would be there, all clean, oiled, and wrapped in a swaddling blanket made of deerskin.

When the Grandmother came into the council house to announce that a new warrior had joined the tribe, Mohe could hardly wait to go see his new son. Waya left at the same time, but went home to give Ah-man-da the news. Kanuna was old enough now to understand that a new baby was at his house and wanted to go see it. Amanda wrapped the children up in warm furs and Waya carried them both home. Amanda went with them to see the new baby and make sure her friend was all right.

When they called out at the door to Mohe's house, he laughed and told them to come in. Tsula was sitting by the fire on a pile of furs nursing the new baby. She looked drawn and tired, but had a huge smile on her face. Amanda immediately went to Tsula and looked at the new babe. Like Kanuna and Hialeah, the new baby was much lighter skinned than other babies in the town. Hialeah even had Mohe's blue eyes. From the looks of it, this baby would have Mohe's eyes and hair. The soft down on its head was not black, but it was very thick and stuck almost straight up. The effect was almost like the baby had a halo around its head.

Mohe and Tsula decided to name the baby Gawonii because of his big voice. It was said he could be heard all over the town when he was born. When Gawonii had finished eating, Tsula handed him to Amanda. As she held the newborn, she felt her own baby kick hard several times. It was almost as if he was jealous that his mother held another child. Amanda had to smile at this thought.

Waya watched her hold Gawonii and there was pain in his eyes. She looked so beautiful holding the baby with the sweet smile on her face. Again, he wondered what more he could have done to make Ah-man-da love him. He could think of nothing and it caused him deep pain. Mohe noticed Waya's pain and tried to distract him by talking about a hunt they were planning for the next week.

Some hogs had been spotted not far from the town. They had grown fat on the big crop of acorns the oak trees had put out this year. Some pork would taste mighty fine and several warriors had decided to hunt together for the whole town. Venison could be smoked, but was usually tough and had to be soaked in water for some time to be tender enough to eat. But pork was tender and tasty after being smoked. The tribe was excited to be getting some nice tender pork to eat. They had built a fire in the communal smokehouse and readied their skinning knives in preparation.

Two days later, Mohe and Waya, along with several other warriors left very early in the morning on a pig hunt. They came back late in the afternoon with eight nice sized hogs. They didn't kill the females, only the young males in the herd.

The older males were gamey and tough, but the young ones were tender and tasty. That night, the women worked long hours to butcher the meat and get it ready to smoke. Amanda joined them, but had a great deal of difficulty bending over so Waya brought her stool outside and she sat and helped to skin the hogs.

After the meat was cut up, the hams, belly, and shoulders were taken to the smokehouse. They would be watched carefully while they smoked for several days. Since the weather was cold, there was less likelihood of the meat spoiling before it was properly smoked for storage. Other parts of the hog were put to boil in large pots to make stew. The fat was rendered from the skin. After it was skimmed, the lard was stored in clay pots for cooking.

The rendered skin was very tasty and the children in the town vied for the best tidbits. The whites called the fried skin, cracklings. They made a very tasty bread with them. None of the Cherokee had ever had this type of bread, so Amanda made some, baking it in a clay pot. The bread was a big success and many women in the tribe had Amanda tell them how it was made. Waya was proud that his wife had contributed something new to his people. Amanda seemed to be happy at that moment as well. That night they dined on crackling bread and hog stew with the rest of the tribe around the big council fire. It was one of the most pleasant evenings they had spent in a long time.

In the days to come, Amanda was more and more uncomfortable. Being so small, it seemed her stomach was about to tip her over when she stood. She had to stand with her legs slightly apart and leaning back. It was very difficult for her to walk for very long as it hurt her back dreadfully. She was miserable and just wanted the baby to be born as quickly as possible. She was thankful the weather held and it didn't rain or snow. Amanda was afraid she might slip and fall in wet or snowy weather. Now that she had begun to care for this child, she didn't want anything to happen to it. Waya was very supportive as well. He also didn't want anything to happen to their baby or his beloved wife.

Late on a particularly cold night in late December, Amanda woke to a strange feeling. Her stomach seemed to harden momentarily and she felt a great pressure in her lower back. Tsula had told her what to watch for and she knew she was in labor. Thankfully, Tsula had prepared her for what was to come. She had explained the whole process to Amanda until she understood it perfectly. Tsula was amazed that no one had told Amanda what to expect when she had a child. She didn't understand the white people. Cherokee children were included in all discussions and no knowledge was withheld from them.

Amanda didn't awaken Waya right away. Tsula had told her it was sometimes hours from the first contractions until the baby was born. Soon though, Amanda needed to go to the latrine. She tried to rise by herself, but just as she was getting to her knees, a much harder contraction hit her. She groaned and Waya was immediately awake and on his feet.

"Are you ill, Ah-man-da? Do you hurt somewhere?"

"Not ill, Waya. I think the baby is coming, but right now I need to go make water really badly and I can't get up. Will you help me?"

Waya immediately leaned down and put his hands under Amanda's elbows easily lifting her to her feet. He was very concerned when she just stood there with one hand on her stomach and the other on her lower back. From the light of the fire, he could see a look of pain on her face.

After what seemed a long time, Amanda straightened a little and took a couple of steps toward the door. Waya came with her putting his arm around her shoulders for support. "Let me get your coat, Ah-man-da. It is very cold out there. Just stay right here and I'll be right back."

Amanda just nodded her head. She had a far away look on her face as if she was concentrating on something very hard. She frightened Waya. He got her coat and helped her into it and then grabbed her cloak and put it around her shoulders. He pulled the door flap back and helped his wife out through the low opening. When they were outside, Amanda stopped again putting one hand under her stomach this time and the other on her lower back. She was biting her top lip with her sharp little white teeth. Again she had that far away look on her face.

"Ah-man-da, can you make it to the latrine? If not, just go anywhere. We're not close to town and no one will ever know."

Still Amanda hadn't spoken, she just nodded her head and edged her way to a bush nearby. She grabbed onto the bush and slowly lowered herself into a squatting position. When she was done, Waya had to help her back up. She only took a couple of steps back toward the house when she had to stop again.

Amanda looked at Waya with worry in her eyes. "I think these pains are already too close together. Tsula said the birthing process usually takes some time, especially for the first child. Something must be wrong. Waya, please go get the Grandmother. Please….I, I."

Amanda stopped talking and hung onto Waya as a huge wave of pain came over her. She felt a gush of water run down her legs. At first, she thought she had urinated again from the pain, but then remembered Tsula had told her that her waters would break when the child was really ready to come. As soon as she was able to walk again, she hurried to their house with Waya's help.

Waya got her out of her clothes and into their bed. By then, she was writhing in pain. Waya covered her with their bearskin and hurried to the Grandmother's house. When he arrived, the Grandmother was not there. He hurried to the council house to see if she was there. There were only a couple of the elders sitting by the fire. They didn't know where the Grandmother was, but had heard there was someone's child sick with a fever. They couldn't remember who though. By this time, Waya was wild with fear for Amanda. He ran to Mohe's house and banged on the side waking all three children. Mohe yelled to wait and finally came to the door opening.

When he saw the state Waya was in, he knew immediately, it had something to do with Ah-man-da. Tsula also had risen and came over too. Waya said as quickly as he could. "It is Ah-man-da's birthing time and the Grandmother is not home and no one knows where she is. The pain is very bad and it just started. I fear something is terribly wrong."

Tsula was grabbing her fur coat and cloak as he spoke. She told Mohe she would go right away and ran out the door. Waya followed her. When they got to the house, they heard a baby cry. They looked at each other in astonishment, then hurried into the house.

Amanda was half sitting, half lying on the fur bed. She was laughing and crying at the same time. She held a wiggling baby girl on her belly still attached to her mother by the cord. The child had a very healthy set of lungs and was letting her displeasure be known. Waya saw all the blood and fluids and felt sick to his stomach. He had butchered untold number of animals in his years as a warrior and had killed some men, but nothing had affected him like the sight of his wife's blood.

Tsula saw right away that he was useless and sent him to get water. She cut the cord and took the squalling baby from Amanda. She set her down on the furs beside her mother and held Amanda up in a sitting position to deliver the afterbirth. That happened as quickly as the child had come. By the time Waya had returned with the water, mother and baby had been cleaned up and the soiled furs had been removed from the bed and replaced with clean ones.

Amanda was wearing a clean shirt and propped up in the bed holding the baby to her breast. She looked up when Waya entered and smiled at him. "Your daughter is like her father, impatient. She couldn't wait to be born. Come and see her. She is beautiful."

Waya immediately went to the bed and sat down. Amanda pulled the swaddling blanket back from the child's face so her father could see her. When Waya looked at the little girl, his heart turned over in his chest. She had Ah-man-da's face! Her thick hair was a darker chestnut than her mother's, but very similar. There were little waves in it just like Ah-man-da's. Her eyes were closed as she nursed, but they were shaped just like

Ah-man-da's. Waya reached out his hand and the baby closed her little fist over one of his fingers and held on. She was a big baby and had a strong grip. Apparently, she got her size from her father, but her face from her mother.

Waya looked up smiling to see the same happy smile on Amanda's face. She said, "I want to name her Leticia after my sister, if that's alright."

"Le-ti-sha. That is a good name. What does it mean in your tongue?"

"It means joy," said Amanda with a smile. "My mother gave us all names with meanings and told us what they were. My name means worthy of love."

"Your name fits you well. And so does our daughter's. She brings me much joy just looking at her." Waya said softly.

With tears in her eyes, Tsula slipped out the door carrying the ruined furs with her. It broke her heart to watch Waya and Ah-man-da right now, knowing that Ah-man-da planned to leave all of them soon. From the look on her face tonight, she wouldn't be leaving without her daughter and that could cause much trouble in the tribe. Tsula feared for her friend.

Soon, there was a knock on the door and the Grandmother came in. "I was told Ah-man-da needed me, but I see I have come too late. Why didn't you come for me earlier, Waya."

"There was no time, Grandmother. From the time Ah-man-da woke me until the time the baby was born, was just a very few minutes. I didn't know babies could come so fast." Waya said wonderingly.

Amanda spoke up, "It's the same for my mother. Most of the time, the midwife doesn't get to our house in time for the birth. She's had ten already with very little trouble."

The Grandmother just shook her head and said, "We should all be so lucky." She shooed Waya out and examined both Amanda and the baby. She pronounced them both fine although Amanda had had some tearing during the birth. The bleeding had already stopped from the tears though. The grandmother told her all was well. She went home, sending Waya back in.

Waya stood in the doorway and looked at Ah-man-da and Le-ti-sha. Ah-man-da held the baby close to her chest crooning softly to her as she gently rocked her. The baby was asleep and Ah-man-da looked very tired.

Waya took the sleeping baby and placed her in the cradle he had made for her. It was lined with soft furs and he took another fur and lay it over the sleeping child. The cradle wouldn't be big enough for long. Waya was amazed at the size of his new daughter. She looked bigger than Mohe's son and he was almost a month older. When Waya turned back to Ah-man-da, she was already asleep. He crawled into the bed with her and took her in his arms. She snuggled against him, but didn't really wake up.

Chapter 23

The next day Waya and Amanda had a steady stream of visitors. Everyone in the town wanted to see the huge baby that had practically birthed herself. Leticia was held and cooed over by almost every woman in town, but Ninovan more than anyone else. She stayed all day cooking and straightening the tiny house. Amanda was still tired and welcomed her help. She could see how Ninovan looked at Leticia with eyes of love and couldn't deny her the time she spent holding her.

Amanda had not had a moment to herself all day and was glad when everyone went to their own homes for the evening meal except Ninovan. Even she, after cuddling the baby one more time, left after cleaning up from the meal. Waya had gone to get water and Amanda finally had her new daughter to herself. She was a really good baby. She only fussed when she was wet or hungry.

However, she was hungry a lot. Amanda was worried she might not have enough milk for a baby this big, but the Grandmother, who had come early that morning to check on them, told her she would generate more milk in the next few days. She told her to just feed the baby when she acted hungry and everything would be fine, so that is what she had done.

Leticia had nursed six times already today. She had emptied both of Amanda's breasts every time. Now she lay beside her mother sound asleep. Amanda was sore all over it seemed. Her private parts were stretched so far, she felt like she walked spraddle-legged as her grandmother used to say. The places where she had torn were very sore as well. The Grandmother had put a healing ointment on them that morning that had helped. Her stomach was still puffy and she felt bloated, but her breasts were the source of the worst pain. They were so tender she could hardly stand to have her buckskin shirt touch them. She wished she could take it off and just lie in the bed naked, but she didn't dare. Instead, she held it away from her chest and turned onto her side with a groan.

Waya came through the door just in time to hear his Ah-man-da groan. He hurried to the bedside and asked worriedly, "Are you alright? I heard you groan. Are you in pain?"

Amanda smiled up at him and hastened to allay his fears. "I'm okay. It's just, well, my breasts are hurting really badly and this shirt feels like it's made of briars."

"Take it off then, if it hurts you. Surely no one else will come this late in the day. It is very cold outside. Hopefully everyone will stay in. There is no reason for you to be in pain. Let me help you get it off."

Waya came to the side of the bed and very gently pulled the shirt over Amanda's head. He lay it on a bench and returned to the side of the bed. Amanda's breasts were red and did look very painful.

"Is there nothing you can put on them to make them feel better? Some herb or something?" Waya asked in a very concerned voice.

"The Grandmother told me I might have this problem since Letitia is so hungry all the time. She said a warm cloth on them might help and also to rub them with some warm grease. This is the first time today this little house hasn't been full of people. I didn't want to do any of that with everyone around." Amanda said with a groan as she started to get up.

"Ah-man-da, stay in bed. I will warm some water and get you a cloth. I will also warm some lard for you. You look very tired. It has been a busy day and you didn't get a lot of sleep last night. Our girl is hungry so often, you were awake half the night."

"Thank you, Waya. I am tired. Leticia is a big girl and she gets hungry often."

Waya went about getting everything ready while Amanda rested. When the water was warm, he brought it to her in a clay bowl with a piece of calico. While she was putting the cloth on her nipples, he returned to the fire and put a small amount of lard in a clay pot to heat. The fire was hot and it only took a couple of minutes to warm the lard. Waya came back and sat on the side of the bed. He took a dry cloth and very tenderly dried Amanda's sore, red breasts. Then with surprising gentleness, he massaged a small amount of the lard into Amanda's nipples.

At first Amanda was embarrassed to have Waya perform such an intimate task for her. But looking at him, his handsome face intent on his chore, his long beautiful black hair hanging down his back, she relaxed and just enjoyed the lessening of the pain she had been suffering for several hours.

When Waya was done, he cleared away everything and then came back to stretch out on the bed beside Amanda and the baby. He raised himself on his elbow and lay staring at their amazingly big baby. She did indeed have Amanda's eyes, except they were blue. When he had remarked on this to Amanda earlier, she had said her own eyes were blue until she was about two and then they changed to green. Waya hoped that Leticia would have her mother's beautiful green eyes.

Letitia's little face was identical to her mother's. The softly winged brows, the high cheekbones, the wide forehead, and the slightly pointed chin were so much like Amanda's it was uncanny. When he looked at her little body, however, he saw himself. Her shoulders were wide, her waist much narrower, and her legs were long. It seemed funny to him that a girl would have his body and he smiled.

Amanda had been watching Waya without his noticing it. When he smiled, she reached up and touched his face and he looked down at her with a question in his eyes. She said, "Why are you smiling?"

Waya smiled broader and said, "Because our daughter has your face and my body. I find that strange and amusing at the same time. She will grow into a tall, strong woman. I wish I could see her when she was grown."

With Waya's words, something broke in Amanda's chest. His voice was so sad, and yet resigned too. Apparently, he had come to the conclusion that she would be taking the baby when she left. Amanda knew, when she left, she would not be able to leave her daughter behind. She loved this little girl with all her heart. She was very confused. Waya had been so very good to her all through the pregnancy, even after he knew she couldn't love him and wanted to go home. Amanda was surprised when she felt her heart hurt at the thought of leaving Waya. She had thought she had no feelings for him, but maybe she had been wrong. Maybe she had not allowed herself to care for Waya just as she had denied her feelings for her baby.

Other than stealing her from her home and family, he had never done her any harm. On the contrary, Waya had been very good to her in all ways. He was a good provider, he was kind, and he obviously loved her very much. He continued to love her even though she had hurt him when she told him she didn't love him and never would. He even kept loving her when she told him she wanted to go home. Amanda had seen the pain in his eyes, although he had never said one word of reproach to her. She had caught him looking at her many times in the past two months with such agony in his eyes, it had hurt her to see it.

Maybe she hurt because she didn't want to cause him pain, she thought. Maybe she did care about him. Looking down at their little daughter, Amanda was shocked to think she didn't want to take this child away from her father and grandmother. She had made good friends here in Tsula and Mohe. She held great affection for their three children as well.

Here her daughter would never have to face the stigma of being a half-breed. Amanda knew that many white people would look down on she and her daughter if she went home, maybe even her own family. Here Leticia would be protected from that stigma and she would be loved unconditionally by both her parents, her grandmother, and Tsula and Mohe, as well as their children. Even if some people here didn't approve of mixed blood children, they were never cruel to them and they were never excluded as they might be if she took Leticia home.

Amanda lay awake a long time thinking after both Waya and Leticia slept. She had been away for over a year and a half. Her family probably thought she was dead. Maybe it would be better to just let them go on believing that. If she stayed here with Waya, she would have a man who loved her and their child. She would have good friends, a warm, snug home, and peace. There was no guarantee what her reception would be at home.

Amanda didn't so much fear her own family, but there were others to be considered as well. Even if her parents accepted Leticia, what about their neighbors and the people who lived in Paris. She had heard the adults talking when they didn't know she was near. She had heard the stories about a girl who had been kidnapped like her. When her family got her back, she had a little boy. Her own father had beaten her because she had a half-Indian child. He told her she should have killed herself before she let an Indian lay with her. He had taken the little boy and given him to some Indian people who were in town trading that day. The girl had killed herself then.

Her mother had been very angry about how the man had acted, but no one had stopped him. Children belonged to their parents. And girls belonged to their parents until they got married and then they belonged to their husbands. Females had no rights and very few had any way to make a living nor were they able to own property unless they were widows. They were dependent on their male relatives for everything. Amanda didn't think a white man would be willing to accept her baby as his own when she was half Indian. And she would never marry a man who didn't accept Leticia. She would never be able to marry if she went back. She would always have to live with her parents and be a burden to them.

The more she thought about the situation, the more upset she became. Amanda ended up crying herself to sleep. It was only a couple of hours before Leticia woke hungry and crying. Amanda roused herself picking up the wet baby. She changed her diaper and then put her to nurse. Her nipples were still so very sore, she groaned when the baby latched on.

The crying baby had wakened Waya, but he hadn't said anything. He just wanted to be able to enjoy watching his wife feed their child for as long as he could. When Amanda groaned in pain, however, he raised himself on his elbow and said, "Is the pain so bad, then?"

Amanda looked up in surprise. "I didn't mean to wake you. I'm sorry."

"There is no need to be sorry, Ah-man-da. I enjoy watching our daughter eat. She's a greedy little thing. I am sorry her feeding makes you have pain. What did the Grandmother say about it."

"It will get better in time. My milk is not very rich right now, that's why she eats so often. My milk will be better in a couple of days and she will not eat as often. Also my breasts will toughen after a time. I will bathe them again when she's done and put some more grease on them. It's not so bad after she gets started. It's just right at first that they hurt really bad."

"I will heat water for you and heat some more grease too." Waya said getting up and stirring the fire. He added more wood and put a pot of water to warm. Amanda watched him with a musing look on her face he couldn't interpret. He noticed her eyes were red and swollen.

"Does feeding La-tish-a pain you so much that you cry? Your eyes are very red and swollen."

"No, I'm not crying now. I was crying earlier though. I am very confused right now."

"Confused, Ah-man-da. What are you confused about?"

"Waya, I….I'm not sure that I should go home after all. I fear how some white people might treat our baby. I love her very much and wouldn't see her hurt for anything in the world. Also, well, although I know she will be safe here, I cannot leave her. I had thought I might be able to, but these last couple of months, feeling her grow inside me, feeling her move, well, I started to have very deep feelings for her. And now that she's born, seeing how perfect and beautiful she is, I love her even more. I fear taking her home with me and I cannot leave her. So, you see why I'm feeling confused."

"Ah-man-da, you don't have to leave. You and La-tish-a will be safe and loved here with me and my people. You know how I feel about you and I feel the same deep love for our daughter. I would never let anyone harm either of you as long as there is breath in my body." Waya said with a fierceness that startled Amanda. She was about to speak when Leticia started to fuss. She had emptied Amanda's right breast very quickly.

Amanda moved the baby to her other breast and groaned again as Letitia latched on. It seemed her left breast was even more tender than her right. When the pain had ebbed, Amanda looked up at Waya. He was so very handsome squatting by the fire in nothing but a breechclout. He was one of the most beautifully made men she had ever seen. His shoulders were wide, his chest was huge, and his arms were heavily muscled as well. His dark eyes shone with the light of love as he looked at her and their baby.

When the baby had emptied her other breast, she cuddled her close and rocked her gently until she was asleep again. Waya took the baby and lay her in the cradle then brought the warm water to their bed. This time he gently bathed her breasts and very carefully rubbed the lard into them. When he was done, Amanda leaned back upon the furs.

When Waya would have turned away, she stopped him by taking his large hand in both her small ones. She started to speak and then stopped, only to start again. "Waya, I am confused about the baby, but I am also confused about my feelings for you. I had convinced myself that going home was the only way I could ever be happy, but now, I'm not so sure. You have been so very good to me, right from the first when we couldn't even speak to each other. You were always gentle with me, even when I ran away and you had to come track me down. From what I have seen here, most men would have beaten their women for running away. You never even raised your voice to me. You are a good and kind man and I have come to ....care for you. It would also be hard for me to leave you behind."

Waya was overcome with joy. His Ah-man-da might love him yet. He reached over with his free hand and gently touched her face. He was afraid to say anything, so he just caressed her beautiful little face and touched his lips to hers in a very soft kiss. Waya put away the things he had treated Amanda's breasts with and came back to bed. He put his arms around his wife and pulled her small body close. They spent what was left of the night in each other's arms, both with smiles upon their lips.

Chapter 24

The following days were spent in Amanda regaining her strength and Leticia growing fat and happy on her mother's much richer milk. The time between feedings got a little longer, but Leticia was still a very hungry baby. Since, at birth, she was as big as a two or three month old baby, her appetite was much larger than most newborns. In just a few weeks, it was obvious that Amanda's milk would have to be augmented with some other type of food.

The Grandmother had never seen a baby this big, so she was somewhat at a loss as to what food they could give a child this young that wouldn't upset her stomach. Amanda told her that white babies usually just drank their mother's milk for the first six months and then were gradually introduced to small amounts of soft foods like potatoes and oatmeal. Neither of those things were available, but they did have cornmeal, so they made a very thin mush from it and sweetened it with honey when Leticia was two months old.

Leticia loved it. Soon she was eating the mush three or four times a day and emptying both Amanda's breasts too. The mush didn't seem to upset her stomach, although she had much nastier diapers for a couple of days until her system got used to the mush.

By the time she was four months old, Letty had four teeth and was trying to eat everything in sight. She was already sitting alone and scooting all over the floor on her tummy trying to crawl. Of course, her parents thought she was the biggest, smartest, most beautiful baby in the world.

Everyone in town loved to hold her. She had a big smile for everyone. Letty, as she was soon called, had an endearing way of looking very closely at the people who held her. When they spoke softly to her, she would hold her little hand up and touch their faces very gently. Ninovan was so proud of her, she could hardly stop talking about her. Ninovan had noticed that there had been no talk about Ah-man-da leaving. As a matter of fact, there were signs that her daughter-in-law was quite happy where she was.

Now that spring had come, Amanda would take Letty with her to work her two plots of land. Ordinarily, the baby would have ridden on Amanda's back in a papoose carrier, but as she was so heavy, it was painful for Amanda to carry her that way for long. Amanda began to lay a blanket on the ground under a tree for the baby while she tilled up her ground for planting. Often she would have to stop what she was doing and put the baby back on the blanket. Letty loved to scoot off the blanket and examine all the interesting things she found in the dirt. Of course, those interesting things would almost immediately go into her mouth. Amanda found herself removing dirt, twigs, rocks and bugs from her baby's mouth. There was no telling what all she swallowed before Amanda got to her.

In desperation, Amanda made a bargain with one of the older women, Ama, to watch the baby while she worked, in exchange for food. She and Waya had more than enough food, so it was no imposition for them, but it was a blessing for Ama. Ama's family was all gone and she was dependent on the charity of others. Her pride wouldn't let her take much charity, so she tried to gather as much food as she could. Because she was old and crippled with arthritis, her pride made her very thin. With the new arrangement, she started to gain weight and the baby no longer ate things she shouldn't. It was a good arrangement for everyone.

Soon Ama had become such a part of their lives, with Amanda's permission, Waya asked Ama to move into a small house he built next to their larger one. She took all her meals with them and proved invaluable to Amanda for many reasons. She not only took care of Letty, but she was very knowledgeable about herbs and plants used in healing. She was the Grandmother's slightly younger sister and had learned much from their mother who had been the healer before she died.

As the weeks wore on, Waya became guardedly optimistic that his Ah-man-da might stay with him. She never mentioned leaving after that one time, just after La-tish-a's birth. She worked her land every day, cleaned their house, played with their daughter, and learned from Ama everything she could. She and Tsula often put their children together in the afternoons to play while they sewed, made clay vessels or carved and painted gourds. The children played well together. Little Hialeah was very motherly and watched the two babies closely even though she wasn't much more than a baby herself.

As the summer wore on, it became hotter and dryer every day. Amanda, Tsula, and all the other women of the town were kept very busy carrying water for their fields. The heat was taking a toll on the older members of the tribe too. Ama no longer accompanied Amanda to her fields, but kept Letty at the house in the shade. Because Letty was a very large baby, she didn't respond well to the heat either.

Sometimes, Waya would take Ama and Letty to the river to cool off in the water. He would help Ama down the bank and she would sit in the shallow water while he took Letty further out and played with her in the waist deep water. Amanda was afraid of the river because she couldn't swim, but soon Waya remedied that. He taught Amanda to swim in the evenings when everyone else had left the river for their homes. Ama would sit in the shallow water with Letty while Waya gave Amanda her swimming lessons.

Once Amanda overcame her fear of the water, she became a very good swimmer. Almost all the Indians swam. They were taught at a very young age. Swimming could possibly save their lives if they were caught in a flood swollen river or creek. It could also save their lives if they were running from an enemy. They could cross the water to cover their trails or even hide in the water, breathing through a hollow reed until their enemy was gone. Waya taught all these things to Amanda.

Finally the long hot summer came to an end with the cooling change to fall. The leaves began to turn orange, red, and yellow and there was a slight nip in the air. The signs all indicated another very cold winter was on the way, so the whole town worked to gather enough wood to keep warm when the cold struck. Those too feeble or old to gather wood, would be given wood by those who could. The same applied to food. The town elders made sure everyone had enough to eat whether they could hunt or grow the food or not. The town's people took care of each other.

The cold was very hard on Ama because of her arthritis. She dreaded the winter, but was soon made happy by Waya and Amanda's invitation to live with them in their small house this winter. Waya had stacked wood all around the perimeter of the small house in case of deep snow. None of them would have to go far to replenish their wood supply. He had also stacked a lot of wood around the interior walls of the small house. The wood didn't take up much room and actually insulated the house and made it warmer. They used that dry wood to start the fire in case it went out. They would use the outside wood after the fire was well started. It was sometimes damp and caused smoke, but it kept them warm.

Amanda had had another good year with her fields. Waya went to the white man's town nearby three times to barter produce for things they either needed or wanted. He brought back salt, calico, thread, needles, cooking pots, and even a toy for Letty, a spinning top. After Amanda showed Ama how to spin the top on a level rock, the baby would spend a lot of time watching it. It kept her occupied while her mother worked around the house and gave a lot of enjoyment to Ama too. Letty seemed to be fascinated with the colors that spun around and around.

Waya also brought a gift for his Ah-man-da. He found a small hand mirror set in a wooden frame at the trading post and thought his wife might like it. When Waya presented the gift to Amanda, she was surprised at his thoughtfulness. She hadn't seen herself in a mirror in almost 2 years. She was now eighteen years old and was surprised at the changes she saw in her reflection. She no longer saw the innocent young girl she had been. She saw a mature woman looking back at her. Her skin had tanned in the sun and the red streaks in her chestnut hair were more pronounced. She was thinner than she had been, but her breasts were much fuller from having Letty.

The biggest change Amanda saw was in her eyes. They were still the same color green with long straight black lashes, below naturally arched brows, but the expression in them was very different. What she saw surprised her because she saw contentment. She had never expected to become not only used to her life in the Cherokee town, but to enjoy that life to the fullest. She had everything she had dreamed of when she was a little girl, even though in a much different place than she had ever imagined.

She had a loving husband, a beautiful child, and people she loved, who loved her back. Amanda had become even closer to Tsula and Ninovan. And now she had Ama as well. It was like having her Granny living in the house with her. Ama had developed a deep and abiding love for the little white girl and her child. She had always been partial to Waya, but now she was even closer to him through their shared love of Amanda and Letty.

The fall seemed to pass very quickly with all the activity of getting ready for the coming winter. Soon, the nights were cold and the days were crisp. In mid October, the tribe celebrated the Friendship Ceremony during which Ama pledged her eternal friendship to Waya and Amanda. Amanda in turn pledged her eternal friendship to both Ninovan and Ama making them both extremely proud. It was her way of acknowledging Ninovan as a mother figure and Ama as a grandmother figure in her life. The Cherokee took these pledges very seriously as they were life long and not taken lightly.

Waya beamed with pride as he watched his beautiful Ah-man-da participate in the ceremony with his mother and Ama. Everything he had wished for had come to pass. Just last night, after some very intense love-making, Ah-man-da had whispered the words he had longed to hear for the last two years. She had told him she loved him. He thought he was the happiest Cherokee alive at that moment.

Chapter 25

The signs portending a very cold winter were true. The north wind howled almost constantly and brought torrents of cold wet snow down on the little Cherokee town. There was very little anyone could do outside. They all huddled in their little houses around their fires most of the days and all of the nights. It was so cold at night, just breathing the outside air was painful.

It became impossible to make it to the latrines because of the ice and snow. The people had to use clay jars for chamber pots. Privacy was hard to come by, but Amanda took a blanket and hung it in one corner of their tiny house to shield the clay pot they used. She had fashioned the pot after the chamber pots she had used when at home. However, she made it taller than normal because of Ama. It was hard for the older woman to bend low because of her painfully arthritic knees. Sometimes Amanda had to help her up from even the taller one they used. At first, Ama was embarrassed to need the help, but as time went by, Amanda was so sweet about helping, she lost that embarrassment and accepted the help in the spirit it was offered.

Normally, it would have been the woman's duty to empty the chamber pot, but Waya took on that daily job. He was tall and strong and could make his way through the deep snow drifts much easier than his tiny wife or the frail Ama. When he would go out to empty the pot, he would also usually go and check on his mother. He had asked Ninovan to move in with them for the winter, but she valued her privacy and wouldn't even consider it.

For the first part of the winter, everyone was healthy and well fed. However, not long after Letty's first birthday, Waya went to his mother's house one morning to find her still lying in bed. She was very hot with fever, but told him she was very cold. He heaped furs and blankets on her, made some tea for her and then went for the Grandmother. The Grandmother was also ill though. It seemed that a sickness was hitting all the older members of the tribe, as well as the very youngest. When Waya went to check on Tsula and Mohe, Gawonii was also ill with a high fever and chills.

Soon Amanda was trudging to Ninovan's house every day to care for her. Waya would walk through the heavy snow first to make a path and Amanda would follow. Ama would make up poultices, teas, and other medicines from the stores she and Amanda had gathered in the spring and summer, but Amanda insisted only she take them to Ninovan and Gawonii. Amanda feared Ama would catch the sickness if she went and bring it home to Letty. She also was afraid Ama wouldn't be able to make it through the heavy snow. Since neither Ama nor Letty went out, they both remained well, much to Amanda's relief. Amanda and Waya also remained well, but many in the town did not.

Ninovan, however, did not fare so well, nor did the Grandmother. Despite all her granddaughter, Yona, could do, the Grandmother died after being ill for two weeks. Her extreme age worked against her. Ninovan, being much younger, pulled through the sickness, but was left very weak. It was several weeks before she was strong enough to care for herself. There were other deaths in the town as well. Two of the elders succumbed to the disease as did two babies. Gawonii, thankfully, had a very light case and recovered quickly and no one else in Mohe's household became ill.

As tradition dictated, the Grandmother was buried on the day she died in the ground under the bed where she died.

Yona, who would be taking over as Priestess, dug the grave under her grandmother's bed. She washed her body in lavender water and anointed it with lavender oil to purify it. Yona buried her grandmother's personal possessions with her and then purified her house with burning sage and lavender.

Yona, as the new priestess, conducted the same ceremonies for all the dead. Family members washed the bodies, but Yona dug all the graves and performed the purification rites for all the dead and the living who had lived in the same house. Amanda could see the toll these ceremonies took on Yona. She had loved her grandmother dearly and yet, she had no time to grieve for her. Amanda did her best to take on as many of the sick cases as she could to give Yona some much needed rest.

Finally, in March the sickness left the town as quickly as it had come. When the time came for the spring ceremony, the people gathered at the council house to look with renewed hope on the new planting year. The omens were good for a new season and the women were eager to get their ground ready and their crops planted.

Letty was walking or rather running by now. She had taken her first steps at nine months and hadn't slowed down since. It had been a trial to keep up with her in the little house. She was bright and curious and into everything. Ama did her best to keep her young charge occupied, but it was a tough job. Ama couldn't move around nearly as fast as Letty and she knew it. Her fat little legs carried her everywhere at once Ama thought.

Amanda began to take Letty with her to her plots while she worked. Ama came along to help keep an eye on the curious little toddler. Since getting off the ground was hard for Ama, Waya placed benches under the trees for Ama and Amanda to rest on. As Ninovan slowly recovered, she would also come to sit on one of the benches and watch her beloved granddaughter play. Amanda took on the job of readying Ninovan's plot of land this year too. Between Ninovan and Ama, they managed to keep Letty out of trouble for the most part.

Waya was busy hunting this spring. Since the winter had been so very long and hard, they had depleted most of their meat supply. Almost every day Waya and the other men would come home with game that needed to be butchered and readied for curing either by smoking or drying. Then the furs and skins had to be dealt with. Mornings were spent in the fields and afternoons were spent readying the meat and skins.

Working three plots of land, running after an active little girl, and preparing meat and skins every day had Amanda exhausted. However, she was never too tired to love her husband at night when everyone was asleep. Tsula was carrying another baby, and Amanda wondered why she too wasn't pregnant again. She had stopped breast feeding Letty soon after her first birthday. Letty had a mouthful of teeth and ate mostly what the adults ate now. Amanda wanted another child, but decided not to worry about it. Letty was a handful right now anyway.

The spring turned into summer and their lives proceeded in their normal pattern. Amanda again had a good crop and in the late summer Waya took the excess to the white man's town to trade. When he came back, he had the things Amanda had asked for plus a little toy horse for Letty. She loved riding on Waya's horse with him.

Life went on and still Amanda didn't become pregnant again. This winter, which was mild, Letty turned two years old. She had grown so much, she looked like a four year old child. Amanda was hard pressed to keep her in clothes. She was taller than all of the other children her age. Her very dark brown hair was waist length and thick. Unlike her father though, her hair was wavy. Her skin was a much lighter copper than her father's, but also much darker than her mother's. She was a bright inquisitive little girl. She rarely cried and was much more apt to be found laughing.

Letty was the absolute center of her parents' lives and her grandmother's as well as Ama's. It would have been easy for her to become spoiled with so much attention, but she neither sought the attention nor seemed to become spoiled because of it. Everyone in the town seemed to love her.

One late summer day when Amanda was coming back from her fields, she saw Ama and Letty coming back from the town. Letty was carrying a beautiful corn husk doll. When Letty saw her mother, she ran over to show her the doll.

"Mama, look what Yona gave me. She made it just for me, she said." Letty said with a huge smile on her face. At almost three years old, she spoke more like an adult than a child. Amanda remembered her siblings still lisping away at that age. Maybe it was because Letty was an only child that she spoke like an adult.

"It's a very pretty doll. It was nice of Yona to make it for you. Did you tell her thank you?"

"Yes, Mama. I did, just like you taught me," Letty said laughing. Sometimes Amanda thought her daughter was old beyond her years. She liked to tease and play, but she could also be serious when she needed to be.

Later that week, Amanda saw Yona on her way to visit with Tsula. She also thanked Yona for the doll. When she started to turn away, Yona stopped her.

"Ah-man-da, the signs for this winter are not good. This will be a very cold winter and it will come early and stay late. I have been warning all our women to put up extra food and prepare extra clothing as well. I don't want to worry you, but I have seen some very disturbing signs lately. Please try to prepare as much as you can."

"I will Yona. Thank you for letting me know. My crops are very good this year and Waya has had much luck hunting. I will make sure I have plenty put away before Waya goes to the white man's town to trade."

Amanda was disturbed by Yona's demeanor. It seemed she was warning her about more than a hard winter, but Amanda couldn't imagine what it could be.

A few weeks later when Waya returned from taking their surplus crops to the white man's town, he had everything she asked for, but he looked worried. When she questioned him, he wouldn't tell her much, but she noticed that he and the other men were meeting at the council house a lot more often and the talks seemed to be serious.

Being so busy preparing for the winter, Amanda didn't dwell on the talks overmuch until Ninovan came to visit one afternoon several weeks later. Amanda could tell that Ninovan was worried about something. Finally, she just asked her point blank, "Ninovan, I know something is going on, but Waya won't talk to me about it. Please tell me what is happening."

Ninovan worried her hands together for a moment and then looked up at Amanda, "You have a right to know. When Waya and the other men were at the white man's town they heard that two Cherokee towns not all that far west of us had been attacked and destroyed by some white men. They also heard that the white man wants all the people to move further west and give up the land of our father's. The young men of our town want to travel to Quallatown to speak to the leaders there, but our elders don't feel they should."

"Do they think our town will be attacked?", Amanda asked worriedly.

"It is possible. That is why the elders don't want our young men to leave. We will need them to fight if the town is attacked."

When Waya came in later, Amanda broached the subject with him. He was irritated his mother had told Amanda about the troubles. He had wanted to spare her until later. He knew she would be worried and upset.

"We want to travel to Quallatown to seek the wisdom of our leaders there on how to best prepare for and repel an attack if it should come. The elders don't want to leave the town unprotected for the time it would take for us to go and come back. I have suggested that only one or two of us goes. The elders on the council are deciding now what they will do. If I am chosen to go, I will be gone for about two weeks. I would have you, Ama and Letty move in with my mother until I return. Our house is outside the town and I would feel better if you were in the town itself in case of trouble."

Amanda didn't want Waya to leave them. She had an uneasy feeling about his being gone for so long. She said, "Must you be the one to go? I have a bad feeling about this, Waya. I fear for you if you leave."

"Since it was my idea for just two to go, I am almost sure to be chosen. It is for the good of the whole town that we go. We must know exactly what we are dealing with in order to be prepared. We could not get much information in the white man's town. They treated us differently this year when we went to trade. Mohe overheard the white men talking about all Cherokee being pushed out of this area and sent further west so they could have our lands for themselves."

Amanda was very worried already and Waya's last words made her more so. She had heard men who visited her father talking about what they called the "removal plan" before she had been kidnapped. They had been talking about exiling all Indians from Tennessee and Kentucky and sending them west. She told Waya what she had heard, but the information was over two years old now.

The next day, Waya came home to tell Amanda that he and Mohe would be leaving the next morning early to travel to Quallatown. Mohe was going to translate for Waya if they met whites on the trip. He would also eavesdrop on any white's they might encounter. Waya would represent the town to the tribal chief in Quallatown. Amanda helped him pack food and waterskins, but she did so very reluctantly. She could not shake the bad feeling she had about Waya leaving.

That night Amanda lay in Waya's arms and tears rolled down her face. He tried to console her, but she could not be consoled. Finally, she cried herself to sleep. Waya lay awake for hours after Amanda slept. He too had a premonition that something was very wrong, but he felt he had to try to reach the chief in Quallatown and try to get information and maybe even warriors to help.

The next day dawned bright and cool. Amanda stood outside and watched Waya and Mohe's horses disappear with a very sad look on her face. Tsula also was upset that Mohe was leaving. Her time was drawing near and she wanted her husband to be at home when their new baby was born. Ninovan also watched her two sons leave with a sinking feeling in the pit of her stomach. Something was not right, but she couldn't pin down exactly what it was.

The next two days passed without incident. On the third day after Waya had left, Amanda woke with a fierce headache. Ama made her some herbal tea and told her to lie down again for awhile. Ama took Letty to visit with Ninovan. Amanda had fallen back to sleep when she heard the sound of gunshots and screaming.

She grabbed the long rifle Waya had left for her and loaded it quickly, picking up the shot bag. She also took her skinning knife and the small dagger she kept in her moccasin. Since their house was a little way out of town, she was able to skirt the town to Ninovan's house without being seen by the raiders. She could hear rifle shots, white men's voices, and screams from the residents of the town as she crept through the trees and brush.

Just as she got close to Ninovan's house, she saw Ama hobbling toward her carrying Letty. There was blood running down Ama's face from a scalp wound. Amanda rushed forward and took the screaming baby. She shushed Letty as quickly as she could and examined Ama's wound. It was a deep ugly gash.

Ama told her she had been hit by a white man with a rifle butt, but she had managed to crawl behind Ninovan's house with the baby. Ama urged Amanda to take the baby and run to the river. "Go get into the river with the baby and try to get to the other side or hide in the reeds until the white men are gone. Most of the young men are already dead and the white men are burning the houses with the old people, women and children still in them. Hurry, hurry, before they see you." Amanda tried to get Ama to come with her, but Ama said she would just slow her down.

She pushed Amanda away when she tried to care for her wound. "Go, my little white daughter. These men won't see your whiteness and will kill you just like they are killing everyone else. They are mad with drink and hate. Run, save our baby, run."

With those words, Ama turned and hobbled back towards the town. Amanda watched her for just a moment and then turned and ran toward the river. She hid the long rifle and shot bag in the bushes on the river bank and carefully slid down to the reeds that grew thickly near the bank. She waded past the reeds and then made her way carefully back toward the bank in the middle of the thick stand of reeds. She didn't want broken reeds to show her trail for the men to follow.

Amanda crouched down in the reeds and held Letty close to her chest. The baby had exhausted herself with crying and now snubbed softly as her little eyes closed and she slept. Letty was a very big three year old and quite heavy, but Amanda had wrapped her little legs around her own waist to alleviate some of the weight and the water added buoyancy as well. Amanda could see spirals of smoke climbing high in the sky from the town. It looked like every building was on fire. The flames leaped up into the trees surrounding the town. The fall leaves were soon burning as well, catching the trees in turn.

Amanda had no idea how long she squatted in the cold water holding her baby while her home burned. She could still hear the white voices calling to one another as they rampaged through the town shooting and beating the hapless people who ran from their burning homes. The tears rolled down her face as she swallowed her sobs lest she give away her hiding place.

Finally, the only sound was the crackling of the fire and the blowing of the wind. Amanda slowly made her way up the river bank and recovered the long rifle from the bushes. She made her way to the edge of the town where she had lived for almost four years. There were smoldering bodies and houses everywhere she looked. There was not one person, man, woman, nor child alive in the town. The white men had not only killed everyone and burned their homes, they had pulled their possessions from their homes and what had not been stolen was destroyed.

She saw a multitude of broken clay jars and baskets filled with vegetables crushed under men's boots and horses hooves. The beasts had left nothing. What they didn't destroy, they stole. Amanda and Waya's house had also been set afire, but was only partially burned when she came upon it. She was able to pull some furs out as well as some food. She spread out their bear fur and piled everything she could salvage on it. Then she rolled the bear fur up and tied it to a large limb with strips of deer hide.

Letty was awake now and looking around trying to figure out what had happened. She comforted the child as much as she could. Then, Amanda put the limb over her shoulder, picked up the long rifle and encouraged her little daughter to walk beside her. She was afraid the men might come back and wanted to get as far away from the town as she could. She didn't know where she would go, but she knew which direction Waya and Mohe had gone and followed their trail.

Amanda walked for hours before she took a break. She left the trail, making for a thicket she saw nearby. She didn't dare to rest on the trail. She was actually afraid to even walk on the trail, but feared she would get lost in the woods without it. Amanda circled the thicket of bushes and then made her way into it from the back. She didn't want any visible trace of her passage. Letty had become exhausted several hours ago and Amanda had fashioned a travois from the furs she had wrapped the supplies in and another limb. She had placed the supplies on the travois. When Letty got tired, she put her on it also and pulled her along. The travois also served to wipe out her footprints on the trail.

Amanda unwrapped the bear skin from the travois and took out some dried berries and smoked pork. The baby couldn't chew the dried deer well, but the pork was different. Amanda chewed a strip of dried deer and fed the baby bites of the pork with little bits of dried strawberries. She had also been able to salvage two waterskins and had filled them at the river before she left. She gave the baby a long drink and took one herself. After putting away the uneaten food, she gathered Letty into her arms and sat down on the bear skin to rest.

Letty was soon asleep. It was still a few hours before dark and Amanda didn't want to stop for the night yet. However, she couldn't carry the sleeping baby, the long rifle and the supplies. She rebuilt the dismantled travois. This time she attached the travois to her belt with strips of deer hide so she could pull it behind her. She also used strips of hide to loosely tie Letty to the travois, leaving her own hands free to carry the long rifle and shot bag. She needed her hands free in case she needed to use the rifle and reload it. She would not hesitate to shoot anyone or anything that threatened she or her child.

Amanda had only been on the trail a couple of hours when she heard a noise behind her on the trail. She quickly left the trail taking cover in some dense bushes nearby. Luckily, Letty hadn't awakened. Amanda watched fearfully as three white men passed riding horses. She hadn't really seen any of the men who destroyed her town, so she didn't know if they had been among them. Not wanting to take any chances, she kept quiet until they were far down the trail.

Using what daylight was left, Amanda walked parallel to the trail, but not on it. She kept it in view as much as she could. She couldn't take a chance on using the trail again now. She knew she would have to stop soon herself. The emotional and physical toll of the day was telling on her. She was so exhausted she could barely put one foot in front of the other. She knew her exhaustion might make her less aware of her surroundings and she couldn't afford to be lax in any way.

Finding a large rhododendron patch, she walked to the back side of it and burrowed her way in under the large plants.

It was dry and warm there. She managed to pull the travois in behind her. Though she couldn't sit straight up in her hiding place, she could half recline enough to untie her child and her supplies. Letty slept through the whole process for which Amanda was thankful. She put some meat and berries wrapped in a deer hide close to hand then rolled herself and Letty into the bear skin and lay down. Sleep claimed her very quickly.

Letty's little hands on her face awakened Amanda. It was still dark, but she could see the first vestiges of sunrise in the sky. Letty was hungry and needed to make water. Amanda took care of both hers and Letty's physical needs and then sat Letty down to talk to her.

Amanda was very glad she had taught her daughter to speak both Cherokee and English. She cautioned Letty in English that she must not speak Cherokee unless her mother told her it was okay. Tears came into Amanda's eyes when Letty said, "But, Mama, the bad men spoke English. I'm not bad."

"No, my sweet one, you are not bad. All people who speak English are not bad, even though those men who hurt our people were very bad. Remember Uncle Mohe speaks English and so do Hialeah, Kanuna and Gawonii. They aren't bad either."

Then Amanda remembered that Tsula, her unborn child, and all three of her children had been murdered by the white men and tears started to stream down her face. Letty reached up and touched her mother's tears in wonder. She had never seen her mother cry.

"Don't be sad, Mama. I will speak English."

"Thank you, my little one, but I'm not crying about that. I miss your edoda and elisi."

"Me, too, mama." Lettty said climbing into Amanda's arms and snuggling against her.

Amanda held her baby close against her. She was so very sad at the loss of so many people who had been important to her. She didn't know if she would ever see Waya and Mohe again. She had seen the bodies of Ama, Ninovan, Tsula and her children before she had left the town. She had wanted to purify their bodies and bury them, but she feared staying in the town any longer than absolutely necessary. She hoped their spirits found peace.

All that day, Amanda walked parallel to the trail. She would leave her supplies and Letty hidden occasionally so she could carefully go to the trail to make sure she hadn't strayed too far from it. Amanda was so thankful that her child, who was not quite three years old, seemed to understand the need for quiet. Letty made hardly any noise and spoke in a whisper when she needed something. She walked until her little legs could hardly carry her another step before saying anything to her mother. Then Amanda would put her on the travois again and pull her as long as she could.

Amanda had no idea how far they had gone in the day and a half they had travelled. She had no idea how far she needed to go to reach another Cherokee village or a white farm or settlement. She was so angry with the whites right now, she hoped she would find another Cherokee town first. At least with another group of Cherokee she might have some chance of finding Waya and Mohe some day. She feared she would never see her husband or the man she considered a brother again.

Chapter 26

Amanda was wrong. She did see Waya and Mohe again, but not as she wished to. Around midday the next day, Amanda noticed buzzards circling in the air not far off the trail. She slowly walked toward the carrion birds. When she got near enough for the smell of death to reach her, she stopped. She hid the travois, with a sleeping Letty on it, behind some bushes. Then, very slowly and carefully she crept forward.

When Amanda pushed through the final bush, her heart stopped beating in her chest momentarily. She saw Waya's horse lying on the ground writhing in pain. He was badly injured and couldn't stand. The buzzards were feasting on something else nearby and the horse was panicked because he knew he would be next. Amanda scanned the area very carefully before she emerged from her hiding spot. What she saw next made her stomach heave, but she forced down her gorge.

Her beautiful husband lay not far from his horse. However, he was not moving. It was he the buzzards were feasting on. He was dead. His black eyes were open and staring up at the sky. His chest was bare and covered with blood. It looked like he had been shot several times. Mohe lay near him, their hands were outstretched toward each other. It looked like Mohe had tried to crawl to Waya, but hadn't quite made it. Someone had stabbed him in the back numerous times and he had been shot as well. It was all Amanda could do not to scream hysterically at the sight. She ran quickly and shooed the carrion birds away from their bodies.

Whoever had killed them had apparently taken everything they had with them including Mohe's horse. Their long rifles were gone, as well as all the supplies they had taken. None of Waya's knives were there and he had taken five in all. Waya's horse was in terrible pain and from the looks of him, wouldn't last much longer. Amanda had to put him out of his misery, but she didn't dare shoot him with her long rifle. Finally, in desperation, she took her skinning knife and cut his throat. Her presence had scared away the buzzards temporarily, but they hadn't gone far. They were perched in the trees above the grisly scene.

Amanda forced herself to touch Waya. His body was cold and hard. He must have been dead for some time. Mohe must have died soon after as well. Amanda feared staying with her husband and Mohe, but she couldn't just leave them there. She had to bury them, but first she had to purify their bodies the best she could. She pulled first Waya and then Mohe away from the place they had died. They were both very heavy, but Amanda expended all the strength she had to get them away from that horrible place. She knew she was violating Cherokee traditions by not burying Waya and Mohe where they fell, but she couldn't bring herself to stay any longer in the blood-soaked area.

Amanda went back to check on Letty and thankfully the child was still sleeping. She took one of the water skins and a calico shirt she had brought. She washed Waya and Mohe the best she could. She did find some late herbs growing nearby and lay them on the clean bodies. It was the only form of purification she had and she hoped it was enough. She had no shovel or hoe to dig with, but she used her skinning knife to sharpen a thick limb. She dug in the soft dirt until she had a shallow grave for each of them.

Amanda pulled and tugged with all her might until she got both bodies in their respective graves. She knew the graves weren't deep enough, but her strength was almost gone and it was the best she could do. She covered them with what dirt there was and then scoured the area for rocks to make a cairn. Amanda spent a couple of hours looking for rocks and carrying them to the graves. She was finally satisfied that no animals would be able to dig them up.

Amanda hadn't even realized it, but she had been crying the whole time she had cared for her husband and Mohe. Her clothes and her body were covered in dirt and blood. She couldn't go back to Letty looking like this. She took what was left of the water and washed herself as much as she could. She had extra clothes with her and left her badly soiled shirt and skirt hidden in some bushes and went back to the travois naked.

Letty woke when Amanda lifted her off the travois. Although she was so small, Letty could tell something had happened to make her mother even sadder. She didn't know how or what to ask, so she just lifted her little hand and caressed her mother's face. Amanda started to cry again although she tried very hard not to. She couldn't face telling her daughter her edoda was dead. There were still a few hours before dark and Amanda wanted to put as much distance as she could between the place her husband and Mohe had been killed and her stopping place for the night. She couldn't bear the thought that wolves or some other animal might try to dig their bodies up. She would not be able to bear hearing such a thing. She had done all she could, but she feared it wasn't enough.

Just before dark, Amanda noticed a small densely packed copse of trees well off the trail. She pulled the travois into the trees until she found a very small clearing. She fed Letty, but couldn't bear to eat anything herself. It seemed she could still smell the blood and other smells of death. When she thought of food, her stomach turned. After Letty had eaten and drank, Amanda spread out the bear fur. She took Letty in her arms and lying down, rolled them in the fur. Although Letty had a long nap earlier, she had become very tired from walking the few hours before they stopped for the night.

It was many hours before sleep claimed Amanda. The baby had walked a great distance that day and had fallen into an exhausted slumber almost immediately. Amanda lay under the stars thinking about Waya. She felt guilty that it had taken her so long to realize she loved him. He had loved her from the beginning with an unconditional love. Nothing she did turned him against her. Not running away, not telling him she had tried not to love his child, not even when she told him she was leaving him and going back to her own world.

Amanda had learned many valuable lessons while she lived with the Cherokee. Not just the everyday lessons of how to survive, but important life lessons as well. The Cherokee had taught her that people should be judged by how they treated you and the ones you loved. The Cherokee weren't perfect, but no people were. They had their trials and tribulations like any other people. However, their ability to integrate other people and cultures into their towns was remarkable. They didn't show the bigotry and racism so blatantly displayed by the whites. The Cherokee simply thought of the people brought into their villages as other Cherokee and treated them that way,

Sleep finally claimed Amanda and she slept until the sun started to rise on another clear cool day. After feeding Letty and making herself eat as well, she loaded the travois again and took off, still not knowing or really caring where she was headed. She had no knowledge of the geography of the area where she had lived for well over four years or the area where she had lived for all of the years before that. She castigated herself for not paying more attention to what both the Cherokee and her own people had said about the areas surrounding her two homes.

Since she had found Waya and Mohe dead, her original plan to try to make it to Quallatown was abandoned. She had no idea in which direction her home lay nor did she have a deep abiding desire to even go back home. Her emotions had been so severely damaged by the horrible deaths of all the people she had known and loved since coming to the Cherokee, she was basically just numb. Her feelings toward her own people, the whites, was very confused after what she had witnessed in the past few days. The thought of someone white maybe trying to hurt Letty made her considerable temper rise. That she would not abide if it took her dying breath.

After three more days of travel, Amanda knew she would have to find help or at least shelter soon. The days and nights were getting colder quickly. Yona had warned her that the signs had promised this winter would be another cold one. She had Letty to think of now, not just herself. As far as she was concerned, if she had been alone, she might have just lain down in the road and died. Her depression was so deep, it took the first snowflake to drag her out of her inner turmoil.

She had been trudging along pulling the travois with Letty walking beside her when she heard her child say, "Look, Mama. Snow, pretty."

Amanda stopped and looked around her. There were just a few snowflakes, but the gray forbidding clouds in the sky promised more. The wind had changed directions to due north and it was several degrees colder than it had been when they left their last sleeping place this morning.

Looking down at Letty, Amanda almost panicked. Where was she going to find shelter for her baby from the snow? They were literally in the middle of nowhere travelling in an easterly direction. Leaving Letty with the travois, she crept quietly toward the trail. At first, she couldn't find the trail. It had grown less distinct it seemed. Had she missed a cross trail somewhere? What she found now was little more than a deer trail. She would have to backtrack to find a more heavily travelled trail.

Going back to Letty, she attached the travois again with the baby on it and headed back the way they had come staying on the deer trail this time. After three or four hours, Amanda came to a T in the road. The deer trail she was on was barely travelled, but the roads leading both right and left showed heavier use. Amanda had no idea which way to go and finally just turned left because she didn't know what else to do.

Chapter 27

Amanda had travelled on the left fork for several hours now and it was near dark. She had to find shelter soon. The snow had steadily gotten harder and the wind had continued to blow making the air colder and colder. She had stopped and put Letty inside the bear skin wrapping her in furs, several hours ago. Letty's teeth had been chattering, but she had not said she was cold. As a matter of fact, Letty had said little today at all. That fact worried Amanda as well. There weren't a lot of supplies left so there was ample room for the child.

Amanda herself was cold. She had only managed to salvage a calico shirt and a deerskin skirt for herself from their house. Having left her heavier deerskin shirt and skirt behind after ruining them burying Waya and Mohe, she only had the clothes she wore now. Letty had on a deerskin shirt and leggings with long moccasins, but she would be freezing if she wasn't under the bearskin and wrapped in furs.

With scant food and very little protection from the elements, it wasn't long before Amanda began to feel weak and disoriented. She trudged down the trail without even being aware of her surroundings for hours. Finally, the sound of a cow lowing brought her out of her stupor.

Amanda's head jerked up at the sound. She looked wildly around and saw a sight she never thought to behold. Sitting a short distance off the trail was a log cabin. There was smoke coming from the chimney. The sound of the cow was coming from a small log barn some short distance behind the cabin. Amanda just stood there for several minutes in shock. She had never expected to see a house here in the middle of nowhere.

Amanda was finally brought to her senses by the door of the cabin opening. She saw a man, who appeared to be in his late thirties or early forties, come out the door carrying a bucket. He was tall and lean with reddish-blond hair showing out of the bottom of his hat. He came down the steps of the porch and turned toward the barn. Amanda made an involuntary noise and his head jerked around toward her. Amanda didn't know whether to try to run away or to go toward what might be shelter for she and her child.

The man took the decision out of her hands when he dropped the bucket on the ground and hurried toward her. "Och lassie, where have ye come from? Ye look froze to death. Come in the house and get warm. I got some stew on the stove and I made bread yesterday. Here, let me take that travois for ye. You don't look strong enough to pull it another inch!"

The man said all of that in such a rush and with such a thick brogue, Amanda didn't understand him or know how to answer him. She had been speaking Cherokee so long, his English was indecipherable to her at first. By the time she understood he was welcoming her into his home, he had already divested her of the travois and gripping her arm, lead her toward his cabin.

Amanda pulled away and rushed to the back of the travois. The man looked very surprised by her actions, but just stood and watched her. When she pulled the bear skin back and picked up Letty, a huge smile lit his face.

"Ye've got a young'un. Well now, ain't that fine. Been a long time since there's been a young'un around this place. Come on now. I'll put yer travois in the barn after I get ye settled in the house. What's yer name, child?"

"Amanda….Amanda Whitworth.", was all Amanda could manage through her chattering teeth. She was just about done in from all the walking, the cold, the worry, the grief, and the lack of food over the past few days.

"Well, Amanda, come on in and set by the fire. I'll get ye a plate of stew and some bread and butter. Havin' cows is a lot of work and a right pain in the winter, but one of the blessings is fresh butter and milk."

Amanda carried Letty to the stone fireplace and sat on a small stool near the fire. She was still shaking with cold, but rapidly began to warm up. Soon, she unwrapped the furs from Letty and hugged the baby to her. Letty turned to her and said in Cherokee, "Who is that man, Mama?"

The man turned rapidly from what he was doing and looked at Amanda in shock. "Did that young'un just talk to ye in Cherokee, child?"

What Amanda had feared appeared to be happening already. Letty had forgotten to speak English, probably from being so tired and hungry. The man looked shocked that her baby spoke Cherokee. He looked at Letty closely now. He could see her very thick dark hair and her darker than normal complexion now that she had been unwrapped from the furs. All he had noticed when Amanda first picked her up was that she had her Mama's beautiful green eyes and very pretty face.

"Well, I'll be durned. That baby is part Cherokee, ain't she?"

Amanda wrapped her arms more tightly around Letty and said, "Yes, her father was Cherokee. He was my husband."

Amanda watched the man closely to see how he handled that information. He just shook his head and slowly walked over to them. He reached out his hand and Amanda shrank back from him in fear.

"Och, child, don't be afeared. I won't hurt ye or this beautiful little girl. I had a Cherokee wife once, myself. The smallpox took her and both our boys over ten years ago. I haven't heard Cherokee spoke much since. Hearing yer young'un brought it all back to me is all. Now, let me get that food ready."

With those words, the man turned back and walked to the table. His face was a study in sadness and yet, he had a small smile on his face. Amanda couldn't figure him out. He was a contradiction, it seemed to her. She was glad he didn't hate her baby though. She had almost expected him to do something bad to Letty at first or tell them to leave.

When the food was ready, Amanda took Letty and they sat at the table. The man also sat down and encouraged them both to eat all they could hold. He talked to them about everyday things while they ate. It seemed strange to Amanda to sit at a table and eat with a metal spoon on a pewter plate. And poor Letty hardly knew what to do. However, she was a smart little one and just started copying her mother.

At first Letty had a hard time handling the metal spoon, but soon was eating with gusto. When she first tasted the bread and butter, her eyes grew large and round and the smile on her little face was priceless. Amanda had forgotten how good fresh bread spread with creamy butter tasted. She savored the slice of bread she had been given and took tiny bites, smiling all the while. It was the first time Amanda had smiled in days.

When the meal was finished, the man started to take the dirty dishes from the table. Amanda jumped up and took the dishes from him looking around to see if there was a sink or bucket in the little cabin. She truly hadn't noticed her surroundings until now.

The cabin was small, but very well provisioned. There was a sink on the back outside wall with a pump handle attached to it. Even back home, they had to carry water from their outdoor well to heat for dishes and washing. The pump was a convenience, Amanda had never seen. She walked over and looked at the apparatus in wonder.

The man came over and showed her how to work the contraption. She pumped water into a pot and put it on the still hot stove to heat. Then Amanda went back to the stool by the fire. Sitting down, she drew Letty up into her lap. The man came over and sat in the rocking chair on the other side of the fire.

"Well, I'm glad to see ye two ladies get full and warm. Och, where are my manners. I haven't even told ye my name yet. I'm Nathan Fraser. I've lived here in West Tennessee for almost twenty years. I came to this country from Scotland when I was a young'un. I fought in the war against the British. Then I heard about the trappin' in this part of the world. I came here and never left. Don't do much trappin' these days though. I quit that when I married. My wife didn't like me bein' gone so much. I farm some and sell my extra produce in Paris to the store there."

Amanda almost jumped out of her skin when she heard Nathan mention the town of Paris. He noticed her expression. "Do ye know someone in Paris, Amanda?"

"No, but my folks used to go there sometime for supplies. We lived about ten miles from there. I...I haven't been home in almost five years. I don't even know if my family is still there."

"Taken by the Cherokee, wasn't ya. I remember now. About five years ago a man named Whitworth rode into Paris with his grown sons and some other family members telling about his daughter being took by the Cherokee. That was ye, wasn't it?"

"Yes, it was me. So my father is alright? He was struck with a rifle butt the night I was taken. I'm so glad to hear he's okay. Do you know whether my mother is alright as well? She was knocked out when she was pushed and her head struck the bed post."

"Well, now, I don't know for sure, but I didn't hear bout no one being killed when ye was took. It looks like I would have heard about that. She must be okay too. Yer family looked for ye for weeks, but then the weather changed and any signs that the Indians might have left was covered by the snow. There was a late blizzard that year and it was a rough one."

"Yes, it was rough where I was too. I don't know exactly where the town I was taken to was. I never paid much attention to the land around our farm or around the Cherokee town and I didn't leave it except once. I sure have been sorry that I didn't pay more attention. I tried to run away once the first year, but I didn't get real far. When they found me, I had gotten only a day's ride away, though it took me three or four days to make it that far on foot."

"Ye run away and lived to tell about it. Lass, yer verra lucky. Most Cherokee would have skinned ye alive or at least beat ye senseless for running. Don't tell me they didn't do nothin to ye."

Amanda hung her head in sadness, "No, nothing was done to me. The man who took me, Waya, loved me very much. He would never have hurt me or allowed anyone else to hurt me either."

Nathan could see the abject sadness in Amanda's eyes. He reached over and put his hand over hers and gave it a squeeze. He wondered about the rest of the story, but now was not the time to ask. This young woman had been through enough. He would see that she and her baby were taken care of tonight and when she was ready, she would tell him the rest, if she was of a mind to.

Nathan left Amanda and Letty sitting by the fire and went out to milk and take care of his cows and other livestock. When he came back in, the dishes had been washed, dried and put away. Letty was asleep in her mother's arms and so was Amanda. She had leaned her head against the stone of the fireplace and not been able to keep her eyes open.

Nathan took care of the bucket of milk. He took the milk into his little pantry and then down into the cold cellar under his cabin. The entrance to the cold cellar was not noticeable from the main room of his cabin. He had planned it that way. One could never be too careful in this day and age. The cold cellar could be barred from below as protection against attack. Since it was full of food and Nathan kept water there also, the cellar could be used for some time, just in case.

There were always Indians to contend with, as well as roving whites too lazy to work, but not averse to stealing. Nathan never had trouble with the Cherokee. They knew he had been married to one of their own and he had never participated in any of the white men's raids on Cherokee towns. He still spoke quite a bit of the Cherokee tongue, though he was rusty these days. That didn't keep other tribes from giving him grief occasionally though. So far, he had been able to barricade himself in his house and shoot from the windows when he needed to. There hadn't been an attack in a couple of years. It seemed the Indians were slowly being pushed further west by new settlers and old.

Nathan picked up a hunk of bacon and some eggs for breakfast from the cellar. Just before going back up the small staircase, he thought of the canned peaches he had and grabbed a can of them as well. That baby would really like peaches he bet. Nathan hadn't been around a small child in a long time, but he remembered how his boys had loved peaches.

When he came back into the main room, he woke Amanda and lead her into the little bedroom his boys had once shared. There was a comfortable bed in there with a well stuffed corn husk mattress on it. He kept it made up with clean sheets and quilts in case he had visitors. Visitors were rare, but not unheard of for Nathan. He had friends in Paris who liked to come visit occasionally and once in awhile a stranger came through.

After he got Amanda and Letty settled, he went to build up the fires so they would burn all night. It had gotten a lot colder outside. It looked like they were in for the first bad snowstorm of the season. The wind was howling and the snow was coming down hard and fast. Nathan was very glad

Amanda had found his little home when she did. He didn't like to think what might have happened to her and that baby if they were caught out in this weather.

When Nathan climbed into his big four poster bed, made with his own hands, he lay awake for a long time thinking about the young woman who had stumbled into his life that day. He could see from the pain and sadness in her eyes that she had known great grief, and it was recent. He had heard about the group of wastrels who were raiding Cherokee towns to the west and killing everyone in sight, then stealing everything they could. He didn't know if that was what had happened to Amanda, but he thought it might have been since she had come from the west.

The last time he was in Paris, he had spoken to his good friend, Ray Talbot, who owned the general store about the latest raids. He and Ray were both of a mind that the men perpetrating these raids were no good scoundrels just out for whatever they could steal. They rarely left anyone alive to identify them in the Indian towns. After stealing everything they could, they would burn the towns to the ground as well. There was no organized law in West Tennessee, but there were good people who didn't condone such practices. Nathan Fraser was one of those good people.

Nathan also wondered about the man Amanda had married. He must be dead as well for her to be wandering alone with the baby. She hadn't told him much about her time since she was taken from her family, but she had mentioned that she *was* married to a Cherokee man. From Nathan's knowledge of the Cherokee tribe, he was very surprised that she had not felt at least some reprisals from running away. The man must have loved her very much indeed.

The next morning Amanda awoke to the smell of bacon frying and the sound of Nathan singing Yankee Doodle horribly off key. She had to smile at the sound and the smell. She was very hungry and the smell of the bacon was making her salivate. She looked at Letty and saw that her little daughter was awake as well. She smiled at her Mama and Amanda's heart melted. She loved her baby so much.

However, Amanda was afraid for Letty. They were very lucky that Nathan Fraser was not the sort to hate a child because of its parentage. The fact that he had been married to a Cherokee woman and had children with her was amazing to Amanda. She had heard of such a thing happening, but it was a rarity. Most white men who were married to Indian women lived with the Indians and were trappers or guides. That Nathan had married an Indian woman and she had moved into his world was mystifying to Amanda. She had never thought of that possibility before.

Letty reached over and touched her mother's face gently. Then she said in Cherokee, "Mama, will the big man give us some more of the bread with the gooey stuff on it today?"

Amanda had to smile at her daughter's description of butter, but then she realized she would have to caution Letty to speak only English from now on. The Cherokee tongue would only bring her grief in the white man's world.

"Letty," Amanda said in English, "we have to speak Mama's tongue now. And only Mama's tongue. The people we see from now on will probably all be white. They don't know or understand the Cherokee tongue. It would be rude to speak to them in Cherokee since they don't know it. So from now on, English only, okay?"

Amanda didn't want to scare Letty. After all, she was little more than a baby, but she also didn't want her to be at any more of a disadvantage than her mixed blood would make her. Speaking English might not alter people's attitudes toward her, but it would make it easier for her to fit in in the white world.

Letty didn't seem to mind speaking English. She had been speaking both languages since she started to speak. Amanda had made sure that Letty knew both languages for every word she was taught. She had also asked Mohe to speak English with the baby when he was around so she would be as fluent as his children were. Amanda hadn't planned to leave the Cherokee town, but she wanted her daughter prepared in case Letty ever decided to leave and go to the white world.

Amanda rose needing to urinate. She knew Letty needed to go as well. She remembered that the chamber pot was kept under the bed at home and took a look. sure enough, a plain white chamber pot was sitting under the bed. She set Letty on it and had to laugh at the quizzical look on her daughter's face. "It's to make water in, sweetling, like we used to do in the winters at home. People use it when it's too cold or rainy to go outside. This one is made of a different kind of material, not clay" Letty just smiled and used the pot. After Amanda relieved herself, she saw there was a pitcher of water and a bowl on the little table across from the bed.

She showed Letty how to wash her hands in the cold water and then took an edge of the towel lying beside the bowl and washed Letty's face as well as her own. She finger combed Letty's long hair and plaited it into a long braid down her back. Doing the same to her own hair, they were now ready to face the day. Then taking Letty by the hand, they walked into the main room of the cabin.

Nathan turned when he heard them come into the room. He smiled his big smile and said, "Well, look who's up so early this mornin. I thought ye might sleep in since ye was both so verra tired last night. But, I'm some glad yer up. Ye can help me eat this bacon and eggs I been cookin. I made a pan of biscuits too and I was thinkin about making some gravy. How does that sound, little Letty?"

Letty smiled at the tall white man and said in perfect English, "It sounds very good to me. I'm hungry."

A shocked look passed over Nathan's face. He looked at Amanda in surprise. "So, ye taught her English, didja? Right smart of ye."

Amanda smiled and said, "Yes, I thought she might need it some day." Then Amanda's face almost crumpled, but she swallowed her grief and said, "Unfortunately, that day came a long time before I thought it would."

"I'm sure it did," said Nathan with sympathy. "Come on and set yerselves down. The biscuits are almost ready and it won't take long to make a pan of gravy with these bacon drippins."

Amanda and Letty sat at the table and watched as Nathan moved around his kitchen. Amanda hadn't really noticed much the night before except the unusual pump, but the kitchen area of the main room was set up very efficiently. The cook stove was in the corner of the room. It wasn't large, but it had three big burners, an oven and a warming oven and kept that side of the fairly large room warm. The fireplace on the opposite wall kept the rest of the room nice and toasty.

Amanda could see it was still snowing outside and the wind was still high. She could hear it moaning around the eaves of the snug little cabin. She knew she and Letty would have perished if she hadn't come upon this nice man's house when she did. She was very grateful to Nathan Fraser for taking them in and proceeded to tell him so.

"Mr. Fraser, I want to thank you from the bottom of my heart for taking me and Letty in last night. I don't know what would have become of us if you hadn't. I knew the weather was turning, but I sure didn't expect a blizzard so early in the winter."

"Och, lass, don't you worry yerself about all that, Miss Amanda. Yer both welcome to stay with me as long as ye like. I get right lonely being here all alone, especially in winter when there is less to do. It's my pleasure to have ye both here. And the name's Nathan, not Mr. Fraser."

"Alright, Nathan. Thank you for allowing us to stay here at least until the weather breaks. I will need to try to find out if my family is still in this area soon. I'm anxious to see all of them. It's been a long time." Amanda said with a worried look on her face.

Nathan thought she might be apprehensive about how she would be received by her family since she was coming home with a half-Cherokee child. He hoped they were good people who wouldn't want to punish a child for being half-Indian. If they weren't good people, he would offer Amanda a place for her and Letty to live. He had the room and he could well afford it. No way would he sit back and watch someone punish that beautiful little girl by word or deed if he could help it.

Nathan had had his trials and tribulations being married to a Cherokee woman, but he had loved his wife, Ayita, and their sons with all his heart. After some years, people had gotten used to seeing his family in town and stopped pestering them. When his boys got old enough for schooling though, he had taught them what he knew himself rather than subjugate them to possible taunts from the town kids. His heart still mourned the loss of his beloved wife and sons even though it had been over ten years that they had been gone.

After a big breakfast which culminated with the canned peaches, which Letty did indeed love, Amanda again did the washing up and cleaned off the table while Letty sat with Nathan by the fire. While she worked, Amanda listened to the two of them chatting like they had known each other for years. She was so proud of her smart little Letty. She had always been a bright, happy, giving child with an irrepressible spirit. She had played so well with the other children in the Cherokee town. Her mixed parentage had made no difference to the Indian children, anymore than Kanuna, Gawonii, and Hialeah's had, but Amanda had much fear about her acceptance by other white children and their parents.

When Amanda had finished her work, she came over and sat with Nathan and Letty by the fire. Nathan was obviously curious about her, but didn't ask her any questions. She was very glad for that. She intended to tell him everything, but she didn't want to do so in front of Letty. She wasn't sure exactly how much Letty had seen when their town was raided, but she didn't seem to be adversely affected by it. Possibly Ama had been able to keep her from seeing too much before she got her out. Amanda dearly hoped so. She was traumatized by what she knew had happened and she hadn't even seen any of it until afterward.

The day progressed slowly. When Nathan rose to begin the mid-day meal, Amanda rose as well. "Ye don't have to help me with dinner, child. Ye still look mighty tired to me. I have to admit I don't mind cookin, but I really do hate washing up afterwards. If ye just keep doin that, I'll be one happy man."

"I don't mind washing up. I've been doing it since I wasn't much bigger than Letty, but I can cook too. It's the least I can do in return for your letting us stay here with you until the weather clears."

"Well, now that's fine, but I think I'll take you up on that offer tomorrow when ye've had some time to really recover from your trip. How long was ye on that trip, anyhow?"

"To be honest, Nathan, I'm not sure. I think it was four or five days. They started to just blend into each other after awhile. I...I wasn't able to take much when I left our town. There, well, there wasn't much left. What little I found I pulled on the travois and Letty too when she was tired or sleepy. I have to admit I am still tired. I really appreciate your kindness and thoughtfulness."

With those words, Amanda went back to the fire. Then she thought to ask, "What did happen to my makeshift travois? My long rifle, shot bag, and a few other things were still on it along with a good bear skin."

"You had a long rifle? Do you know how to shoot it?"

"Yes, I do. I found it in a cabin when I ran away. The man who lived there was dead when I got there. He looked like he had been dead a long time. When I left the cabin, I took it with me. I had practiced loading it like I had seen my father do while I was holed up there during a blizzard much like this one. That cabin saved my life. The long rifle did too a few days later. I had to shoot someone. I wasn't even sure I had loaded it right, but it fired and he fell dead. He was an Indian from a different tribe. I'm not sure which one. Waya and Mohe, his brother, found me right after it happened."

'Well, child, ye have been through some rough times. Yer travois is in the barn. I didn't mess with it. It's just like it was when ye took Miss Letty out of it. I probably should bring that long rifle in when I go milk later though. It shouldn't be out in the damp cold barn."

"That would be fine, Nathan. I hope I never need to use it again on a human being, but I would if I had to to protect myself or Letty,' Amanda said with a grim determination.

Nathan didn't doubt for a moment that she would indeed shoot anyone who tried to harm her or her child. He understood exactly how she felt. Later that evening when Nathan went out to milk the cow and see to his livestock, he went over to the travois and pulled the bear skin open.

Laying there, far to the left of where the baby had lain, was a nice looking long rifle, a bag of shot, a corn husk doll, and some earrings made of bone, feathers and beads. He took everything except the skin with him when he went back to the house. It was an awkward load to carry along with the full milk bucket, but he didn't mind.

Nathan had strung a rope from the house to the barn the day before because of the deep snow, so he just kept his side against the rope and trudged through the deep snow back to the house. When he got on the porch, the door opened for him and Amanda took the heavy bucket of milk from him. He got into the house and laid the other things on the table. While he was taking off his heavy fur coat and outside boots, Amanda stood at the table with her head bowed looking at the earrings.

When Amanda raised her head, Nathan saw her beautiful green eyes were filled with tears. She glanced at Letty who was playing on the floor in front of the fire with some blocks Nathan had made for his boys. She visibly tamped down her emotions and taking the doll from the table went over to her daughter.

"Letty, look what Nathan brought in. It's Betsy. Would you like to play with her too while I help Nathan with the milk?"

Letty looked up with such a sweet smile on her face, Nathan's heart lurched in his chest. "Yes, Mama. I love Betsy. It was very nice of Yona to make her for me." She hesitated and then said, "I miss Yona and Ama, and well everybody." she said with a sad smile. She took the little doll and hugged it close to her little body. In a few moments she was sitting in the rocking chair, rocking the baby and singing to it in a high clear voice.

When Amanda turned away from her daughter, Nathan could see that the tears she had so valiantly held back earlier were on the verge of falling for sure now. He said in a bright voice, "Amanda, come see my cold cellar where I keep the milk overnight. I need to separate the bucket I took down yestiddy to make butter. I know Miss Letty sure does like butter. Let's go down and bring some more up for supper later."

Amanda started toward him, but almost stumbled when her foot caught on a chair leg. Her vision was impaired by the tears that were now running down her cheeks. Nathan caught her arm and lead her into the pantry and then down the few steps into the cellar. When they were down the steps, he simply took her into his arms and let her cry.

It was quite some time before Amanda had cried herself out. She wouldn't allow herself to cry in front of Letty, but seeing the doll and the beautiful earrings she had worn on her wedding day was almost more than she could handle. She was very grateful for Nathan's kindness and understanding. She pulled herself back from his embrace and wiped her eyes with her fingers. Nathan took a big brightly colored handkerchief from his pocket and handed to her without saying a word.

Then he took the bucket of milk over to a work table and set it down next to one just like it. He put cheesecloth over the other bucket and slowly poured the milk through it into a stone crock. The cream left in the cheesecloth, he put into another stone crock with a churn. He then picked up the churn crock and turned to Amanda.

"If yer alright now, let's take this upstairs and do the churning up there. It's really cold down here."

Amanda just nodded her head and turned to go up the stairs ahead of Nathan. She really appreciated his kindness and also his willingness to let her tell her tale in her own time. She thought she owed him an explanation and she would give it to him tonight after Letty was asleep.

When they were upstairs, Letty joined them at the table. She was fascinated by the churn, especially when Nathan told her that's where butter came from. Since Amanda had been churning butter since she was a small girl, the chore came back to her immediately. She moved the plunger up and down in the crock while talking to Letty and Nathan until she could hear the sound she had been waiting for. She pulled the lid off and there was butter collected on the lid. Then she took a scraper and scraped the butter off the lid and the sides of the churn. She took the churn over to the sink and carefully poured the thin milky water down the sink. She pumped water into the churn and moved the plunger some more. She repeated this process until the water she poured off was clear.

In the meantime, Nathan got a stone out in readiness for the butter to be worked on. He brought out another clean cheesecloth. When Amanda was done at the sink, he wet the cloth in the cold water spreading it over the stone. Amanda scraped the butter onto the cheesecloth. Nathan carried it to the sink and wrung all the water out of it.

When he brought the butter back to the stone, Amanda worked a little salt into the butter and then portioned it out into blocks. She and Nathan then transferred the blocks to small covered butter dishes to be stored in the cellar. Nathan asked Letty to help him carry the small dishes down to the cellar. She was thrilled to be asked to help and was very careful not to drop her two dishes.

While Nathan and Letty were putting the butter up, Amanda heated some water and cleaned the churn. By the time Nathan and Letty had come back up carrying food for supper, Amanda had the churn clean and ready to be taken back downstairs. While Nathan took the churn back downstairs, Amanda began preparations for supper.

Nathan and Letty had brought up a small ham that Nathan had smoked, some peas he had dried, and several apples. Amanda soaked the ham in some cold water and then sliced it to fry in bacon grease left over from breakfast. The peas she seasoned with small pieces of bacon and one of the onions Nathan had hanging from his ceiling and put them to boil. The apples were going to be the real treat of supper.

Amanda took some of the butter they had churned and quickly made a flaky pie crust for the apples. She cut the crust into circles. After pealing, slicing, and seasoning the apples with brown sugar and more butter she cooked them for a few minutes in the butter. She placed a couple of spoons on each crust and folded them over to make fried pies. After frying the pies in a mixture of lard and butter, she drizzled them with honey and butter she had mixed together.

Nathan was sitting by the fire playing with Letty while Amanda cooked. He usually just ate bread and meat himself. He was thoroughly enjoying the smells coming out of his kitchen. It had been a long time since a woman cooked for him and he could tell just from the wonderful aromas that Amanda was a fine cook.

When Amanda called Letty and Nathan to the table, Nathan was amazed at the spread she had made in such a short time and with only the few items he had brought from the cellar. His cellar was full, he thought, and at this rate, if he could get Amanda to stay awhile, he would be fat as a bear by spring.

Amanda blushed at Nathan's extravagant praise for her cooking. It had been a long time since she had cooked in a real kitchen. She had been cooking over an open fire so long, she had forgotten how much easier it was with a real stove. "With all the food Nathan has in his cold cellar, we sure won't starve." she thought.

Amanda was shocked at her thought. She was surprised she was thinking about staying here when she hadn't even been invited. "I guess I've been so scared that the first place I feel safe, I want to stay," she thought to herself.

Later after Letty was asleep, Amanda and Nathan sat in front of the fire. They were quiet for some time and then Amanda began speaking. She told Nathan everything that had happened to her since she had been kidnapped by Waya almost five years ago. Well, almost everything. She didn't go into detail about her feelings for Waya and how she had tried not to love her baby. Those things were too private to tell anyone.

After Amanda had finished her tale, Nathan spoke for the first time since she had started. "Amanda, I know ye wanta find yer family, but I would like to ask ye and Letty to stay here with me until spring. I think ye need time to sort through all that's happened to ye and come to grips with yer grief. Ye've been through a lot. The weather may not break for some time anyway and I think we're in for a bad winter.

I have plenty of food put up and lots of wood chopped. And to tell ye the truth I could use the company. I've been alone here a long time except for a few visits from friends from Paris and it's been quite awhile since I had one of them. So, what do ye say?"

Amanda sat for a few minutes without speaking. She was surprised that Nathan had invited her to stay so quickly after she had been thinking the same thing. She almost felt like she was taking advantage of his loneliness, but then again, she wasn't ready to face her family yet. She needed time and she and Letty definitely needed shelter for the winter.

Finally Amanda looked up and said, "Nathan, I appreciate your offer more than you can know. You're right. I'm not really ready to face anyone else, even my family. To be honest, I'm not sure how they will take my having a child and that child being half Cherokee. My folks don't cotton to Indians much. They've had trouble with thieving and the like, like a lot of folks. So, yes, I would very much like to stay here until spring."

Nathan's face was almost hurting from how big his smile was. "Now, that's good, Amanda, that's real good. Ye've made an old man very happy."

"Oh, Nathan, you're not old. You can't be more than thirty-five or so." Amanda said with a laugh.

"Well," said Nathan, "ye'd be surprised. I'll be forty-five on my next birthday in March. I'm old enough to be yer Pa. My boys woulda been eighteen and twenty this year. They was eight and ten when the smallpox took 'em," Nathan said sadly.

"I'm so sorry you lost your family like that, Nathan. I know how it feels to lose someone you really love," Amanda said with tears in her eyes.

Nathan reached over and patted her hand which lay in her lap. "It's been a verra long time fer me. Yer sadness jest happened. It don't never stop hurtin, but ye do get used to it after a time."

Amanda hoped Nathan was right. The pain in her heart at the loss of so many people she had grown to love and care about was almost more than she could bear. Later when she lay in bed next to Letty, she thought of Waya and couldn't stop herself from crying for her tall, handsome husband. He had been so good to her and had loved her so much. She didn't expect to ever have that kind of love again.

Chapter 28

The winter lived up to everyone's expectations. Amanda remembered that Yona had warned her that it would be hard, as had Nathan. They had both been right. The first blizzard lasted almost a week. The snow was so deep it came halfway up the windows of the cabin. Nathan spent a lot of time just getting to and from the barn to take care of his animals. He had to shovel the snow out of the way some days just to get the hundred yards or so distance between the house and barn.

Amanda always had something hot ready for him when he got back from his two daily trips. Nathan usually went out to the the barn very early in the morning and late in the evening before supper. Amanda would hear him go out the door in the mornings. She would rise and start preparations for breakfast. The first thing to go on the stove would be the coffee pot. Nathan really loved his coffee. Amanda hadn't drunk coffee before going to the Cherokee town and of course they didn't drink it there, so she had never developed a taste for it herself, but Nathan really enjoyed the brew.

Nathan soon became used to having the company of Amanda and Letty. Some days it was hard for him to remember how alone he had been before they came. Since the weather was so terrible, they spent almost all their time together in the small cabin. Nathan still had the books he had used to teach his sons their letters and even though Letty was not quite four, he started to teach her simple things from the books. He was amazed at how quickly the little girl learned whatever he taught her.

Amanda was also very occupied that winter. Since she only had one set of clothes, Nathan had offered her some of his wife's clothes. He had never had the heart to dispose of them and had kept them in a cedar chest in his bedroom. When Amanda and Letty had been at his home for a couple of days, he noticed that Amanda still wore the clothes she had arrived in, as did Letty.

"Och, Mandy girl, I could kick myself in the rump," Nathan said one morning over breakfast. He had started to call her Mandy girl not long after they had arrived and Amanda liked it. It reminded her of her brothers teasing ways.

Laughing, Amanda said, "And why would you do that, Nathan."

"Well, after all ye told me about yer escape from the fiends who burned yer town and killed yer friends, it never occurred to me that ye wudn't have been able to salvage any clothes for ye and Letty. I don't have any yard goods, but I do have my wife's clothes. She was a bigger woman than ye, but ye might be able to do somethin with 'em to make ye and Letty somethin to wear."

"Oh, Nathan, that is very kind of you. You're right, we only have the clothes on our backs. If you're sure you wouldn't mind my using your wife's things, I would very much like to look them over and see what I could do. I would need a needle and thread though, and some scissors. Do you have those things?"

"My wife made all our clothes so, yeah, there's a sewin basket in the chest too. I'll go get the chest and let ye have a look."

With that, Nathan rose from the table and soon came back with a large cedar chest. When he opened the top, Amanda was surprised at the amount of clothes in it. There were several dresses, petticoats, and even a corset. The shoes would be too big for her, but her moccasins were still in fair shape. There was also a very well stocked sewing basket with several different colors of thread, needles, and a sharp pair of sewing scissors.

Amanda took one of the dresses, a white flowered print on a red background, and took it to her room to try. The dress swallowed her and drug the ground. Nathan's wife must have been tall and stately. Amanda took off the dress and carrying it, went back into the main room.

"Well, I'll have to do quite a bit of taking in, but I think I can make it fit. I will have to take it apart and pretty much start over." Amanda said with a smile. "Are you sure you don't mind me cutting this up to fit me?"

"My sweet girl would be happy for you to have these things. She had a good and giving spirit. That was one of the things I loved most about her," Nathan said with a sad smile.

It was plain to Amanda that Nathan had loved his Cherokee wife very much. It made her sad that she and his boys had died and left Nathan alone. She reached over and patted Nathan's hand, "Well, if you're sure, I believe I'll get started on this right away. It's going to take me awhile to rework the dress."

Amanda cleaned the kitchen area with water she had been heating on the stove and then began her work. After taking the dress apart, she held the bodice up to her chest and measured it on her own body. She had nothing to measure with so she took a piece of twine and put it around her cutting it to the right lengths for her bust and waist. Then she took the bodice, laid it out on the table, and cut it to the right measurement allowing selvage for seams. The skirt of the dress was very full and had been gathered, so all she had to do was tighten the gathers to fit her waist. The style of the dress was much like the dresses she had worn before being kidnapped by Waya. It had a fitted bodice that ended in a vee just below the waist, a high neck, and loose blousy sleeves that ended in tight cuffs at the wrist. It was trimmed in red ribbon around the neck and cuffs.

Several days later, Amanda was finished with her first sewing project. Nathan surprised her again when he offered to bring up the tub from the cellar so she and Letty could have a bath. Amanda hadn't bathed in anything except the river in so long, the thought of a real bath in a tub with hot water and soap brought tears to her eyes. Nathan was embarrassed by the emotion and was kicking himself again for not thinking of the tub before now. He didn't bathe that often himself in, but he did like a hot bath about once a month or so in the winter and he swam in the creek almost daily in the summer, as much for the enjoyment as for cleanliness. Of course, when he finished working in the fields, he was covered with sweat and dirt, so the swim was beneficial in more ways than fun.

He had bought the big wooden tub when his wife and sons were alive. His wife, Ayita, had been an exceptionally fastidious person. She had kept their home immaculately clean, as well as her person. She had bathed the boys often and had subtly made it known to Nathan that she appreciated it when he bathed as well. They had been an uncommon family in their bathing habits.

Not everyone bathed very often because it was hard work to carry and heat enough water to fill a tub. Most families had to carry water from an outside well and heat it on a stove or over the fire. Nathan had put the pump in for his wife after his friend in Paris, Ray Talbot, told him about seeing one at the doctor's house in town. Ray had ordered some and installed one in his house as well. As much as Ayita cleaned and bathed, the pump had been a huge work-saver for her. Nathan never regretted the amount of work and the expense of putting the pump in.

Nathan Fraser, though he didn't look or sound it, was actually quite well to do financially. He had come west almost twenty years ago and had had much success with his trapping. Since he neither drank nor smoked, he had saved his money. When he had married Ayita, he had bought this land, fifty acres, and built his cabin with his wife's help. Ayita had almost immediately become pregnant, so he had built the cabin larger than most, but not huge. He liked the snugness of their home.

Over the years, Nathan had made many improvements to his little home. After his wife and sons had died, he had wallowed in grief for several months, but then his natural light heartedness had reasserted itself. Since he had so much time on his hands after his work day was finished, and to keep from dwelling on his losses, he had spent that time working on the inside of his cabin in winter and the outside the rest of the year. He had a natural talent for woodworking which he put to good use making furniture for his home. He also took the time to insulate his cabin by making wooden shakes to cover the interior walls. Since the cabin ultimately had two walls, it was easier to heat in the winter and cooler in the summer.

The cabin even boasted real glass in the windows, which was also unusual for the time. Most cabins had wooden shutters over the windows. Nathan had never liked the darkness the shutters brought to the interior of the cabin. As soon as the glass could be ordered and received in Paris, he had removed the original wooden shutters and put in real windows. Ayita had made pretty calico curtains for the windows in bright colors to match the blankets she had woven for their beds and had hanging on the walls in the living area. The Cherokee people loved color and Ayita was no exception. Most of her clothes were made in bright colors as well as the shirts she made for Nathan and the boys.

After Ayita and the boys had died, Nathan left everything as it was. The curtains were a little faded now from many washings and the bright sun, but they still added a touch of color to the wooden walls and brightened up the place. Nathan was proud of his home.

After Nathan brought up the tub, Amanda pumped water into pots and put them on the stove. Nathan also brought out some linen towels and a cake of good smelling soap. Amanda knew the soap had to have belonged to his wife and was touched that he had kept it and offered it to her for she and Letty to use.

When the water was hot, Nathan helped Amanda pour the big pots of hot water into the tub and then went out to tend his animals giving her privacy. Amanda added enough cold water from the pump to make the bath tolerable. She undressed Letty and put her into the tub first. She washed her child all over and then washed her hair wrapping her in one of the linen towels and sitting her next to the fireplace.

Amanda then took off her much soiled calico shirt and deerskin skirt and sank into the tub herself. The feeling of being submerged in hot water felt so good, she couldn't help a long sigh of contentment. She just sat in the tub for a few minutes letting the hot water do its work relaxing her. Then after scrubbing her body and her hair, she stood and dried herself with one of the linen towels.

It felt so different to be putting on a chemise and a real dress. As Amanda fastened the last button on her cuff, she couldn't help but smile. She went to the fireplace and sitting by Letty, dried her long thick mahogany colored hair. Nathan had also handed her a comb and brush when he brought out the soap and towels.

As Amanda's hair dried, she took Letty upon her knee and slowly and carefully combed and brushed the tangles from her daughter's almost black, wavy hair. She had managed to make a little dress for Letty also. She put the little chemise over her head and then slipped the green sprigged calico dress on her baby. She had never seen Letty in this type of clothing and was amazed at the difference it made. She looked almost like any other white child, but with a slightly darker complexion.

She braided Letty's hair in two pigtails instead of the long braid down her back and tied them with a bit of ribbon to match her dress. Letty looked beautiful. Letty was very proud of her new clothes and twirled around the room in her bare feet. Amanda couldn't help but laugh. The sound startled her. She hadn't laughed in what felt like a very long time. The last time had been with Waya just before he and Mohe left. They had been watching Letty's antics with her little friends Kanuna and Hialeah. It seemed like years, but it was actually only a few weeks ago.

When Amanda's hair was dry, she braided it and wound the braids around her head fastening it with some of the pins she had found in the chest. She didn't have a mirror, but she felt like she looked pretty. She got affirmation of that when Nathan came back in from the barn.

He stopped just inside the door and just stared at Amanda and Letty as they sat by the fire. They both looked so different with their new clothes and their hair done differently. He had noticed before how pretty they were, but now they looked absolutely beautiful. Amanda, with her tiny frame, heart shaped face, and huge green eyes looked much younger than her twenty years. And Letty, was like a miniature Amanda with a taller, stockier body and much darker hair and skin. Their faces were almost identical. High cheekbones framed heart shaped faces, full mouths, and large shining green eyes with long straight dark lashes on both of them.

"Well, look at my girls," Nathan said, "ye both sure do clean up fine. Mandy yer a wonder with a needle. Them dresses look like they come off the rack at Ray Talbot's store in Paris."

Amanda smiled at their kind benefactor and said, "Thank you so much, Nathan. We both appreciate all you've done for us. The dresses and well, just everything," Amanda said with a hint of tears in her voice.

Embarrassed again by all the emotion, Nathan headed to the cold cellar with this evenings bucket of milk. While he strained the milk, Amanda emptied the tub down the sink bucket by bucket. By the time Nathan came back up with the churn, the tub was ready to be taken outside to completely empty.

Soon, Nathan and Amanda were again making butter with Letty's help. She had learned to use the churn and loved helping. She could only plunge the churn at the beginning of the process because she wasn't strong enough once the butter started to come, but she really liked to help as much as she could.

Letty was a naturally ebullient child. Though she had seen things no child should ever see, her very young age and her own sweet nature, helped her adapt quickly to new situations. Amanda was very glad she hadn't been emotionally scarred by what had happened to their Cherokee family and friends. She had still not told Letty that Waya and Mohe were dead. She just couldn't bring herself to discuss it yet and honestly didn't know how to tell her she would never see her father again. Amazingly, Letty hadn't questioned Amanda about her father. When she did, Amanda would tell her the truth. She had decided to never lie to her child.

That day came much sooner than Amanda would have liked. About two weeks later, when they were getting ready for bed, Letty looked up at Amanda and said, "When will my father and Uncle Mohe come for us? How will they know where we are?"

Amanda sat on the bed and took Letty on her lap. "Letty, there's something I have to tell you. Your father and Uncle Mohe won't be coming for us. Those bad men who burned our town and hurt everyone there did the same to them. I found them on the trail coming here," Amanda said sadly with tears in her eyes.

Letty looked up at her mother and tears started to roll down her little face. Amanda held her tightly and let her cry. She cried with her for all they had lost. When Letty's sobs stopped, she looked at Amanda and said, "Don't cry, Mama. My dlvl wouldn't have wanted you to cry."

"No, Letty," said Amanda, trying to stop her tears, "he wouldn't have wanted either of us to cry. Your dlvl loved us very much. I want you to always remember that."
"I will Mama, I will," Letty said with a very serious look on her face.

Nathan could tell the next day that something had happened. Letty wasn't her usual self. She was much quieter than usual and had little interest in playing. Nathan looked at Amanda and she was subdued as well. Later that evening, after Letty had gone to sleep, Amanda told Nathan what had transpired the evening before. Nathan's heart ached for both of his girls. He had grown very fond of these two females in the past few weeks. He dreaded the time in the spring when Amanda would attempt to find her family. He didn't want them to leave.

The weeks of that terrible winter dragged slowly by. There was much for all of them to do, but the winter seemed to go on forever. It had started early and looked like it would stay late. Amanda had reworked all of Ayita's clothes for she and Letty. They now had quite a wardrobe. Amanda had four dresses as did Letty. Letty had grown out of her moccasins so Nathan fashioned her a pair of slippers out of pieces of leather he had left from making seats for his dining room chairs.

Letty was so proud of her new shoes. Since there hadn't been any stockings to fit her in the chest, Nathan had gone out to the barn one day and come back with a small box of clothes that had belonged to his boys. Apparently Ayita had saved their clothes from the time they were small because there were three pairs of stockings that fit Letty in the small cedar box.

Letty had turned four in late December. Amanda had made her an apple spice cake and cooked her favorite supper of ham, fried potatoes, and beans, with cornbread covered in lots of butter. Amanda had been working on a surprise for her after Letty was in bed at night. She had made her bonnets to match all her dresses. She had taken small snippets of ribbon to decorate the bonnets making them quite festive.

Nathan had also been working on a surprise for Letty's birthday. He had been carving her a set of figures. There was a horse, cow, pig, a chicken, and a deer. Amanda was amazed at the intricate detail he had wrought in the small pieces of wood. The cow looked very much like one of his cows, Arabella, but he had put a smile on the cow's face. As a matter of fact, all the animals had human expressions on their faces.

After supper on Letty's birthday, Nathan and Amanda gave her her gifts. Letty's face was a so expressive, it was immediately obvious that she loved all her gifts. She put on the green bonnet first. Green was her favorite color. Nathan went into his room and brought out his shaving mirror so she could see herself. She preened like a little queen as she tried on all four bonnets.

When Nathan gave her the animals, Letty ran to him and threw her arms around his neck giving him a big kiss on the cheek. Nathan's lined face turned a bright red and his mouth stretched wide in a big grin. It was the happiest Nathan Fraser had been in ten years.

Chapter 29

The winter held on until the end of March that year. Finally, the sun shone bright and the snow and ice began to melt. The creek behind the house reached flood level pretty quickly from all the snow that was on the ground both on Nathan's place and higher up. The creek was far enough away from the barn and house that they needn't worry about being flooded, but snakes were a big concern to both Amanda and Nathan. Letty loved to play outside and they both feared she would be bitten. Amanda had Letty play on the porch when she worked inside. On most days she played in the yard, but only if Amanda or Nathan could be with her.

Amanda helped Nathan prepare his land for planting as soon as it was dry enough. Nathan had conveniences Amanda had lacked while with the Cherokee. He had a plow and a mule to pull it which made quick work of preparing the ground for planting. He planted almost his whole fifty acres. He planted potatoes, corn, beans, squash and onions. Nathan let Letty ride the mule while he walked behind the plow. Amanda came behind them dropping seed, then Nathan would come back down the row covering the seeds with dirt. They made a very efficient team and before too long all the fields were planted.

Amanda knew it was time she started to look for her family. The winter was over, she and Letty had good clothes to wear thanks to Nathan's generosity. It was past time that she asked Nathan to take her to Paris to start her hunt. Nathan had told her if her folks were still in the area, his friend, Ray Talbot, would know them and could give directions to where they lived. They hadn't discussed what she would do if her family was no longer in the area. That possibility was something Amanda didn't even want to think about.

Later, on the day the planting was finished, Amanda broached the subject with Nathan over supper. "Nathan," she said hesitantly, "Would you be able to take me to Paris in the next day or so? Me and Letty have imposed on your hospitality overlong."

"Och lass, ye ain't imposed on me a'tall. If it wudn't for ye, I wudn't have my fields all planted and I would have been plumb crazy after this long winter if ye little lassies hadn't been here. But, I reckon the time has come for ye to find out about yer folks. What say we go to town in two days time? I got some work I need to take care of tomorra, but we'll leave bright and early the day after."

"Thanks, Nathan. You have no idea how much I appreciate all you've done for me and Letty. You kept us from dying in that first blizzard and you've been so kind and generous ever since. I will never forget that, or you," Amanda said as she rose and walked over to Nathan. She put her arms around his neck and leaning over, gave him a kiss on the cheek.

Nathan's face turned such a deep shade of red, it looked almost purple. Hesitantly, he slid his arms around Amanda's waist and hugged her back. Oh, how he would miss his lassies. He didn't know how he was going to be able to part with either of them. Amanda was like a light at the end of a very dark and long tunnel. He felt about her like she was his daughter. And Letty, oh his sweet little Letty. She was so bright, cheerful, and beautiful. She was the granddaughter he would never have.

When Nathan looked up he could see tears in Amanda's eyes and his felt suspiciously damp too. He cleared his throat and stood up after Amanda had taken her arms from his neck. He couldn't speak he was so emotionally overwrought. He started to say something twice and finally gave up. He took his large, weather roughened hand and patted Amanda on the head, then left the cabin as fast as he could.

Later that night Amanda prepared Letty as best she could. "Letty, day after tomorrow we're going into town with Nathan. I'm going to try to find where our family is. You remember, I've told you about my Mama and Papa and all my brothers and my sister. You're named after my only sister, Leticia. If we can find where they live, we're going to see them."

"Will our Nathan be coming with us?" Letty asked with trepidation. She loved Nathan almost as much as she had her own father. Just like she had loved Uncle Mohe. She was very young, but she had suffered so much loss, the thought that she was about to lose someone else she loved upset her very much.

"Nathan will be taking us to see our family if they still live near here. After that, we will probably stay with our family and Nathan will come back here," Amanda said tenderly. "Hopefully, Nathan will come visit us and we can come back here to visit him sometimes, too."

Amanda knew how much Letty loved Nathan. She loved him too. He had been so kind and thoughtful for all these months. She felt horrible leaving him. Sometimes she was just tempted to stay here with Nathan forever. She and Letty were welcome and much loved here. The future was uncertain at best, but Amanda's conscience wouldn't allow her not to at least try to find her family. She owed them that much and more.

The next day all three of them were quiet. Amanda washed all their clothes and then ironed her's and Letty's dresses as well as Nathan's shirts. Nathan had made her a pair of slippers as well to wear around the house, so her moccasins were still in good shape. She didn't have any type of trunk or bag to carry their things in, so she took a clean flour sack and put their clothes in it.

As Amanda packed all the things Nathan had given them, her eyes filled with tears over and over. It seemed unkind to just up and leave Nathan, as good as he had been to them. She wished she could have her family and keep Nathan too. She knew that was impractical, but she couldn't help how she felt.

That evening, Amanda decided to make them a big supper since it would probably be their last here with Nathan. This time, she cooked all the things Nathan loved. She fried up some bacon extra crispy like he liked it and made a pan of biscuits, She took some of the corn Nathan had dried and added eggs,butter and flour with a little bacon drippings, to make a corn pudding. She sweetened it with honey and baked it in the oven until it was set. She also baked some sweet potatoes in the coals of the fireplace after rubbing them with a little lard. The skins were crispy and easy to remove and the potatoes inside were soft and delicious. For dessert, she made the apple fried pies she had made when she and Letty had first come, drizzling them with honey and butter mixed.

When they sat down to eat, Nathan looked at the well-filled table and said, "Och, Mandy girll, ye done yerself proud on this meal. I sure am gonna miss your cookin. It reminds me of the way my Ma cooked when I was a young'un," Nathan said with a forced smile on his face.

"I wanted to cook all your favorites since this will probably be our last supper together," Amanda said in a small voice.

"Have ye give any thought to what ye'll do if yer folks ain't still in this neck of the woods?"

"I've tried not to, to be honest," Amanda said quietly.

"Well, I jes want cha to know ye and Letty are welcome to live with me forever, if that's what ye want to do. I know yer young and will probably want to marry again, but until ye meet the right feller, ye'd make an old man happy if ye stayed with me."

"Nathan, believe me I have given that a lot of thought. Living here with you has been one of the happiest times of my life. You've made sure we were warm, well fed, and safe from the moment we met you. You're a fine man, Nathan Fraser and I'm proud to call you my friend."

Letty looked from her mother to Nathan and was upset that they seemed so sad. She felt sad too. She didn't want to leave Nathan and his comfy house. She didn't understand why her mother was taking them to see this family she talked about so much. Letty didn't know this family, but she did know Nathan and she loved him.

Even though they were all emotionally upset, they did justice to the fine dinner Amanda had cooked. They had all worked or played hard that day and were hungry. Later after Letty was asleep, Amanda and Nathan sat for a long time not saying much, but staring into the fire, Amanda knew Nathan would be lonely without she and Letty there. She would miss him something fierce, but she felt compelled to try to find her folks.

Nathan sat staring into the flames wondering how he would get by without his lassies. They had brightened up his life so much. He honestly hadn't known how very lonely he was until they had come. Now, to lose them, was more than he could handle, but he had to. He contented himself with the knowledge that he could visit them and they could come to see him sometimes too. He wasn't losing them forever.

The next morning dawned bright and sunny. After a good breakfast, Nathan went out to hitch his mules to the wagon. He returned to the house to find the dishes washed, dried and put away. Amanda had banked the fires in the stove and the fireplace and she and Letty were dressed in one of their pretty dresses. Without saying much, Nathan hefted the flour sack with their belongings and loaded it into the wagon.

He helped Amanda up to the seat and then swung Letty up to her mother. Letty sat in the middle between the two people she loved most in the world. She held her little cow Nathan had made her with the smiling face. It was her favorite of all the animals he had carved for her. Cows were where butter came from and Letty sure loved butter.

It took four hours to make it to Paris. As the wagon pulled up in front of the general store, the owner, Ray Talbot, came out on the porch of his store.

"Howdy, Nathan. Surprised to see you here. Wasn't lookin for you for another month or so. You out of provisions already?" Ray asked as he eyed Amanda and Letty curiously. 'Who's this you got with you? Did you up and marry again?"

"Howdy, Ray. No, not out of provisions and I ain't married. This here is Amanda Whitworth. She's the one took by the Cherokee several years ago. Them no good sidewinders running around burning Cherokee towns hit the one she was livin in just before winter and kilt everybody. I was lucky enough to be able to help her and her little girl out this winter. We've come to see if you had any idea if her folks was still in these parts."

"John Whitworth, right." Ray said looking at Amanda, she nodded affirmatively. "They lit outta here about a year ago like a lot of other folks. They sold up and went to Texas. Mr. Whitworth's Pa, Douglas, got all his grown young'uns to sell out and they all went together. He was aimin' to buy a passel of land near Nacogdoches I heard. It was a regular wagon train by the time all the families got together. There was fifteen wagons in all."

Amanda's face had turned white and Nathan thought she was going to faint, but she got a hold of herself after a few moments. "Mr. Talbot, you said they left about a year ago? Do you know if my older sister Letitia went with them. She was supposed to be getting married not long after I was kidnapped by the Cherokee. She was supposed to marry William Wells."

"I can't say for sure, but from what I heard from your father just before they left, everybody in the family went. The Wells are still around, but I ain't seen William in some time."

Amanda didn't know what to do or say. She was dumbfounded by the news that her entire family had left. They must have thought she was dead to leave like that. Amanda didn't know what to do or say, so she just quietly sat on the wagon and stared in front of her.

Nathan thanked Roy and got down and went inside the store. He wasn't gone long and came back with a box of provisions. He put the box in the back of the wagon and turning to Amanda said, "I figgered I might's well get a few things while I was here. Let's us get on home and we can talk there about what ye wanta do, Mandy."

Amanda just nodded her head affirmatively and kept staring straight ahead. Letty really didn't understand what was going on, but she knew her Mama was even sadder now than before they came to town. Letty took her little hand and lay it on Amanda's arm. At the touch of her child, Amanda turned to look at Letty.

"Don't be sad, Mama. We still have Nathan. He loves us and he ain't gonna go off and go to this Texas place without us. Where is Texas anyway?"

Amanda's eyes filled with tears at her child's words. "Yes, we do have Nathan, thank God," she thought. Getting ahold of her emotions, she smiled at Letty and said, "Well, Letty, I don't rightly know where Texas is, but I think it's a long way from here. Maybe Nathan knows where it is."

Nathan looked at his lasses thinking he was lucky in a way because he still had them. He knew Amanda had been counting on finding her family and he knew she was very sad that they were gone. He looked at both of them and smiled, "Well, from what I hear, Texas is a big place way to the west of here. Lots of folks are headin out there to make their fortunes cause the land is so cheap. Texas is owned by Mexico and the Mescan guvment is both sellin and givin away land to people to get 'em to move there."

Amanda thought a moment and then said, "Well, I guess my grandpa wasn't satisfied with the land he had here. He was always talking about buying more land here, but I guess he figured he could get more for his money in Texas. There's no telling how much land he'll end up with there."

Nathan was busy a minute or two turning the team to head for home, but then he spoke, "Yep, from what I heard your grandpa could get three or four more times the acreage in Texas than he coulda bought here for the same price. I reckon that's why they all up and left like that. A lot of folks have been doing it. Even, old Davy Crockett has been talkin' about going there."

Amanda's head came up quickly when she heard Davy Crockett's name. "My grandpa knows Davy Crockett. He came to my grandpa's place a bunch of times when we were there. If he decided to go to Texas, that's probably why my family went. My grandpa thinks the world of him."

On the trip back to the cabin, Amanda's mind was working furiously for a solution to their predicament. She knew they could stay with Nathan indefinitely, but her heart pulled her toward her family. She wanted Letty to grow up with family near. Nathan had become like a member of her family, but she wanted her mother and father to know their grandchild and for her to know them. Amanda had grown up in a large family with an even larger extended family. She wanted the same for Letty.

However, there was also the problem of Letty's Indian blood. Amanda hoped with all her heart that her parents and siblings would accept her daughter, but she wasn't so sure about her extended family. She knew her grandfather hated Indians, so she was ambivalent about exposing Letty to him or to some of her uncles as well. They had all taken part in Indian wars at one time or another and she knew they especially hated the Cherokee.

Amanda just didn't know what to do. She decided to talk it over with Nathan after Letty went to sleep tonight. After supper, it only took a few minutes for Letty to start rubbing her eyes. The eight hour round trip to town and her hard play when they got home had worn the little one out. Amanda helped Letty undress and tucked her in after telling her a story. The story hadn't even ended when Letty was out like a light.

After Amanda cleaned up their supper dishes, she went to sit by the fire with Nathan. He had made another rocker just for her during the winter. It was a fine oak rocker with a padded seat. Nathan had carved the chair by hand and rubbed a dark stain into the wood until it shone. Amanda was very proud of the rocker because it was not only lovely, but it had been made to fit her small frame and short legs. The other rocker by the fire had been made by Nathan to fit his tall frame and long legs and Amanda's feet didn't touch the floor when she sat in it.

After a few minutes of comfortable silence, Amanda broached the subject most on her mind, "Nathan, I have been thinking all day since we spoke to Mr. Talbot about what I'm going to do. Letty and I love you and love living with you, but I think Letty should know her family as well. I want to write a letter to my folks in Nacogdoches to let them know I'm alive and tell them about Letty."

"Och, that's a fine idea, Mandy. That way ye'll know how the wind blows concerning Letty. Yer folks will know where ye are and how to contact ye. Yep, that's a fine idea."

Nathan got up and went to his room coming back with a quill, ink pot, and some foolscap for her letter. He put them on the table and then returned to his chair. Amanda went to the table and picking up the quill began to write. It took her a few minutes to compose the letter in her head. It had been quite some time since she had used a quill or written anything at all. She found it soon came back to her as she found the words she wanted her parents to read.

Dear Mama and Papa,

I know you probably thought I was dead, but I am alive and well. The Cherokee town where I was taken when I was kidnapped was destroyed by white men late last fall.

My husband was killed, as well as everyone else who lived there. A wonderful woman named Ama got away long enough to warn me and save my baby. I was able to take my daughter, Leticia, and hide in the river until they were gone.

Letty is four years old and very pretty and bright. I was married to her father in a Cherokee ceremony about six months after I was kidnapped. I tried to escape twice, but was caught both times. I wasn't mistreated in any way while I was with the Cherokee. Even though I was taken forcibly and not allowed to leave, I was never harmed in any way by them.

A wonderful man named Nathan Fraser gave us shelter when we wandered on to his land trying to find help. He has been ever so kind and generous to us. Letty and I love him like he was family and that's how he treats us.

Nathan's friend, Ray Talbot, in Paris told us that you had all moved to Nacogdoches. I was trying to find you to come home. I want my daughter to know her family and I miss all of you very much.

Please let me hear from you. I have no idea what I will do now since you are all gone. Nathan has offered Letty and me a home and if you don't want me anymore, Letty and I will probably stay with him.

Love,
Amanda

When Amanda finished her letter, she made an envelope from another sheet of paper and sealed it with some candle wax. She wrote her father's name and Nacogdoches, Texas on it and let out a deep sigh. Now the waiting would begin.

Chapter 30

After Nathan had ridden to town several weeks ago and mailed her letter, Amanda had tried not to think about it. She knew it would take long weeks to reach her father, if it reached him at all. She had told Letty she had written to their family, but she didn't know if the little girl understood or not. Letty had not asked about them at all. She was content to keep living with Nathan forever.

The spring had been wet, but not too wet, and Nathan's crops had grown tremendously since they were planted in late March. It was now late June and the potatoes had been dug, the corn was ready to harvest, the beans had to be picked every day, and there were strings of onions drying in the barn. It looked like they would have a bumper crop of everything. Nathan had bought some slips when he was in town the last time and they had planted a second crop in the potato field, but this time it was sweet potatoes.

Nathan and Amanda worked every day in the fields hoeing and weeding. When the weather became too dry in mid June, they carried bucket after bucket of water to the fields. When they were totally worn out from carrying water, they got a couple of good rains for which they were very grateful.

At night Nathan continued to teach Letty her letters and numbers. She could now read simple sentences and work simple math problems. Nathan continued to be amazed at how quickly the little girl learned. In just a few short months she had learned to read and write quite well, as well as doing math problems both on paper and in her head. It seemed Letty's mind was a bottomless pit that absorbed all the information he could throw at her. Soon, Nathan knew, he would need more advanced books to teach her with. On his last trip to town, he had asked Ray Talbot to order him some.

Amanda was also teaching her daughter the tasks that would befall her as a woman. She had Letty helping her to cook by stirring pots on the stove standing on a little stool, learning to knead bread, and washing the dishes while Amanda rinsed and dried them. She was too small to use the big broom to sweep, but Nathan got the idea to make her a small broom, so she soon mastered that skill as well.

Nathan was very happy during this period. He had what he thought of as his "family" with him. The weather had been wonderful and his crops were growing well. He knew he would have a good profit from his crops this year. His livestock was also doing well. His mare had foaled in March and had twins, another little mare and a colt. One of his milk cows had also calved and he had a new heifer to go with the other four he already had. These were in addition to a young bull he had raised himself a few years ago. His chickens were multiplying and they had plenty of eggs. They would kill the young roosters soon and process the extra meat for the winter.

All was right in Nathan's world, but still he was worried. He had a nagging feeling that things were just too good to last. He knew Amanda still wanted to hear from her family. He wanted her to as well, but he was also selfish enough to hope she didn't hear from them. He was more content than he had been since his wife and sons died and didn't want to lose that feeling again.

Near the end of June, right after their noon meal, Amanda and Nathan were in the cornfield harvesting their bounteous crop when they heard horses coming up the trail from the direction of Paris. Both of them stopped their labor and shading their eyes from the sun looked down the road. They saw two young men astride some good looking horses headed their way.

Amanda's heart nearly stopped when she recognized her oldest brother, John Jr. The other young man looked very much like her younger brother Jacob, but this young man was too tall and too old to be Jacob. He had been barely 15 when she had been taken by Waya. As soon as the men spotted Amanda, they started to ride faster and wave their hats at her.

Amanda took off running through the cornfield to the road. Letty, who had been playing at the edge of the cornfield, didn't know what to make of her mother running towards these two strange men. She saw Nathan walking quickly toward the road too, so she joined the adults as fast as her little legs would carry her.

"Oh, my God, Johnny, it's so good to see you. I never thought I'd ever see any of my family again," Amanda said breathlessly when she reached the men. She quickly looked at the other man and said, "It is you, Jake. You went and grew up on me. Look how tall and broad you are now. You look like a man grown."

Jake laughed and swung down from his horse grabbing Amanda in a bear hug. "I am a man grown, Mandy. I'm over twenty now and married with a little boy. I'm farming my own land in Texas just like John and Jesse."

Amanda shook her head and clung to her little brother, who was no longer little. She turned her head as John got down too. "Johnny, oh, Johnny, it's so very good to see you both," Amanda said as she grabbed John in a big hug with happy tears streaming down her face. "Are Mama and Papa alright? How about Leticia and little Jimmy and all the boys?" Amanda said almost in one breath.

"Slow down, Mandy girl. I'll tell you about the whole bunch of 'em, if you just give me a chance to wash a little of this trail dust off me and get a drink of fresh water. These canteens make water taste awful."

Nathan arrived about that time. He was introduced to both the young men and invited them to the house to freshen up and have some refreshments. Letty had been hanging back hiding behind a bush while she watched the adults hug and talk. She didn't know who these two big men were, but her Mama seemed to like them so they must be alright. She decided to come out of her hidey spot and see who they were.

Amanda caught sight of Letty about the same time John and Jake did. She hurried to her daughter and swung her up in her arms. "Johnny, Jake, meet your niece. This is my daughter, Letty. She's named after Leticia." Amanda said with a nervous smile on her face. She wasn't sure what type of reception her baby would have from her brothers, but she was hopeful they would love her as much as she did.

John walked over to Amanda and the little girl. He reached out with a finger and lifted Letty's little face so he could see her better. She had been semi-hiding against her mother. "Well, Letty, you're most as pretty as your Mama. You got her face almost exactly. I'd know those sparkly green eyes anywhere. My Mama has them too." John said smiling at the little girl.

Jake came over then too and held out his arms to Letty. "Come see your old Uncle Jake, honey. You can ride on my horse to the house."

After a brief hesitation and a quick look for approval from her mother, Letty reached her chubby little arms out and was on the back of the big horse before she knew it. She loved to ride. Jake had made a friend of her immediately. "If this is what family is all about", she thought "I'll like it just fine.

Soon they were at the house. Nathan took the Whitworth boys' horses to the barn to unsaddle them, rub them down, and give them some grain. He wanted Amanda to have some alone time with her brothers. He also knew Letty needed some time to acclimate herself to the two new strangers in her life. He was very glad the two young men hadn't mentioned Letty's darker skin or very dark hair. They seemed like fine young men, but he wasn't surprised since knowing their sister so well.

When Nathan came back to the house, the boys were sitting at the table having some of Mandy's fine honeycake and drinking coffee. Letty was now sitting on John's lap playing with his watch chain. From the look on Amanda's smiling face, all was well between the siblings.

When Amanda saw Nathan come in, she jumped up and brought him a piece of the cake and a cup of coffee as well. She put cream in his coffee just like he liked it. He sat down at the table and looked at the three Whitworths.

"Och, I reckon yer catchin' up on family news. I hope alls well with yer folks and yer other brothers and sister." Nathan said with a smile.

"Yes, sir," said Johnny, "We're all fine. Texas is a big country and there's lots of unclaimed land around there. My grandpa has bought or been granted over a thousand acres and we're all gettin' settled there. We've been some busy gettin' land cleared, houses built and crops planted, but I reckon everybody's got shelter and the crops are doing great now. We had enough rain this year so's everything is growin' great. I see you've had a good year too from the looks of that cornfield."

"Yep, me and Mandy are havin' a good season this year. We already brought in a bumper crop of potatoes and planted the field again in sweet potatoes. We've harvested more squash and onions than we can ever eat and I've been able to sell the rest in Paris to my friend at the general store there. It's been a real good year for us."

John and Jake looked at Nathan a little strangely after that statement. He quickly understood they might have misunderstood what he had said. They may have thought he and Amanda were a couple, so he quickly went on.

"Mandy and Letty came wanderin' up last October and they've been keepin' me company ever since. Yer sister is a fine hand when it comes to plantin, cookin', and keepin' house. She's been like the daughter I never had. My wife and boys died some years ago. Her and Letty have really lit up an old man's life while they've been here."

Looking somewhat relieved, Johnny said, "We really appreciate your taking them in like that. We didn't know what happened to Mandy. We hunted her for months until that late blizzard come up. The winter closed in so hard, we couldn't see to ride. Daddy didn't want to give up even then, but he knew it wasn't no use to keep lookin' when we couldn't even see our hands in front of our faces for the snow. Mama took it hardest of all. Her and Leticia both. They both took to their beds and couldn't be got up for weeks after we quit lookin' that first winter."

"Oh, Johnny," Amanda said with tears streaming down her face, "I'm so sorry Mama and Leticia took it so hard. I wish I could've let them know I was fine. The Indians weren't mean to me at all. They didn't even punish me when I tried to run away to home twice. They adopted me into their tribe and treated me like I was one of them. I never wanted for food or clothes or nothin else."

Jake, whose head had been hanging low while Johnny and Amanda spoke, raised his head sharply. "You tried to run away and they didn't do nothin'. That don't sound like the Indians we heard about all our lives. Most of the captives that did get away said they was beat bad if they was caught when they first tried to run."

"I might have been too, but my husband, Waya, loved me and never raised a hand to me. Not even when I was at my meanest. And I have to admit, I wanted to come home so bad, I was mean more than once. You both know my temper."

"Well," said Johnny looking at Amanda again, "how did you get away? Mama told us what you wrote, but you didn't give much detail."

Amanda looked at Letty and said, "I'll tell you all about it after supper this evening," she said rising from her chair. "Right now, there's a field of corn that needs to be picked. If you boys ain't too tired, maybe you'd like to help us make short work of it. I'll cook some roastin' ears for supper if we get it all picked today. I'll even make corn pudding and the one who picks the most, gets the biggest helpin'," Amanda said with a grin towards her brothers. She knew neither of them could resist a challenge and they both really loved corn pudding.

The boys tried to beat each other out the door to the cornfield while Nathan and Amanda laughed at them. Amanda grabbed two more big baskets off the porch and when she caught up with her brothers handed each of them one.

In just a few hours all the corn was picked. Amanda left several ears in her own basket and put the rest in the wagon for the men to take to the barn to be stored. She took Letty's hand and they headed up to the house to start supper. Amanda set Letty to shucking corn while she got the stove hot again and sliced some fresh backstrap from the deer Nathan had shot the day before. The deer had been trying to eat up their cornfield.

Amanda floured the backstrap and set it to frying in some bacon grease and lard. Then she went to work on the corn. She cut the kernels off a good amount of ears and then got busy making the corn pudding. She got it into the oven and then started on the biscuits. Before long, she had steaming ears of corn in a bowl on the table along with a big bowl of sweet butter, a bowl of mashed potatoes, a big plate of biscuits, a bowl of gravy, and the fried backstrap. The corn pudding she left on top of the stove toward the back to stay warm until dessert time when she would pour even more honey on top of it when it was served.

The men came in looking freshly washed and sat down at the table. Since there were only four chairs, Amanda had Letty sit on her lap to eat. It got very quiet around the table as four hard working people and one hungry little girl made short shrift of all the food on the table. When the men were almost finished, Amanda sat Letty in her chair and went to serve up the corn pudding. She took the bowls back to the table and sat the fullest one in front of Jake. She poured extra honey over it, adding cream too. Then she gave him a quick one arm hug.

Johnny looked at Jake's portion and started to complain, "Hey, I picked as much corn as that young'un did. How come he got the most?"

Amanda laughed and said, "I counted, Johnny, and I had Letty counting too. Jake got two more ears than you. Nice try though."

Johnny laughed good naturedly and started in on his own bowl of the delicious treat. "He's only faster cause he's skinnier than me. My wife must be a better cook."

When Jake started to protest, Nathan broke in with a grin, "I bet both yer wives are great cooks. Neither of ye look thin to me. It's probly his youth, John. I sure can't pick corn like I did at twenty."

Before long Letty started to rub her eyes and yawn. Amanda took her into their room and washed her up for bed. Letty looked up from her little pillow and said, "Mama, I like your brudders. Is they our family?"

"Yes, honeybunch, they are a part of our family. We have a lot more. I have ten brothers and a sister and a bunch of nieces and nephews now too. That's not even counting all the aunts, uncles, and cousins. We have a huge family."

Letty's little eyes drifted closed and then she said sleepily, "Well, I hope they're all like Uncle Johnny and Uncle Jake."

Amanda smiled down at her baby girl and silently hoped the same. She wasn't truly worried about her immediate family now that her brothers were here. Obviously, her family still wanted her and her baby. However, it was her grandpa and some of her uncles she wasn't any too sure about. They were such Indian haters, she just didn't know how they would take to Letty.

When Amanda went back into the room, she could tell the men had been talking about her. She sat back in her chair and picked up her coffee cup. Looking at her brothers, she said, "I know you're both curious about how Letty and I ended up here with Nathan. Just know this, Nathan has treated us both like we were his family from the start and we both love him very much. We had been wandering for several days when we got extremely lucky and wandered up to this place. The snow had just started falling. It turned out to be a huge early blizzard. We would have both died if we hadn't found Nathan and he hadn't taken us in. We owe this man our lives."

Both the Whitworth brothers looked at Nathan. His face had turned red from embarrassment and his big adam's apple bobbed up and down in his throat as he tried to swallow his emotions. He didn't say anything, but the love shining out of his eyes for their sister was plain to see.

Johnny and Jake both stood and shook Nathan's hand and thanked him for all he had done for their sister. When everyone was again seated, Amanda took up her tale again. She told her brothers of her time in the Cherokee town. She made sure they understood that she was well treated and well loved by not only her husband but most everyone in the town.

She told them about the white men who had raided and burned the town and how Ama had gotten Letty to her and then had gone back to meet her own fate, throwing off the white men who might have seen her run away. She described how she found Waya and Mohe a day or so later beside the trail. When she talked about Waya, it was very obvious that she had loved the Cherokee man. Her sorrow on his passing and the way she described their lives together was touching to her brothers.

When she was through, Johnny reached over and took her hand. "Little sis," he said quietly, "you have been through Hell and back in the past few years. I'm so sorry we weren't able to find you right after you were taken. Maybe we could have spared you that heartache."

Amanda looked at him and said, "Yes, you might have spared me some heartache, but I would also not have known the great happiness I had with Waya. Nor would I have had my Letty. And believe me, big brother, there is nothing I wouldn't do for that child."

Both Johnny and Jake knew she was speaking the Gospel when she said those words. Amanda's big green eyes held a new maturity that hadn't been there before. They also held a huge sadness as well.

Amanda had looked down after her last words, but she now looked up quickly. She couldn't help but see the pain in Nathan's eyes. He knew she would want to see her family and that meant she and Letty would have to leave Tennessee and go to Texas with her brothers. She had grown to love this tall wonderful Scotsman, as had Letty. She couldn't bring herself to hurt him so she said, "Nathan, you know I both want and need to go see my family in Texas. What would you think about coming along with us?"

Nathan had a shocked look on his face. He hadn't thought about leaving Tennessee and following Amanda and Letty to Texas. He sat in silence for several minutes letting this new thought settle. When he looked up, he saw three questioning faces looking at him.

"Well, Mandy girl," Nathan said hesitantly, "I hadn't give it any thought before now. There ain't nothin holdin me here since my family's all gone. I just stayed here cause I didn't have nowhere else to go. I'd have to think on it a might, but I reckon I just might take ye up on that invite, if yer brothers think I could get some land in Texas."

Johnny spoke up first. He had taken a great liking to this man and was very grateful for all the help he had given Amanda and Letty. "Nathan, there ain't nothin but land in Texas. You could probly get a grant from the Mexican government easy. There's land for sale there too. There sure ain't no scarcity of land. We'd sure like for you to go with us, if you was of a mind to. Our folks would certainly like to thank you for all your help to Mandy and Letty in person. I know you'd be welcome at any of our homes."

Jake piped up, "Hell, Nathan, we could use a fine man like you in Texas. There's folks comin' in ever day to Nacogdoches. If you didn't want to stay there, there's millions of acres west of Nacogdoches needin' to be settled. The ground's rich and there's plenty of water too. You oughta think real hard about comin' with us."

When Nathan looked around the table all he saw were shining eyes and smiling faces. He looked right at Amanda and said, "Och, Mandy girl, is that what ye want?"

"Oh, Nathan, it would make me so very happy if you would come with us. Letty and I have come to love you very much and we wouldn't be happy in Texas without you. Please, please say you'll come with us."

Nathan swallowed the huge lump in his throat and said, "Well, I'd do jest about anything for my gals. Okay, Mandy girl, I'll go to Texas.

If you liked this book, or even if you didn't, please go to Amazon.com and leave a review. This is the first part of a trilogy. The second part - "I'll Go To Texas - The Revolution Years" - has been finished and is being edited. I hope to publish it in late April, 2016. The third part - "I'll Go To Texas - The Civil War Years" should be completed and published by the summer of 2016. I hope you enjoyed this book.

Author's Note - This book is a work of fiction, but was very loosely based on some of my ancestors who left West Tennessee for Texas near this same time period. Our family's Cherokee heritage came from an abduction much like Amanda's. My family also participated in the revolutionary war with Mexico that made Texas an independent country, as well as in the Civil War. One of my great-great uncles, Jesse Walling, served as a Texas senator, as well as fighting in the Texas Revolution alongside his brother, John Walling, who was my great-great grandfather. Our family is extremely proud of our Texas heritage.

Made in the USA
Middletown, DE
03 August 2023

36178476R00144